ASCENSION:

Invocation

BRIAN RICKMAN

For my family; without whom, this series would have been completed long ago.

Thanks to Kendall, Mike and Dean.

CHAPTER ONE

A sixteen year old girl ran frantically down an empty, paved road in the foothills. The green pines and grass were a blur as she raised her hand to her face and checked the monitor she clutched tight.

"34.666597, -87.757279"

It was less than a mile now, but time was running out. She desperately picked up her pace as sweat stung her eyes. The black tar of the road clung to the soles of her shoes in the Alabama heat, and she could smell the jasmine on a slight breeze. It was pretty, she thought.

"34.665741, -87.757823"

Faster now, she made her way up an incline and felt her muscles stretch like elastic bands. In the distance, she could see a farmhouse and a pasture with horses; down the drop to her left, a creek. The yellow fog; she could taste it on her tongue. Something was wrong.

"34.665105, -87.758338"

She stopped. The girl fell forward, placed her hands

on her knees and struggled to catch her breath. She brushed her hair away from her eyes and looked at the monitor one more time. 1:45pm. She glanced up and saw no cars before her in the distance. She spit on the road and wiped her mouth with her sleeve. The calculations were off. Perhaps she was early.

ᘓ

At Noon, Central Standard Time, the studio monitors crackled with static and Graham began to fade the end of a John Mayer track. He placed a pause in the automation software and, for a few moments, dead air hung on the frequency. He set the volume on the board and removed his headphones. There was nothing more to do. He sank back in his chair and waited with the rest of the world.

In the next room, formerly a production studio, a gang of men and women monitored their computer screens, documenting all activity from this point forward. They recorded the silence with precise care and watched the real-time monitors of seismic and atmospheric activity. Outside, the small town of

Tuscumbia, Alabama had become a parking lot. Station vehicles representing every major media organization could be seen for miles. It was unclear why a fifty thousand watt FM radio station in Northwest Alabama had been chosen as the flagship for this broadcast, now being beamed worldwide. For the moment, however, it was the most listened to transmission in the entire universe, and as the radio-silence blanketed the airwaves, the blinking lights on its tower measured the heartbeat of every man, woman and child on the planet. Finally, a familiar voice broke through the static.

"Good day. We thank you for your patience. It is our pleasure to be with you. Foremost, allow us to state that we mean you no harm; quite the contrary. For today begins a great evolution in your world. We bring glad tidings and offer you peace."

With this, one could feel a great, collective relief as those huddled to hear this message grew ever calmer. The voice penetrating the air was reassuring. It was friendly, and it sounded as if it were smiling. The voice had been heard before. It had been analyzed, reversed, and synthesized. Yet, only now did the voice seem to embody a sentient, living being. Reporters that had been typing feverishly at first now stopped and simply began to listen.

"Many of you are confused, and you do not understand. Some of you are frightened. Still others possess great confidence that may now be misplaced. Please know that these are all valid emotions. It is in your very nature to fear that which you cannot explain. Our advice to you is to go inward now. Listen. Become like a child, full of wonder. We shall explain to you the great changes taking place in your world but first your history must be atoned. Do not fear this. As we have assured you, the Dark Age is nearly complete, and today begins your reawakening."

Graham looked outside his studio window. Amongst the crush of media, he saw pockets of citizens. He recognized a woman as one of the check-out girls at the local grocery store. She stood with her young son held close as tears streamed down her face. A man next to her knelt on the ground praying. Two men behind him stood, arms-crossed, with pistols strapped to their belts. Two teenagers sat on a blanket in the grass, holding hands. Above them all, a great tear in the sky; a deep, black rip through an otherwise blue canvas that had centered above them only days before. The voice continued.

"As you live in a world of polarity, it must be understood that with great leaps forward come the great responsibility of knowing. Your world is poised to undertake its most profound evolution. There is no one among you with the knowledge that today will be shared. But soon, your very existence will become clear. You are on the precipice of your enlightenment. We invite you to embrace this. We will teach you the great way forward."

No one was working now. The reporters stood motionless, and the scientists abandoned their statistics as the computers processed seemingly inconsequential data. The mild vibration that had engulfed the Earth since the rip appeared remained the only constant. It felt as if all life stood atop a purring engine, now transfixed on a hole in the sky and a disembodied voice; a vibration itself. Was this the voice of God, extra terrestrial life, a conspiracy? It didn't matter for the moment. A powerful connection seemed to overtake all humanity.

"The genesis of your world is not for you to know today but you will understand this very soon. Know that when we speak of your world, we speak of your universe. You occupy but a small space in your vast, ever-expanding world. Your world is your very creation, but you do not remember. Fear not. In time, you will. As the Dark Age leaves you, so shall your amnesia. The planet on which you live is the womb. And just as a child has no memory of its conception, so you cannot recall your origin. Your great teachers have taught you the story of your creation. You may rest assured that these stories are rooted in truth. Have faith, for you have not been misled. Yet, your history has evolved into many stories. It is time now that all souls know their very origin."

A cell phone rang in the distance. The voice continued.

"You exist as one universal mind; a collective consciousness that spans your dimension. You have had among you from the beginning great, ascended masters. These masters have placed upon you the path of ascension and led you to this very moment. You have once before been in this moment. In that instance, you did fail. It is now evermore critical that you succeed. Soon you will understand. Today begins your great step forward. You will be guided, but before your new birth can begin; your world must first straighten its spine. The universe will now exhale. The Dark Age is nearly complete. You will soon be counseled further. For now, it is time for celebration! Enjoy the music."

The message ended abruptly. Dead air. Graham instinctively rushed to the board in his studio and fired off the next song: "What I Got" by Sublime.

"Early in the mornin'. Risin' to the street. Light me up that cigarette and I'll strap shoes on my feet..."

Graham cringed. Somehow this song didn't seem appropriate, given the gravity of the situation. Yet it was being broadcast worldwide to millions. His heart sank with the revelation that this song would be forever remembered as the one played immediately following contact with aliens or God or whatever had been speaking to humanity only moments before. He blew it. Just as his mind began racing to think of another, perhaps more thought-provoking track, a collective roar could be heard outside the building. Graham walked to the window and watched as the world danced in celebration as it had been instructed. In a way, he thought, it was apropos.

ଔ

Outside, amidst the dancing revelers and within the swarm of reporters, the Alabama National Guard joined the local and state police in monitoring the crowd. Now, there were fewer of them than ever. Since the appearance of the tear, many officers and soldiers had abandoned their positions. Some left to be with their families. Some left to drink. Others left to pray. Throughout the world, this was steadily becoming an issue of concern. Despite governments urging their citizens to maintain their daily routines, in the weeks leading up to today's invocation, shops had gone vacant, and crime had increased. While it could not be said that anarchy reigned, one could sense that chaos might be only a few steps behind.

The news media speculated as they will often do and this day would be no exception. Milan stood in a dollar store parking lot just blocks away from the radio station, staring intently at the tear in the sky. He knelt to the ground as people danced above him and he felt the Earth, the hum that now emanated from the ground and clung to air. It felt to Milan as if he were wearing a light jacket of elements, walking through a vibrating breeze. He stood up and was immediately summoned from the doorway of the dollar store.

"Milan! Two minutes, man! Get in here!"

It was the producer. Milan walked toward the entrance of the dollar store, which had been commandeered by the news network and made into a makeshift studio. It was the closest location they could find to "ground zero," and word was that the network had paid an incredible sum of money to broadcast their 24 hour news coverage from a position still littered with generic colas, cat litter, and dandruff shampoo. Milan excused himself amongst the dancers and made his way inside. The producer gently shoved him in the direction of the cameras. He sat down next to a gorgeous redhead, professionally attired, with flawless skin. She smiled at him as Milan attached the lapel mic to his jacket.

"Isn't this exciting?!" she nearly giggled.

"Yes," Milan agreed. "This... is certainly unlike anything I've ever seen."

"Biggest news story ever and I'm on the front line," she whispered. "It's a career maker."

Milan stared at her for a moment, but before he could respond, the on-location director began the countdown. "We're live in five... four... three..."

"We're in a commercial break? Who's sponsoring the end of the world?" Milan wondered.

The graphics on the screen in front of them exploded, and the music crescendoed. The anchor in Los Angeles began his solemn recap. "Just moments ago, all of humanity came face to face with an other-worldly life form, or the OWL as it has come to be known..."

"OWL? What the fuck is OWL?" Milan thought, "And it wasn't exactly 'face to face'."

"We're joined now by our panel of experts alongside the most trusted news team in America as we bring you this world-changing news story. We begin with Alicia Parker, joining us live in the small town of Tuscumbia, Alabama where this first contact has remarkably taken place. For starters, Alicia, what is the mood at Ground Zero?"

The director pointed to the redhead next to Milan. Her school-girl composure suddenly evaporated as she took on the air of an accomplished professional. "Jim, right now it's pure elation; there is a literal 'party in the streets' atmosphere as citizens of this tiny hamlet celebrate. They are dancing and singing and enjoying themselves. We're seeing this happen world-wide as the OWL suggested that all Earth's residents quote enjoy the music end quote."

The director gave a signal and the red lights atop the cameras fixed on Alicia and Milan went out.

"We're in a cut-away? It's a cut-away?" Alicia asked and the director nodded as she quickly reached for her bottled water, and took a drink. She then fixed herself in the monitor and straightened her jacket. On the monitor, Milan watched as the network replayed the final moments of the invocation. "You will soon be counseled further. For now, it is time for celebration! Enjoy the music."

The monitors now segued to footage of world-wide celebrations. Italy. China. Scotland. Egypt. The red lights on the cameras lit up again. Milan and Alicia sat up straight, and the anchor posed another question.

"So, did these alien beings travel light years to begin a worldwide dance party?" he laughed. "What is their motivation? For insight, we turn to Dr. Milan Janáček, a world renowned theoretical physicist, futurist and author. Doctor, why are the aliens here?"

"Well, foremost, Jim, I don't think that we know that this is, in fact, contact with an extra-terrestrial life form; at least not in the Hollywood sense."

"Expand on that, please, Doctor."

"It seems more logical to me that what we're experiencing today is contact with a life form in another dimension. Perhaps a fifth or sixth dimension based entity. The tear that we see in the sky may, in fact, be the opening of what is known as a traversable wormhole; a tear in dimensions. This could represent contact with a parallel universe."

"Kind of like Star Trek?" Jim asked.

Milan took a deep breath. "Kind of like Star Trek, yes. But, again, I don't think that Hollywood has really prepared us for what we may witness going forward. What we are seeing today is unlike anything we have ever experienced in terrestrial or extra terrestrial science. It's quite remarkable."

"I see. Let's take a listen to the speech from the OWL once more." The lights on the cameras went off, and the network began a replay of the invocation. Milan and Alicia each took a sip from their bottled water.

"The OWL," said Alicia. "Who the hell came up with that?"

"I know, right?" Milan smiled. He was glad to hear

that the sensationalism of this important event was not lost on her.

"It's fucking genius. Was it Anderson?" she asked the director. He shrugged.

Or maybe not. The replay ended; red lights on. Jim, the anchor, picked up his cue. "Our military expert, Retired Colonel Patrick Nelson joins us now as well. Colonel what do you make of today's events?"

"I can't make heads or tails out of the speech, Jim," the Colonel grumbled. "I think, without question, we have to be on guard. While it was a lot of mumbo-jumbo, I think that there was a clear indication of a threat. I don't know whether the threat is from the OWL or if they are invoking our assistance in some way to fight an outside threat. That may-"

Milan had to interrupt the Colonel. "With all due respect, Colonel, if we have made contact with an inter-dimensional entity, it is not likely that they require our assistance."

"How so, Doctor?" asked Jim the anchor.

"If this entity does, in fact, occupy a parallel universe and they have found a way to make contact with us, then their intellect and technology is far superior to our own. It's not likely that we would have anything that they need."

"The OWL mentioned a failure in our past and that we must now reconcile that failure with victory," the Colonel misquoted. "That, to me, sounds like a call to arms."

"I don't think that's what the voice said," Milan corrected.

Jim grabbed his notes and read aloud. "The actual quote from the OWL was 'In that instance, you did fail. It is now evermore critical that you succeed. Soon you will understand.'"

"There was more to it than that, Jim," said Milan.

The Colonel agreed. "There certainly was. I guess we just heard two different things. And what about this constant buzz? It feels like we're on the verge on a massive quake of some kind. We need to talk about that."

"Colonel, the vibrations we're feeling could be the result of a dimensional tear. String theory suggests that each dimension is a string or a membrane if you will. If they have breached our 'string', it would be equivalent to plucking a note on a guitar, for example. We could be feeling the reverberations of that note being struck. That may be why they told us to enjoy the music," Milan said, giving a nod to Alicia.

"Interesting indeed. Let's bring in our theology expert," the anchor swung around in his chair to face his new panelist. "Dr. Robert Pembrooke. What did you hear today?"

Dr. Pembrooke paused for a moment. "I heard the voice of God. And I would suggest you stop calling Him 'Al'."

Milan couldn't help it. He laughed out loud, on camera. Dr. Pembrooke smiled at him through the monitor as Jim quickly gave a summation and went to commercial. The red lights went out. The director gave an all clear, and the producer began to shout to the team.

"Okay, we're done here for now, people. Let's get some new footage of the tear and the town. Milan, can I see you?" The producer walked to Milan as he removed his mic. He was anxious to get back outside. "L.A. would like for you to do more about string theory. We have something in the can that you did last year with Larry. Do you remember that?" the producer asked.

"Faintly," Milan said as he briskly walked to the door.

"Can you be back in an hour to talk with Jim about the advances in the theory since last year?"

"Advances?" Milan checked his cell phone. He had no signal. It was working before he thought.

"Yeah, like... has anyone solved it?" the producer said, his voice shaking. Milan looked up from his phone and saw the middle-aged man brush tears from his eyes with his shirt sleeve. "What's happening?" he asked, trying to catch his breath. The producer had now thoroughly broken down and was crying as silently as possible, so not to attract the attention of his staff.

"No one really knows at the moment," Milan said,

putting his hand on the man's shoulder. "But we'll figure it out. Let me see what I can find out at the site. I'll come back in about an hour, and I'll try to explain things further, okay?" The producer nodded and worked to regain his composure. "Walk outside with me," Milan told him. "Get a little air, clean yourself up. You'll be okay."

"I can't even call my family," the producer said.

"I'll try to see if I can make arrangements for that, okay?"

Again, the producer nodded. Milan began to walk away toward the radio station, disappearing inside the crowd dancing now to Paul Simon's "You Can Call Me Al". It was ridiculous. Milan left him with that. He felt terrible. He didn't even know the producer's name.

α

Alicia made her way past the remaining aisles of goods in the dollar store to her makeshift office, which consisted solely of a desk and her iPad. She took off her jacket and draped it across her folding chair. She checked herself in the reflection of the computer screen and tapped a key to wake it up. First stop: Facebook. She had thirty friend requests. Not bad. She updated her status. "It's a party in Tuscumbia, Alabama! Crazy here. Going to talk to the locals. Will update more details as they happen. Stay tuned to Triton! Blarrgh! Need coffee!!!"

She then surfed to the competing networks. CNN had a terrific shot of the tear. "God, they've got the best graphics," she thought as she made her way to Fox, then ABC, CBS, and finally MSNBC. No one had anything new. This was good. Everyone was focusing on ground zero, the radio station. She needed a different angle. Maybe she'd go for the fringe. "Oh, wait," she thought. "Mama fears for her family. Sweet!" She'd find a rattled backwoods family and do a piece on them and their response to the aliens. Southern kids had adorable accents. This was Alabama. There had to be some dust bowl-era-looking barefoot family somewhere. Potentially hilarious. Perfect.

"Brady!" she shouted.

"Yeah?" was the response from the wash room

directly in front of her desk.

"You ready?"

"I'm taking a dump, babe."

"Hurry up. We've got to go."

"You got a lead?"

"I've got an idea, yeah. Finish jerking off and let's get out of here."

"I love it when you fantasize about my junk." The toilet flushed, the water ran and Brady emerged drying his hands with toilet paper.

"Are we out of paper towels?" Alicia asked.

"I couldn't find any."

"We're in a fucking convenience store, Brady. Aisle six."

"This is a fine." Brady tossed the wet paper in the trash can. He stepped to the corner and picked up his camera and remote bag. "Where are we going?"

"To the sticks. We need to find a redneck family."

"Can't we just do that in the parking lot?"

"No, no. I want to find a dilapidated house. No running water; that kind of shit."

"It's Alabama, Ali, but I'm pretty sure it's not 1936."

"You know what I mean. Let's go. You got the keys?"

"We're good. I don't know how you think we're going to drive through this mess."

Alicia and Brady walked toward the exit. Alicia stopped at the cold remedy aisle. "Wait a minute." She found a box of generic Sudafed, ripped it open, popped four red pills from the blister pack and swallowed them down. She put the rest in her pocket and made her way to the door. They took two coffees from the hospitality table on the way out.

Outside, the music was deafening. Alicia led the way and shoved past the revelers to the back of the building and the rented SUVs. They got in, Brady fired up the truck, and they began the slow trek out of the parking lot. A sea of people eventually parted to let them through the city streets.

"What do you know about this Milan guy?" Alicia asked.

"The scientist?"

"Yeah."

"I don't know. This is the first time I've met him. Seems like a good guy. Why? You crushin' on the geek?"

"Whatever. I'm not that kind of horny. I think he slighted me in the last break."

"He's smarter than you, Ali. Get over it. He's not the only one."

Brady glanced over to Alicia in the passenger seat and noticed that she looked a bit sad. This was rare. In the year that they had been partnered together, he had only known her to be a brash, hard drinking, pill popping, redheaded, wonderful nightmare. He was somewhat surprised to see her ego, which was epic, deflated.

"Hey," he said, gently punching her in the arm. "You can't be the prettiest girl in the room and the smartest chick. Leave a little something for the rest of us, huh?"

"Fuck you, Brady" she said, punching him harder. "I'm smart."

"Never said you weren't."

"Maybe not doctor-of-fucking-physics smart but smart enough to win a Murrow."

"Oh yeah? When did that happen?"

"It's going to happen. It might just be this story."

"Fuck yeah," Brady smiled. "Let's get it."

They were a solid pair, albeit a mismatched one. Brady was an overweight, balding 37 year old industry veteran. He had shot film in both Gulf Wars and on 9/11. His wife hated his job and worried that he put himself in harm's way far too often. After all, he had two young kids at home in Colorado. Truth be known Brady would rather have been playing golf but as he often told his wife, "golf won't pay the bills." He ate too much junk food and was probably one cheeseburger away from his first heart attack.

Alicia, on the other hand, was 10 years his junior, stunning and an upstart in the business. She landed at the network a year prior after cutting her teeth in Portland and Seattle, first as a beat reporter and then an anchor. Brady often thought that she was meant for another time. He was a fan of old movies, and she reminded him of Bette Davis or Katharine Hepburn. She had a dignity about her. She could be competitive to a fault though, which alienated much of the staff. Alicia was driven, and Brady sometimes worried that the work consumed her. He didn't dare tell her to slow down. It was like working with a woman possessed, and she would have ripped his head off. Still, he knew a side of her that most missed. She was genuinely charming when she wanted to be and she made the work exciting.

"Jesus Christ, this place is weird. Everyone here is drunk and packing a gun," Alicia said.

"Then there's that whole alien thing," Brady shot back as he navigated through the crowd, periodically honking the horn.

"Yeah, there's that." Alicia paused. "Is that what you think this is? Aliens?"

"Who the hell knows? What? Are you worried you're going to get probed?"

"It might be the best part of the trip."

☙

Milan made his way through the streets. The radio station was only a few blocks away from the dollar store. A month prior, he suspected that he could have made this walk in fifteen minutes or less. Now, he struggled to move a few feet per minute. The roads were just packed. It was like navigating through some insane street festival, he thought. The music was incredibly loud, and every kind of crazy was represented here. The whirling hippies, the religious zealots, the tin-foil hat crowd. This coupled with the presence of armed police, news media of all sorts and ordinary civilians sipping beers and talking about their mortgages amidst a dimensional crack in the sky was a new sort of surreal. He pressed forward.

Nearly a half hour later, Milan finally made it to the

block where the station was located. The military had barricaded the perimeter several days before. Milan knew that getting past would be a challenge. He approached a soldier, flashed his press credentials and waved the gentleman closer. They would each have to shout in each others' ear to be heard.

"No press!" the soldier yelled.

"I understand! I'm a scientist! I'm not a reporter!"

The soldier looked him over for a moment and finally shouted "Stay here!"

With that, the soldier left the line and walked behind one of the armored trucks that guarded the city block. Milan saw snipers on the surrounding buildings. Behind the line, ambassadors from throughout the world, military minds and scientists like him huddled in the old Victorian home that doubled as the radio station studios where this entire debacle began weeks before. Milan desperately wanted to be a part of whatever was happening behind those closed doors. It was moments like this, however, that he cursed the day his agent had talked him into signing the consulting agreement with the network. Sure, the money was fantastic. The shot to his credibility amongst his peers, though, made it hardly worth it. He had become a "Mr. Wizard", as his colleagues often joked. It was unfair. His credentials were impeccable. They knew this.

One of the soldier's superiors appeared from behind the truck and approached Milan. Since his arrival in Alabama, earlier that morning, Milan had detected a palatable fear in the eyes of everyone he encountered. Even the new age freaks welcoming their new, next dimensional masters with drum circles and crystals held a spark of terror in their gaze. This man's cold stare was fearless. Something about that was reassuring to Milan who was, admittedly, as nervous as the next by-stander.

"What is your business here, sir?!"

"I want to help! I'm a doctor of physics! I have a few theories about what is happening!"

"We have plenty of physicists working on this!"

"I can't imagine that one more would hurt! My name is Dr. Milan..."

"I know who you are," the man interrupted. He paused for a moment and finally waved Milan through the gate. "Follow me."

Behind the perimeter was a flurry of military activity. There were several tents set up and Milan could see a number of personnel working diligently at their computers. It was a relief to leave the mass of people behind. Milan followed the man down the block and up the concrete steps of the yellow house. On the porch, they were greeted by two armed guards who parted immediately at the sight of Milan's escort, saluted and opened the double doors to the home.

Inside, the house boasted high, ornate ceilings. An elaborate chandelier hung above them in the entryway. A mahogany staircase to their right was full of traffic as people ran up and down the stairs, carrying files and various pieces of equipment. To the left, was a conference table now occupied by a number of dignitaries, apparently awaiting a presentation of some sort. The soldier told Milan to stay put, and he vanished around the corner, into the conference room.

He emerged a few moments later, this time accompanied by a familiar face. "Milan! Welcome to the war zone," he said. It was Dr. Charles Trumboldt, an astrophysicist. He and Milan had attended several conferences together in the past. Both were in-demand speakers. Milan smiled and shook his hand.

"Let's hope it's not a war zone," he joked.

"Yeah, I suppose that's debatable. You have to admit, though, it does feel like something out of H.G. Wells. Are you in town with the network?"

"Yes. I just arrived this morning."

"I'm surprised they let you in. No one here wants to leak anything to the press until we have a better understanding of what's happening."

"I understand, but I'm not here as a reporter. I want to assist in any way that I can."

Charles knew that Milan would bring a unique perspective to the assembled group. He was, after all, an accomplished physicist. His theories were sound and, truth be told, he might be useful as a trusted spokesperson should the need arise. Still, Charles had been given strict orders to avoid leaking information. That said he felt he could trust Milan.

"You'll have to quit the network. Effective immediately. No more reports."

Milan didn't hesitate. This was the chance of a lifetime. "Consider it done."

Charles shook his hand again. "Welcome aboard. Come on back."

Milan followed Charles to the conference room. Along the way, he removed his press credentials and tossed them in a nearby trash can. He simply wouldn't return in an hour as he had promised. This probably wouldn't come as a shock to the network as they had employees abandoning their jobs by the hour. What were they going to do? Sue him? Milan was pretty sure he would win whatever court battle he'd be facing given the circumstances. In fact, it was strange, he thought, that this concern even crossed his mind.

Almost immediately, Charles and Milan were stopped. A stern-looking woman with piercing eyes halted them as soon as she caught sight of them. "Where's this man's clearance?" she demanded.

"He's only just arrived. This is Dr. Milan Janáček. He's a respected theoretical physicist. His input will be very helpful. We're fortunate to have him," Charles pitched.

She paused and seemed to quickly size up Milan. She didn't appear to sense a threat. "I'll need to run him through," she concluded.

"I'm sure that will be fine. Milan can you please follow Ms. Hendrix? She needs to run a background and security check on you."

"Certainly. That will be fine," Milan smiled. Ms. Hendrix didn't smile back but waved him into an adjacent office.

She instructed Milan to have a seat and he sat on a couch amidst boxes of what appeared to be radio station business. Commercial orders and spreadsheets were messily stacked in white cardboard, labeled with black marker. His OCD kicked in. He felt a compelling urge to begin organizing the files but that would be clearly inappropriate. Instead, he folded his hands in his lap as Ms. Hendricks sat in front of a laptop computer and began asking him questions: full name, social security number, address, etc.

"Where were you born, Doctor?"

"Chicago, Illinois."

She began to read from her computer screen. "Your parents were Czech immigrants; your father a pianist, your mother a home-maker. You received your B.S. in physics from Columbia College in 1976 and your doctorate in theoretical physics from The Rockefeller University in 1981 under Professor Spalding Ianthe. You later worked with Professor Yashmir Andropov of Tel Aviv University. You've since authored ten books, numerous articles on quantum mechanics. Your books are equally praised and criticized for their informal style, and you are routinely credited by both fans and critics as having a talent for communicating highly abstract scientific concepts in ways that are accessible to everyday readers. This talent led to your being hired as an on-air science consultant for the Triton

Broadcasting Network. You currently hold the Ivan Acker Chair and Professorship in theoretical physics at City College of New York, where you have lectured for more than 20 years."

"Wow," Milan laughed. "All of that from a few keystrokes. Are you in some sort of government database? At least it's all good, right?"

"It's Wikipedia. You were arrested in 1982 for driving under the influence, you have five outstanding parking tickets in three cities, you have three active memberships to online adult websites including..."

"I get it. Wait. That's on Wikipedia?"

Hendricks shook her head 'no' and just then Charles ducked his head into the room. "We're ready to begin. Are you finished, Ms. Hendricks?"

Hendricks continued typing on the laptop and spoke as her eyes darted around the screen. "He looks okay. No major criminal history. I'll give him a pass."

"May I go?" Milan asked.

She nodded, and he got up to follow Charles. The

conference room was now especially crowded. Milan vaguely recognized a few faces in the crowd, but this didn't seem to be the right time for introductions. The shaking air was beginning to irritate Milan. It was as if he were surrounded by sub-woofers, all rattling out the same silent, steady bass note. The curious thing to him was that this nonstop vibration did not appear to influence sound waves. He would assume that this should somehow affect the way he heard noise; the rate at which the voices in the room would travel. Also, the hum appeared to create an illusion that the oxygen in the room was heavier than it had been prior to the rip. The vibe was just an irritant, albeit one that had appeared to increase its velocity in recent moments.

The general that had escorted Milan to the house stepped to the front of the conference table. "Ladies and gentlemen, we're ready to begin. I believe a recap of sorts is in order." The lights in the room dimmed, and a power-point presentation began with the general narrating each slide.

"On May 22nd, the radio station which we now occupy began experiencing signal interference. This began as minor static charges inhibiting their broadcast. A local radio DJ reported the discrepancy to the station's engineer. Upon investigation, no equipment failure was found nor did there appear to be any local interference from other licensed stations. As the engineer continued to search for the issue, the interference became stronger until finally a voice appeared on air. Here is a recording of the voice that most of you are already familiar with."

The sound clip played from the laptop computer. It simply sounded like a long distance radio broadcast bleeding into the station's frequency, but what the voice was saying was clear: "The Dark Age is nearly complete. Stand by."

The general continued. "This occurred on May 24th. The following day, the local DJ was engaged in conversation by the voice on-air. The voice was much clearer now. Again, many of you will recognize this recording."

"Graham, we can hear you."

"Hello?"

"Hello, Graham."

"Look, I don't know what's going on, but you're interfering with our station. This is an FCC violation.'

"We look forward to your return."

A new slide appeared on the screen. It was a photo of Graham on the cover of a radio industry trade magazine, ten years old. The general explained that Graham Barry was once a successful major market radio disc jockey, popular in Detroit and Dallas. At the height of his fame, he developed issues with alcohol which eventually led to him losing his job, etc. It was a typical fall from grace story. At 35, Graham eventually landed in Tuscumbia, Alabama five years ago, settling for a much lower paying job as the afternoon drive talent and Program Director for a Rock station.

"These brief conversations continued in much the same way for several days," the general said. "The community began to take note, and it was assumed that this was some sort of radio stunt being executed by Mr. Barry. He assured the radio station owner that this was not the case. It was the following exchange that began to alarm citizens and began the official FCC investigation at the request of the radio station owner."

The general played the recording as a transcript appeared on the screen:

Graham Barry: Where are you located?

Voice: Just as you are located in your universe, we are located in ours.

Graham Barry: So, I'm speaking with a voice from outer space?

Voice: This is inaccurate.

Graham Barry: Well, if you're a space alien how do you know our language?

Voice: You know our language.

Graham Barry: We speak your language?

Voice: This is correct.

Graham Barry: Mind blowing. Dude, seriously, I hope you understand that there are huge fines and even jail time associated with this kind of...

Playback was interrupted, and the General advanced

to the next transcript slide. "The next exchange brought the communication to the attention of Dr. Trumboldt as the assumed pirate broadcaster revealed an equation considered to be of great scientific value. During this broadcast, it should be noted, the local DJ took a call from an audience member who asked the voice how one might travel at light speed..."

Voice: Travel at light speed is not possible. Your theory of relativity is correct.

Graham Barry: Well, thank you. Score one for Einstein!

Voice: Universal law dictates that if one were to travel at light speed, the mass of your traveling vessel would increase exponentially over time. It would cease to exist prior to reaching your destination. This is not practical.

Graham Barry: I would agree. Ceasing to exist prior to arrival would take all of the fun out of traveling.

Voice: Interstellar travel is best facilitated by bending space. This is perhaps better known to you as warp speed.

Graham Barry: Okay. So, how do we do that?

Voice: You are not prepared to utilize this information.

Graham Barry: Spill it. What's the harm in passing it along? You said we're evolving. Give it up, man.

Voice: It is predetermined. Consider this:

$$ds^2 = -\left(\alpha^2 - \beta_i\beta^i\right)dt^2 + 2\beta_i dx^i dt + \gamma_{ij}dx^i dx^j$$

Graham Barry: Okay. That meant nothing to me. Next caller.

The General began speaking again, "Of course, it should be noted that Mr. Barry, at this point, still assumed that he was speaking with a pirate broadcaster. As stated previously, the FCC began an investigation and could not determine the origin of the broadcast. Over the course of two days, the incident was picked up by a popular national late night radio talk show,

Graham Barry was interviewed, and worldwide interest in the story spread, leading to coverage on a number of news outlets and widespread chatter on the internet. At this point, however, it was still assumed that this was a hoax executed by Mr. Barry."

Milan had thought this as well. Why would an extra-terrestrial being choose to make contact via one radio station in one town? Why radio at all? Wouldn't it make more sense to take control of one of our communications satellites or, for that matter, the Internet? A colleague had sent Milan an email about the events in Tuscumbia, Alabama, and the two had scoffed about it, making jokes. The aliens must have made an unfortunate, wrong turn to end up in Alabama, they laughed.

"Contact was lost until May 31st," the General stated. "On that day, Mr. Barry was once again briefly engaged in conversation."

Voice: Do not fear this. The Dark Age is nearly complete.

The recording ended, and the next slide occurred. It

was a photo of the tear.

"Thereafter, what we assume to be an inter-dimensional tear appeared in the north-east sky above Tuscumbia, Alabama," the General explained. "Clearly, this is related to the transmissions, but we're not entirely sure how. The voice was heard once more prior to today simply indicating that it would address the world at noon on June 2nd. The tear is only visible here. So, if this is an inter-dimensional rip, it is, for some reason, centered here. Again, we don't know why. The tremors in the air that seem to be associated with the tear can be felt worldwide. You're all here today to hopefully assist us in answering some of these questions. So, let's begin the conversation."

The lights came up, and immediately hands were raised. The General began taking questions from the assembled group. "Am I correct in understanding that we cannot make contact?"

"That's right. Our efforts to contact the voice have been unsuccessful. We seem to be at their mercy for contact."

"Why have we not yet explored the vortex?"

"As we speak, pilots are preparing to visit the tear."

The room began to grumble. Milan spoke up. "Forgive me, sir, but isn't that incredibly dangerous? If this is, in fact, a traversable wormhole, we don't have ships capable of entering it. That's a suicide mission to say the very least."

"We don't intend to enter it. We simply want to get a closer look."

Another scientist spoke up. "That's just the thing, General. This isn't an 'object', per se. It's not something tangible. It is literally nothing. You'll be trying to get a closer view of..."

Suddenly, the hum in the air became almost unbearable. The Earth began to shake, and screams could be heard both inside and outside the building. It lasted for less than thirty seconds, but it felt like an eternity. When it subsided, it was utter chaos. Shots could be heard outside; more screaming. Everyone at the table followed the General outside to the front porch of the house.

In the sky, what appeared to be a bright, yellow cloud was emerging from the black tear. Very slowly it began making its way across the sky. A soldier came up to the general from inside the house.

"Sir, Mr. Barry has contact."

The shouting outside began to silence as Graham's voice could be heard over the loudspeakers as it had been before. "Will you please explain to us what is happening? What is this yellow cloud?"

"Soon, we will be visible to you. Your world must first be cleansed. Do not be afraid."

"But what do you mean 'cleansed'?"

"An elemental rain will fall. Bathe all biological life in this rain."

"Everything? Animals, plants... people?"

"All that wishes to progress forward."

"What will become of anything that doesn't get washed in this rain?"

"These things will not advance."

"You mean these things will die?"

"There is no death as you believe it, but these things will not coexist."

"When will this rain fall?"

"Soon."

The transmission concluded, and silence fell over the planet. Within hours, the world would be plunged into war.

CHAPTER TWO

The Rock radio station in Tuscumbia that the world was listening to was owned and operated by Mike Gregory. It coexisted alongside two sister stations, a Top 40 formatted station and an AM talk radio station that aired continuous, right wing national programming and news. Mike had inherited the properties from his father, the founder of the stations. All three frequencies had been long-standing members of the North Alabama community and were generally successful. It was a rarity in American radio, however. Privately owned stations hardly existed outside of small-town America and those that did were barely able to hang on due to the exceptional operating costs.

Mike was an accomplished salesman, though, and an engaging personality. He was well liked in the community, and when the offers came in from the radio conglomerates to purchase the stations during the radio boom of the 90s, Mike refused to sell. As a financial decision, he sometimes regretted this; but as a matter of integrity, he wore it as a badge of honor. Most stations that had been swallowed up by corporate America during the boom were shadows of their former selves. Mike's stations still functioned as they always had, since his father first flipped the switch on the first one in the early 1950s. He was proud of this.

Mike paid better than most small town operators; that is to say that his employees were slightly above the poverty line. Radio DJs were not unlike musicians, writers and other artists. They were willing to accept a small salary in exchange for the creative freedom Mike allowed them on the air. As Wall Street had taken over most U.S. radio stations, creativity had been exchanged for profits. This led to voice tracking stations with generic talent, homogenized play lists and typically bland radio. A lot of talent had been displaced, and many Djs were willing to work in markets once thought below their stature, for smaller salaries, in order to avoid selling used cars for a living.

To a degree, Mike benefited from this, of course.

Yet, he made a point of treating his employees well. Whatever he couldn't provide in the way of financial stability, he tried his best to make up for with hospitality and a genuine sense of family amongst his team. He often had his employees over for Sunday dinner, he gave bonuses for a job well done and he had even been known to trade out necessities like groceries for jocks down on their luck.

Radio was certainly not the lucrative business it had once been. Gone were the days when even small town clusters were million dollar profit centers. The Internet had happened, and radio had been slow to react. Rather than embracing the technology immediately, the corporate monoliths relied on their outdated Wall Street strategies to turn a profit and, consequently, had left behind an entire generation of potential listeners. This trickled down to private owners like Mike as well. As advertisers discovered new, more cost effective ways to advertise via the Internet, the newspapers were rendered irrelevant. Radio was next in line to fall, and while it wasn't dead yet, most owners were scrambling to play catch up with technology in a last-ditch effort to survive. Couple this with the fact that a great deal of the industry's talent pool had migrated to satellite and online radio gigs and a perfect storm of mediocrity had crept in.

Graham didn't know Mike from Adam when he applied for the gig. He had just been unceremoniously let go in Georgia thanks to budget cuts, and he began shot-gunning tapes and resumes. Mike was the only one who called. Graham was immediately struck by his smooth, Southern charm and his penchant for telling long, compelling stories about his adventures in the industry. As they swapped philosophies and anecdotes, something seemed to click. Mike hired him over the phone. It was the first time that Graham had accepted a gig sight unseen, but he was behind on his rent in Georgia and eviction was imminent. It was best to high tail it out of there, and Mike was the first to throw him a paycheck.

When Graham arrived in Tuscumbia, he was impressed. It was a beautiful small town. There was an enormous park with a waterfall, a big fountain, and even a train for the kids to ride. The town actually had an old time drug store with a malt shop inside. When he drove up to the address Mike had given him, he was surprised to find the yellow Victorian house. He was even more surprised to find Mike on the front porch, wearing an apron and flipping ribs on a large grill, surrounded by billows of white smoke. It was lunch time, after all. When Graham introduced himself, Mike smiled, gave him a slap on the back and handed him a tall glass of sweet tea.

"Welcome home, Graham," he said.

It did feel like home. In fact, for a few days it actually did become Graham's home. He had not yet found a place to live, and since Mike was unable to arrange a hotel trade, he had set up a cot in what was to be Graham's office. It could have been weird but given the fact that this office was actually a former bedroom in the home, it felt somewhat appropriate. There was a complete kitchen downstairs, his office had cable TV, a fireplace, and a large desk with a computer. After 10pm, all of the stations were on the bird, so Graham had the place to himself. The only inconvenience was the lack of a shower at the station. Mike had solved this problem by insisting that Graham join him and his wife for dinner at his home every evening until he found a place to live. He could shower there.

The two became fast friends as Mike toured Graham around the town, introducing him to local business people and showing him the sights. He visited the Helen Keller homestead, which was located only a block away from the radio station and saw a live performance of "The Miracle Worker". He went to the Alabama Music Hall of Fame and learned about the region's vast musical heritage. He and Mike even went fishing on the Tennessee River one Saturday, and Graham caught a fish for the first time. It was fun, and the work was rewarding.

Graham's major market knowledge was an asset, and he soon became a mentor for the rest of the on-air staff. He had been hired to host afternoons on the Rock station, but, in time, Mike put him in change of the format. This eventually led to him also overseeing the other two stations and while he didn't see an increase in pay for the new responsibilities, Graham was content. He eventually had a small apartment in a complex not far from the stations. He could pay his bills and thanks to Mike's introductions he had a close circle of friends. It was a pretty good gig, and it was relatively quiet until recently.

In the fall, the Rock station was coming off a lousy book. The ratings had dipped considerably and although Graham insisted that poor diary placement in the market was the cause for the slip, Mike was adamant that the station needed something to build Cume. They needed to cast a wider net. He had given Graham the responsibility of coming up with a promotion that would propel the station back to its dominant, Male 25-54 share. Without these ratings, the station would suffer financially as the regional advertising dollars would go elsewhere. Mike was confident that he could maintain the cash flow until the next ratings period but he needed Graham to make a splash in the spring book; otherwise they were all in for a grim holiday season. So, Graham began to brainstorm concepts.

He approached Mike with a number of ideas ranging from outdoor marketing and direct mail to insured promotions, wherein the station would give listeners an opportunity to win one million dollars. Mike hated the last idea. Of course, no one ever won these things. Graham argued that while this was true, the spike in listenership might be just the thing to increase the numbers. Mike didn't want to do this with a sham so he sent Graham back to the drawing board.

Shortly thereafter, the interference began. When Graham first noticed the problem, he immediately alerted the station engineer and Mike. It was, at first, assumed that this was just another station bleeding in to their frequency. Someone in Memphis, perhaps, had throttled up their power. It may also have been inversion. Atmospherics could sometimes be just right for a far off frequency to accidentally interfere with another. When Graham worked in South Carolina, for example, he had received a call from a listener in Florida who was able to pick up his station clear as a bell, albeit temporarily. Radio hobbyists loved this trick, but broadcasters were less enamored of the phenomenon although there was little that could be done to prevent it.

When the interfering broadcast began to call

Graham by name on the air, things changed. Mike had called Graham into his office. He was all smiles. "You sonofabitch! What have you got goin' on?"

"Mike, I think we have a pirate in the area..."

"Yeah, and I think that pirate is you! What have you got planned?"

"No, Mike..."

"Wait. You aren't changing the format up, are ya? You know I told you that we have to discuss things like that prior to going on the air with them. I've got sales packages I have to change and stuff."

"It's not that. The format stays. I think we've got a listener playing a gag here."

"All right. All right. I'll let ya run with it..."

For a time, there was no convincing Mike that the pirate broadcast was anything more than a brilliant plan concocted by his favorite employee. Graham became incredibly frustrated. His past had come back to haunt him. During his heyday in the big markets, he had become rather famous for stunts not unlike this one.

Except this wasn't a stunt and, for a time, no one would take him seriously. Word on the street was that the cross-town competition was even listening intently to see what he'd do next.

Over the years, following the decline in his career, Graham's on-air persona had changed quite drastically. Partly, this was because Graham had grown up. He was no longer the drunken kid in his mid-20s shouting insults at callers and locking listeners in dirty porta-johns for the chance to win Ozzfest tickets. Also, that sort of radio had become tired. Listeners eventually got fed up with shock jocks and, as Graham had discovered, shock jocks lost their jobs. He had adapted his style over time to become a much more sophisticated jock. He was 40 years old, after all, and there came a time when it was no longer "cool" for him to have the naked, 19 year old strippers in the studio with him; it instead became "creepy". Graham didn't want to be that guy.

As the pirate broadcaster became more cryptic in his messages to Graham, word began to spread via the web and eventually he was contacted by the syndicated late-night, aliens and monsters radio talk show. It was only following this appearance that Mike began to understand that Graham was not responsible for the broadcasts. During the interview with the talk show host, Graham continued to insist that it was a pirate broadcaster; not a stunt on his part and certainly not a representative from outer space. It wasn't the interview the host was hoping for, and it seemed to suddenly click with Mike that this was something the FCC needed to investigate.

Thereafter, things really got strange. Despite the lackluster interview, Graham's program became one of the most listened to broadcasts on the Internet. He received absurd fan mail from all over the world and as the FCC launched their investigation only to come up empty handed, one conversation in particular catapulted his program into the mainstream national spotlight. It occurred one afternoon when Graham was particularly exasperated. The pirate flipped a switch in his brain and shadows of Graham's former self began to appear.

"105.5, the Point. We-"

"Good afternoon, Graham."

"Yeah, I figured as much. Hello. You... just... just hello."

"You appear weary."

"Do I? I wonder why that might be. Maybe it's because I'm trying to do my job and you keep making my life a nightmare."

"This is regretful. That is not the intention. You should not feel sad."

"Sad? Is that what you think I feel? Sad? How about pissed?!" Graham was genuinely losing his temper. "You know what? Look, I don't know what your deal is. I'm not going to pretend to understand what's going on inside your crazy head. For you, this is just a prank. It's a good laugh. I get it. But, for me and for everyone else listening to this station, it's an annoyance. I can't make this any more clear. Go. Away."

"The Dark Age is nearly complete. Your progression is dependent upon this broadcast. It is predetermined."

For a moment, Graham said nothing. It was obvious that the pirate had no intentions of calling off the gag. Graham gave a glance at his phone bank. Once again, the lines were lit up. "Fine," he thought. "This guy wants to be a radio star? I'll throw his ass in the fire."

"All right," Graham said to the voice. "If you're not going to go away, we're going to do this my way."

"I understand," said the voice.

"You're on my show and I say we take some calls from the audience."

"This is acceptable."

Graham half-expected this. Every green jock he knew thought that working the phones was a breeze. It was one of the toughest parts of the job if you did it live on the air. It was like walking through a mine field wearing clown shoes. Like a stand-up comic, dealing with some callers was not unlike handling a heckler. You only got skilled at it with practice. Everyone sucked at their first at-bat.

"Good. I'm glad it's acceptable to you," Graham said

sarcastically. "Got a question for the little green man from outer space? Pick up the phone, listeners. 1-800-256-POINT. Go ahead. Ask it anything. For, it knows all." Graham punched line one and potted up the caller. "Hey, The Point, who's this?"

"It's J.D.", said the caller.

"Where you calling from, man?"

"I'm in Muscle Shoals."

"Got a question for my special guest?"

"More of a comment, really."

"All right. Go ahead, J.D."

"Dude, cut this out. I just want to hear some tunes, you know? If I wanted talk radio, I'd listen to talk radio. Why don't you just knock it off and go back to playing Warcraft with your homo friends?"

"Okay. Thanks, J.D. So, why don't you just go back to gaying off?" The voice didn't respond. "It's a valid question, sir." Still no answer. "All right. Fine. We'll just assume that you're busy gaying off right now and take the next caller. Hey, The Point, who's on the line?"

"This is Chrissy."

"Chrissy, what'cha got?"

"If you're from outer space, like, where's your spaceship?"

"Ahhh. Good question, Chrissy. So, let's get an answer for the big money. Sir, where did you park?"

A female voice answered the question. "Interstellar travel is only now being developed on your plane. In its most remedial form, this travel would, in fact, require the use of an additional vessel. On our plane, however, these vessels are not required. You are most fortunate as your evolution, which is nigh, will propel your world beyond such vessels. In time, you will understand this. For the moment, your understanding of space, even in your most elaborate concepts, is quite finite, which is incorrect."

"Nice," said Graham. "Your Mom sounds hot. Chrissy, did that answer your question? A spaceship is not required, and you don't know squat about space."

"Yeah, I guess. Hey, can I request a song?"

"Sure, kid, what do you want to hear?"

"Play anything by 311."

"Okay. I hope to get to it eventually. Next caller. The Point, who's this?"

"It's David."

"David, what's up?"

"Okay. So, dude just said that he's beyond using a space ship. So, I guess he wouldn't mind sharing with us exactly how we can travel at light speed?"

"Yeah, that's a good point, David. If this is such an arcane technology in your world, lawbreaker, why not just tell us how to build the star ship Enterprise so that we can come visit you? But, be warned, when I get there, I'm gonna totally mess up your radio show."

The familiar male voice responded. "Travel at light speed is not possible. Your theory of relativity is correct."

"Well, thank you," said Graham. "Score one for Einstein!"

"Your universal law dictates that if one were to

travel at light speed, the mass of your traveling vessel would increase exponentially over time. It would cease to exist prior to reaching your destination. This is not practical."

"I would agree. Ceasing to exist prior to arrival would take all of the fun out of traveling."

"Interstellar travel is best facilitated by bending space. This is what you may refer to as warp speed."

"Okay. So, how do we do that?"

"This is irrelevant. You are not prepared to utilize this information but you have asked the correct question."

"Great. Do I win a prize? Spill it. What's the harm in passing it along? You said we're evolving. Give it up, man."

"It is predetermined. Consider this:

$$ds^2 = -\left(\alpha^2 - \beta_i \beta^i\right) dt^2 + 2\beta_i dx^i dt + \gamma_{ij} dx^i dx^j$$

"Okay. That meant nothing to me. Next caller. Who's up?"

"Hi, it's Mateo."

"Why do I think you're foreign, Mateo? What is it? Your accent? Your name?"

"Probably both."

"Go ahead, man."

"¿Cuál es el significado de la vida?"

The male voice responded in Spanish. "Esto es complejo. El significado de tu vida es diferente del significado de la vida de otro. Cada alma sirve a sus propios fines, por el bien del universo entero. Usted ahora existen para servir a su padre que está enfermo. Su alma es muy necesaria y debe transición bien. Tu alma está en esta tierra sólo para este fin. Sin embargo, su alma ha tenido tareas mucho mayor antes de esto y han contribuido en gran medida al mundo entero. Usted debe estar orgulloso y que esperamos con interés sus contribuciones en el futuro. Por favor, dile a tu padre que tanto anticipar su regreso."

"I have no idea what he said, Mateo. I don't speak Mexican. Satisfactory?"

There was a pause, a sigh and finally "Is this a joke?"

Graham cringed. He had never uttered a racial slur in his career. Was that a slur? "I'm sorry; I didn't mean any offense..."

"My Dad is in the hospital dying of cancer right now."

"Okay. I'm sorry to hea-"

"How did you know that?"

The question was directed to Graham. "Mateo, I didn't understand anything that was just said. I don't speak Spanish."

"I'm not mad. I just don't know how you knew that."

"Everyone, I'd just like to make it clear that this is not some sort of joke. I have no control over the other voice you're hearing. This is a pirate broadcast that is bleeding in to our frequency. I'm not involved. Mateo, maybe you know this guy?"

"I doubt it. I don't know anyone who could pull that off."

"I'm sorry, man, that's my best guess. I'm sorry if he said something cruel during this difficult time."

"It wasn't cruel. Kinda nice, actually. Just weird."

Thanks to the Internet, the world now moved at warp speed, so it was fitting then that the short equation on Graham's show landed in Charles Trumboldt's email box within a few hours. He had been taking a day off and using it quite productively, he thought. He was in line at a Boston deli, stocking up on Pecorino Romano and bread when he received an email with the subject line "WTF" on his phone. It was from a colleague at Cal Tech and simply read "Have you seen this?" and attached the equation. Charles read it and quickly stepped out of line.

He called the sender who explained that a student of his had heard this on a radio program a few hours prior; something to do with Alabama. His first thought was that this theory must have originated at NASA in Huntsville, Alabama, but had not yet been published. A call to a few friends there assured him that they knew nothing of the warp equation. It was stunning. Whoever had come up with this had just made a tremendous scientific leap. Surely, the future of space travel didn't originate with a radio disc jockey. Where did he get this?

Charles made a few more calls, surfed the net, located the radio station in question and placed a call. He got Mike on the phone. "Yeah, I just got off the phone with the NASA boys," Mike explained. "Like I told them, we don't know where this guy's at, who he is, nothin'. All we know is that he's impeding our broadcast."

Mike explained the entire situation to Charles who now became even more intrigued. After a call to his chair at Harvard, Charles was on the next flight to Alabama. He had arranged a meeting with Mike and Graham for lunch the following day. By then, the world's scientific community was buzzing about the equation. Certainly, astrophysicists like Charles were thrilled and intensely curious about the author.

During lunch, Graham explained how the interference began and that the station's engineer initially suspected that the pirate broadcaster had discovered their MARTI frequency, which was utilized for remote broadcasts, and had been tapping in to this to gain access. They had confirmed, however, that this was not the case. Most perplexing was how the pirate could take over the station at will without Graham or any other DJ raising the volume on any particular channel on the mixing board. For whatever reason, he only appeared interested in speaking with Graham.

"Here's the thing," Charles said. "This equation that he gave you. Well, it's scientifically sound. This is plausible."

"I suppose this guy could be some kind of genius." Graham offered.

"He would practically have to be."

"He's figured out a way to hijack the station and hide in plain sight," Mike said. "He's eluding the feds. I'd say he ain't no dummy."

"Would you mind if I tried talking to him this afternoon?" Charles asked Graham.

"Feel free. Just be at the station by three and we'll do it."

Charles returned to his hotel while Mike and Graham went back to business as usual. Mike went on sales calls while Graham went to his office to schedule music for the next day. His trance at the computer was interrupted by a boisterous voice in the open doorway.

"Fucking brilliant, Graham!" It was Chris, one half of the Top 40 night show on the station down the hall. "I knew you were holding out, but this is above and beyond. Literally! Now you've got NASA investigating the show. Where'd you find the scientist? Dude, sweet!"

Chris was a young kid, early twenties and this gig with Mike was only his second stop in the business. He was good. Graham thought he had a lot of potential. He had told Mike that he thought he was a nice choice for the job when he was reviewing air checks and resumes almost a year ago. Graham didn't anticipate that Chris would come complete with an encyclopedic knowledge of his entire career. To be fair, it wasn't just Graham's career that Chris knew by heart. It was practically every jock that Graham had ever known and many more that he had only heard of. He was a rare find: a young kid that truly loved radio. Still, the initial awe that Chris attributed to being in the same room with Graham eventually seemed to turn to disappointment. It appeared to Chris that Graham was a shadow of his former self. To a degree this was true, but what Chris couldn't comprehend was that Graham was content with his new found, quiet life.

"I'm not doing anything, Chris," Graham protested. "It's a pirate bleeding in to the station."

"Whatever, dude. I get it."

"I'm serious. This isn't a stunt."

"Strange that it has classic Graham Barry written all over it," Chris smiled. "It's cool, man. I'll keep it under wraps. I'll play along just like Mike."

"Whatever, man." Graham noticed new ink on Chris's arm. "Is that a new tat?"

"Yeah, check it out." Graham took a closer look. It was a vintage microphone with a snake circling it. "I get color in a few weeks if it heals right."

"It's nice," Graham noticed a peculiar odor. "What's that smell?"

"Prep-H," Chris produced a tube from his pocket. Graham must have appeared confused. "You don't have any tats?"

"No. I never did get any."

"The Preparation-H is to keep the swelling down."

"Oh. That's unfortunate."

"Yeah, buying it sucked hardcore. I think I'm going to do a phone bit about it tonight. 'Most embarrassing thing you've ever had to buy'."

"That's a good idea. You can do a prank with that too. Call the pharmacy; explain that you've lost the box and instructions. Ask the clerk to read the directions to you over the phone. Then, begin to apply it as he instructs you. Sound effects and all."

"Oh! That's great! You're on fire, G!"

"It's an old bit. Mad Max did it years ago. I think I heard it on an old air check of his."

"Sweet! I'm totally stealing that. Whatever happened to Max?"

"Last I heard he was in Myrtle Beach."

"Which cluster?"

"NewMedia, I think."

"Is that the old Four Stables?"

"Think so."

"A buddy of mine was there before the buy-out by Helix."

"Before or after the Quad merger?"

"Right after."

"Shit."

"Yeah. He said it was a freakin' bloodbath."

ଔ

At three, Charles arrived as promised and Graham got him comfortable in the studio. He explained that the voice typically interrupted him during his first break. The conversations might last for a few minutes or they could go on for as long as an hour.

Graham noted that he appeared to be in control of how long the talks lasted. The pirate would continue chatting until Graham deemed the conversation over, at which point, it would respect his wishes and go away for the remainder of his show. Charles sat across the console from Graham and observed as he began his broadcast. A song faded, and Graham opened his mic.

"105.5, The Point with the Red Hot Chili Peppers. It's Graham, North Alabama, good afternoon. It's seventy eight degrees with a high..."

"Good afternoon, Graham."

Charles held his headphones close to his ears and kept an eye on Graham. He didn't see him press any buttons or do anything that would seem to cue the new voice.

"Hello, space man, I'm actually glad to hear from you today."

"This is most fortunate."

"Yeah, it would seem that you've caused an even larger stir than normal. You're starting to annoy more people than just me."

"The intention is not to disturb you although this is, we are afraid, an inevitable consequence."

"Sure. You don't mean to be a pain in the ass. You just are."

"Charles is with you today."

With this, Graham and Charles looked at each other incredulously. Each seemed to be briefly accusing the other of being involved in the prank in some way. Graham also thought about the conversation he had earlier with Chris. Was he involved in the stunt? Maybe it was Mike? Regardless, it was all going too far.

"Dr. Charles Trumboldt is with me this afternoon, space man. How did you know that?"

"It is predetermined."

"Uh huh. Of course. Well, he's taken an interest in your equation. It would seem that a great many scientists have as well."

"This is understandable. This represents a great leap forward. It is irrelevant, however."

"He wants to ask you a few questions."

"This is acceptable."

"Go ahead, Doctor.”

"Um. Yes. This is Charles...”

"Hello, Charles."

"Hello. What is your name?"

"We have many names, as do you."

"No seriously," Charles said. "What you've come up with here is nothing short of extaordinary. We'd like to know who to attribute this equation to. So, what is your name?"

"Regrettably, your question is irrelevant, Doctor."

"While I'm impressed with your modesty, you should really accept credit."

"There are a great many more things that you will learn in a short time. The knowledge in this equation will not serve you. It will not be relevant to your world."

"Then, why share it with us?" Graham asked.

"It was your request."

"So, all we have to do is ask? Maybe the doctor should quiz you." Graham smiled at Charles.

"This is acceptable."

"Okay, Doc. Hit him with your most pressing questions."

The Doctor paused for a moment and thought. He didn't want to embarrass the broadcaster. After all, he was clearly a formidable scientific mind or, worse, a very clever, deviant mind. Either way, he didn't want this person as an enemy. He thought going vague might be his best option.

"Well, what is the origin of our universe?"

"Eons ago, under spiritual guidance of the masters of wisdom, the creators of your universe, prepared your plane for the development of higher forms of biological life and for the reincarnation of the souls of Lucifer."

"What?" Graham interrupted. "Lucifer? You mean the Devil? Satan? We're the spawn of Satan?"

"You have asked three questions."

"Well, what are the answers?" Graham asked.

"The answer is that it will be best to refer to the world of Lucifer as Maloan. Your mythology dictates this."

"We are the descendants of souls from the planet Maloan?" asked Charles

"It is best that you refer to Maloan as a world; not a planet. You are not the descendants. Your world is of your creation. It is one and the same." Graham's phone lines began to light up. This was trouble. Certain topics were always off limits on the radio. Religion, especially in the Bible belt, was never a proper topic to breach. "In the beginning, the divine hierarchy's mysteries were known, and you were aware of your planet's inner logos whose consciousness gave birth to unique soul groups, each able to incarnate at different times. You possess within you the great universal records of your genesis. You were once before called upon to release your amnesia, but this was not to be. Now, it is of paramount importance that you progress forward. It will soon be time for your great awakening, and we very much anticipate your return."

"So, if I understand you correctly," said Charles, "you want us to join you in your world?"

"It is predetermined."

"You said we failed before. What makes you think we're ready now?"

"It is different now. You will not proceed in your entirety, this much is true. Regrettably, only you may determine your ascension. We may only facilitate your awakening."

"What role do you play in our world? Who are you? Are you God?"

"We are no more God than you are God. We no less you than you are us. We are of the same kind."

At this point, Mike flung open the door to the studio and promptly gave the "cut" sign. Graham and Charles could hear the office phone lines ringing in the hall. Graham had been down this road before, and it usually ended with him renting a U-Haul. He fired off a song.

"All right. I think that's just about enough out of you

for today, law breaker," he said over the ramp of the song. "Snow Patrol, Dave Matthews coming up next. Right now, it's Arcade Fire on the Point."

Graham and Charles took off their headphones and turned around to face Mike.

"What's all this new age bullshit?" he wanted to know.

"Apparently, this guy is some sort of cult leader. I don't know," Graham shrugged.

"For the record, some of the things he referenced have been written about before. The planet Lucifer or Maloan, for example," Charles offered. "According to some mythologies, it was a planet that once existed between Mars and Jupiter. It was supposedly destroyed in an atomic explosion. The remnants of the planet are said to be the asteroid belt that exists between the two planets in the solar system as we know it today. Some have theorized that this is where the Bible story of Genesis originates; that the Bible scripture was influenced by this tale."

"All I know is I got advertisers threatening to pull

spots," Mike said. "We've got some angry listeners."

Charles requested copies of all of the previous broadcasts featuring the voice and returned to his hotel to listen. Graham completed his show without further incident but stayed clear of the phones. Mike, meanwhile, dealt with an avalanche of phone calls from angry listeners, clients and the local newspaper. Toward the end of the day, he entertained a visit from the local police chief.

"Mike, I'm going to have to arrest him if he doesn't quit."

"Oh hell, Dewey, arrest him for what?"

"Disturbing the peace, inciting a riot..."

"Graham is doing nothing of the kind. That's a load of crap."

"Look, Mike, I'm getting phone calls at all hours of the night complaining about this. People are riled."

"The Church of Christ people are who's riled."

"It ain't just them. I've got a stack of complaints a mile high down at the office. They want him to stop."

"Dewey, how many times have I got to tell you? Graham ain't the one doing this. Our broadcast has been hijacked. I've filed a complaint with the FCC. You want to see it?"

"I don't need to see it. I believe you. How long is it going to take them to fix this?"

"Well, they got to find the guy illegally broadcasting first. We haven't been able to track him down."

"If you take Graham off the air, will the hijacker in question go away?"

"I don't know and why would I want to do that? Think about it. I should just hand over the frequency to the nut job you want me to silence? If Graham's doing anything, he's preventing this lunatic from going full bore."

Dewey now hushed his tone. "Mike, are you sure Graham ain't involved in this in some way?"

"Yes, I'm sure. He's just as alarmed about this as you are."

"He sure don't sound alarmed on the radio."

"That's his job. He's a professional. Professionals don't sound rattled even when they are."

"That may be, but look... we all know his history."

"Now, I'm gonna stop you right there, Dewey..."

"I'm just saying that he's had a problem with the liquor..."

"So did your Mama, Dewey, God rest her soul, and I don't recall her ever inciting no riot."

"I'm only asking if you're sure this ain't some kind of on air play he dreamed up. I been listening to his tapes on the internet."

"That was a long time ago. He don't do stuff like that no more. I can't believe we're talking about this. You know the man, for crying out loud. He's a member of your church. Hell, go ask him yourself."

"I'm an officer of the law and these are questions I got to ask. You're his employer, so I'm askin' you."

"He's a good man, Dewey. A family man. He's taken to that little girl just like she was his own. Graham Barry is an upstanding member of this community. You ain't ever found him in any trouble around here. Last year alone, he raised over five thousand dollars for your battered women's shelter. You really think he just now went off the deep end for no good reason?"

"I don't, Mike. The truth is I don't. It's just that a lot of people are thinking that maybe he did."

"Well, I know that better than any of you. I'm losing a lot of money right now."

"I'm sorry to hear that, Mike."

"Jimmy even pulled his advertising for the new car lot."

"That ain't right. Y'all got history."

"Well, he can't be associated with this kind of talk and I understand that."

Dewey paused for a moment and then reached out to shake Mike's hand. "All right, Mike. I'll keep them at bay, but I'm going to need you to keep me updated on the FCC. Let me know what they find out. It also wouldn't hurt you to take those calls from the paper. Tell your side of the story. Explain what's really happening here."

"I'm thinkin' I might have to."

"The whole town's havin' a come apart. I don't want you to lose any more business."

Mike walked Dewey toward the door. "I appreciate that, Dewey, and I will keep you in touch."

"Thank you, Mike. You think Bama's gonna do it again this year?"

"Lord willin' and the quarterback don't choke."

"I hear ya. Roll tide, Mikey."

"Roll tide, Dew."

⚃

The next day, Graham and Mike awoke as the most unpopular men in town. Typically, Graham would stop by a local gas station on his way in to the office to purchase a cup of coffee. He was accustomed to being greeted with a warm smile and even a bit of small talk. Today, the mood was inside was decidedly different. When he walked in the shop, the room, typically abuzz with conversation, fell quiet. Graham stood awkwardly in line and waited to pay for his coffee. "Guitar lessons. Free cats. Donate your pennies for baby Lucinda." Graham read every flier on the cashier's wall in an effort to avoid eye contact. The clerk coldly handed him his change, and as he left, he could feel their stares upon him. This was familiar, but in the past when he had angered a city, Graham had been far too hung-over to notice or even care. On this day, he finally felt disapproval in the icy chill of sobriety. When he arrived at the station, things were different, though. Mike greeted him at the door and had obviously been waiting for him to arrive.

"Is everything okay?" Graham asked.

"Well, I'd say we got ourselves another situation," Mike said, beaming.

"Is the station off the air? I didn't see any missed calls."

"No, no. Everything's fine. Just fine. We've got us a visitor that you're going to want to see!"

"Another scientist?"

"Just come up to my office for some excitin' news, son!"

Graham followed Mike upstairs to his office. Inside, a guy in a suit sat chatting on his cell phone. He smiled when he saw the two of them and quickly wrapped up his conversation. He hung up the phone and met Graham in the doorway.

"Graham! How are you, man? I'm not sure if you remember me..."

"I'm sorry..."

"Steve Seagal. Steve. I was V.P. of Programming for Northstar!"

"In Phoenix?"

"Yeah! We were competitors. Well, technically, I went head to head with your V.P., Pugs Kelly, but, hey, you gave us a hell of a fight, bro."

"Thanks."

"Going against you in morning drive sucked, dude! You know Ramirez had a nervous breakdown, didn't you?"

"What? No. I didn't know that."

"Fuck yeah. That week during the fall book when Chase, the night guy, took over mornings?"

"Oh. Yeah. I thought that was weird."

"You put him in the fucking hospital, he was so stressed out. He was convinced that we were going to can his ass," Steve laughed.

"Shit. I'm sorry to hear that."

"It's a shame your run ended the way it did. You weren't given a fair shake in the papers out there, man. That was brutal."

"Yeah. I know."

"We almost called you when we cut Ramirez but you were pretty fucked up back then."

"Yep."

"Hey, anyway, have a seat. Did Mike tell you why I'm here?"

"Well, he said it was 'excitin' news'," Graham gave a smile to Mike, who gave him a fist bump. Steve became quite serious. "I think it is. Graham, what would you say right this moment if I were to offer you national syndication?"

"Doing what?"

Steve and Mike laughed heartily. "Doing your show, man!" said Steve. "'Doing what' he says!"

Graham shifted in his chair and waited for the hilarity to settle. What was happening on the air wasn't syndication-worthy. He knew that. "Guys, what you're hearing on the air right now... it isn't my show. It's a hijacked broadcast. I can't control what's happening in there."

Steve's eyes lit up. "That's why it's so fantastic! Graham, you know the state of radio. You read the trades, right? We're dying. Dying on the vine, bro. The Internet is fucking killing us. And why? Because radio has become so fucking predictable. Stale. The same five hundred songs played ad nauseam and devoid of personality. No life. No pulse."

"No pulse," Mike echoed, sadly shaking his head in agreement.

"What's happening right here, right now, today on your show is absolutely thrilling."

"It's damn exciting," said Mike.

"Dude, you've got a fucking space man on the air with you. Your second chair is motherfucking E.T. That's genius!"

"It's clever," Mike nodded.

"It's clever, and we know it's marketable. How many times has your stream crashed in the last two days?"

"A lot. I don't think I know exac-"

"The listeners have spoken! They want this kind of programming. I'm with Regal Networks now."

"Oh, yeah? When did you land there?"

"About two years ago after the bottom fell out of Prestige. Y'know, after they got swallowed up in the Stratus-RedComm merger. Fucking brutal."

"I bet. Sure."

"Anyway, we're confident that we can place you on at least thirty six stations in the first week alone.

Hundreds within a month."

"What?"

"I know! We're talking Stern shit here, and you do nothing. Change nothing. Broadcast right here, we beam you nationwide, handle the stream, the website, place you in iTunes and develop the app, the works. You just come in to work every day and do what you do."

"That's just the thing... Steve, I'm not really doing anything. Mike, you know that..."

Mike shook his head. "You're being modest, Graham."

"I'm calling bullshit, too, Graham," Steve said. "I've seen you in action. When you were on your game, you were a motherfucking titan, man. I would have put you up against any jock in any top twenty market without thinking twice. But the pressure got you, bro. It happens. It happens to the best." Steve's cell phone began to ring. "But now you're back, Graham and we're willing to pay handsomely for a piece of the action. Look, I've got to take this. Mike, can you fill him in on what we talked about?"

"You got it," Mike said as he followed Steve to the door and closed it behind him.

"Mike...”

"I know what you're going to say, Graham, but you just hold on one minute because I got somethin' to say myself, ya hear?"

"Ok."

"This man is offering you and, yes, me a lot of money. A lot of money, Graham." Mie laughed. "Moneygram. Anyway, I don't think we can pass up this opportunity."

"Mike, you know as well as I do that this could end at any moment. Hell, you're trying to put a stop to it right now yourself."

"I can call off the dogs."

"What if he stops broadcasting?"

"Then we replace him with a new spaceman. Happens all the time and then you can control the script. Start talkin' more about boobies and less about math."

"If this goes national, he's going to want a piece. He could sue."

"He ain't gonna sue me. I'll eat his ass alive in a court of law. You think any judge is gonna allow someone to break every FCC regulation on the books, plus cost me a generous amount of revenue? I'm just a poor, defenseless, small-town businessman, Graham." Mike smiled. "And if the sonofabitch wants paid, we'll pay his butt. We'll have more than enough."

Mike handed Graham the agreement and pointed to the offer with his pen. It was more money than Graham had ever made. Double what he was making in Dallas; five times what he was making now. Mike's share was just as much plus they each got a split on the ad revenue.

"This feels weird, Mike."

Mike got up, walked slowly over to Graham and sat on his desk. "Graham, you know I'm on your side, right?"

"Yes, Mike. I do. I've always appreciated..."

"I know. I know. I think highly of you too. It's a mutual respect. And I mean no disrespect when I tell you what I'm about to tell you, son. You ain't gonna get another chance like this, Graham. You and I both know that this is your last stop. You're gonna grow old here, and I'm happy to have you. But don't kid yourself. Assholes like this boy Steve don't come around Tuscumbia, Alabama sniffin' for syndicated talent. It just don't happen. Hell, I ain't gotta tell you that. You know it. So, don't be a fool. Take the money. And, as for me..." Mike flashed that winning grin. "Well, Graham, I do think you owe me a payday right about now. I'm losin' my ass, son. Throw me a bone."

ଔ

The Graham Barry Program went into syndication within a week. As Steve had promised, the show launched with thirty five affiliates nationwide. However, Graham was terribly concerned. For three days prior to the launch, he had not heard a word from the voice. He expressed his anxiety to Mike; their worst-case scenario of having to replace the voice with a paid actor might come to fruition. Mike assured him that this wouldn't be a problem and even advised him to begin the process of searching out potential talent for the role. In the days leading up to the maiden broadcast, Graham made a regular point of reminding listeners, hopefully including the pirate, that the show would soon be broadcast nationwide. They ran promos throughout the day letting listeners know and even went so far as to cross promote the show on the other stations in the cluster.

Everyone at the station was excited. Mike bought a keg and some fried chicken and held an after-hours party to celebrate the news with the rest of the small staff. The station's engineer seemed to enjoy rigging up the satellite dishes and new equipment necessary to facilitate the show. In all, it was a happy whirlwind.

However, a number of residents of the town didn't see this as good news, for obvious reasons. In the week leading up to the nationwide debut, they picketed the radio station with signs reading "Broadcasting Blasphemy!" and "Missing the Point - God". The newspaper ran an article on the launch but focused more on the controversy surrounding the show and Graham's checkered past. The Church of Christ continued their boycott of the station.

Quietly though, a string of sponsors began to get on board and the syndication guys loved the bad press. They used it to their advantage got as much mileage out of it as possible. They called Graham's show "shocking" and "in-your-face" and even "groundbreaking". It was titillating. The radio industry press was kind. They referred to Graham as the "comeback kid" and told his story with reverence and lively humor. Former bosses came out of the woodwork to sing his praises and tell funny stories about Graham's drunken tenure at their respective stations. To hear them recount it now, Graham was always more of a lovable, good-natured drunk in the mold of Dean Martin rather than his previous, more notorious, persona. It turns out that deep down; Graham was actually just a tortured artist, battling demons that he finally conquered. Everybody loved him now. All was forgiven. Of course, Graham didn't buy it, but he did allow himself to enjoy the redemption.

The show was to include music, but the primary focus, of course, was to be on Graham's discourse with his otherworldly co-host. The day of the first national broadcast, Graham arrived scared to death that the voice might not make an appearance. His backup plan was essentially a reversion back to his former, major market program. He had even spent a considerable amount of time listening to his own old air checks in an attempt to re-learn his own shtick. It wouldn't be hard to get back on that horse if need be, he finally concluded. He was convinced, however, that it would, most likely, alienate much of his local audience. When the clock struck 3pm that day, buttons were pushed, and Graham's voice was now heard not only in Alabama but Atlanta, his old Dallas stomping grounds, and thirty three other markets nationwide. He took a deep breath and cracked the mic as his theme music began its fade.

"Good afternoon and welcome to the Graham Barry Program. I'm Graham and, well, welcome to the inaugural nationwide broadcast. Most of you don't know me. Some of you do. Hello, Dallas. What I'm hoping you'll hear today is an unusual piece of folly as I'm typically joined by a man from outer space. Yes. You heard correctly. My co-host is a being that claims to..."

"This is incorrect."

Graham breathed a sigh of relief. For the first time, he was happy to hear the voice, but a cheesy music bed came up under their conversation. Apparently, this was something the network had planned.

"And there he is now. What did I get incorrect?"

"We are not of your world but you are of ours."

"That's what I said. You're from outer-space."

"This is incorrect."

"Okay, fine. How about explaining what you mean?"

"When we speak of your world, we speak not only of your planet but your solar system and your universe."

"So, you're not from our universe."

"This is correct."

"Where exactly are you?"

"This will be complex for you."

"Again with the insults? Friends, the voice insults me a lot. Try me."

"It is not to be an insult. Our bodies exist on separate planes. In a short time, this will change."

"Ahhh, yes. The great evolution you keep speaking about."

"This is correct."

"When exactly can we expect this evolution to begin? I, for one, am ready to get evolving."

"This is good. Time is relative but, as you measure it, it will begin in one hour."

Graham paused for a moment. The pirate was setting up some sort of stunt, and he felt more than a little helpless. His mind began to race, concerned that now he would be expected to launch a nationwide promotion with zero preparation.

"One hour? Well, that's not a lot of time, buddy. I'm not sure I can evolve that fast."

"This process will be gradual. You need not evolve immediately."

"Well, that's good news. What exactly will happen?"

"Our worlds will be joined."

"I knew it. You're invading us. Watch out, everybody, here come the spacemen."

"This is incorrect."

"So, is this going to be, like, Bam! Our worlds are joined or will this be more of a 'they are already among us' sort of thing?"

"We are not physically among you, but will be, in time. Your world will be aware of our presence."

That sounded rather ominous. Graham wasn't sure if he liked where the pirate was taking this. The last thing he needed was to be accused of using his show to make terrorist threats. "Are we talking explosions and great distress in the streets? Rainbows and unicorns? What?"

"We mean you no harm. Quite the contrary. There

are no unicorns."

"You heard it here first, folks. There will be no unicorns at the apocalypse."

"This is correct."

It didn't sound like the pirate was joking. This was going in a weird direction. Graham looked out the studio window to the hallway. He saw Mike and Chris at the window. Mike gave him a kindly smile and thumbs up. Chris mouthed "take some calls". He was right. "Okay, spaceman, let's take some calls, what do you say?"

"This is acceptable."

"Ladies and gentlemen, it's your opportunity to speak to a man from another world. Here's how this works. You call 1-800-256-GRAM. I put you on the air. You ask him whatever you like. He changes your life."

"This is correct."

"Well, aren't you confident as hell? Y'know, I didn't think you were going to show up today. I figured you'd screw me on the first day national."

"This broadcast was predetermined."

"I see. And the last three days weren't?"

"This is correct."

"Whatever. To the phones we go. Caller, you're on the air."

"Graham Barry!! It freakin' rocks that you're back on in Dallas, man!" said the caller.

"Thanks, dude. Who's this?"

"You can just call me... The Muffin Man." The caller began to laugh uproariously.

"Oh, hey. I remember you." This guy had been a regular on Graham's Dallas show. He was kind an odd dude. He'd fit in nicely with his co-host.

"Hell, yeah, brother! We've missed you out here. Last time I saw you, you were hella drunk, pissing on a cop car outside the Melody Bar."

"Lovely. I'm glad I could grace you with such a memory."

"You still party, man?"

"Of course. Only now I party with the spacemen, bro. I've upped my standards. So up yours!"

"Hahahahahaha! Niiiice, dude!"

"You got a question for said spaceman?"

"Sure. I got a question. Hey, spaceman, when you come to party are you bringing the space drugs?"

"We bring enlightenment," said the voice.

"I guess that's a yes," the caller laughed. "G.B. you freakin' rock, dude. You're cray!!"

"Okay, Muffin Man, take care. Line 2, what's up?"

"Romans sixteen, seventeen and eighteen. 'I appeal to you, brothers, to watch out for those who cause divisions and create obstacles contrary to the doctrine that you have been taught; avoid them. For such persons do not serve our Lord Christ, but their own appetites, and by smooth talk and flattery, they deceive the hearts of the naive.' What does your spaceman have to say about that, heathen?"

"The caller makes a good point," Graham said.

"How do you respond, blasphemous spaceman?"

"The pending events are not contrary to your scriptures."

"What do you mean by that?" the caller demanded. "Now you're claiming to be my Lord Jesus Christ?"

"This is incorrect."

"Well, that's only person I'm expecting to descend from the heavens and He will do so on a day of great judgment."

"You may shortly be troubled in your world. Do not fear this for it has been predetermined."

"There ain't nothin' in the Bible about spacemen landing and evolving us."

"This is correct."

"You sayin' the Bible is wrong?"

"This is incorrect. It is unfortunate that your sacred scriptures have been altered. However, this too, has been predetermined."

"Oh, this is stupid. Somebody re-wrote the Bible

and took out all of the stuff about spacemen?"

"This is incorrect."

"I hope you enjoy your time burning in hell." The caller hung up.

"All right," said Graham. "We're off to an interesting start. So, Spaceman, why do we have to evolve now? How about next Tuesday? That works better for me."

"It must happen at this time. It is predetermined."

"Why so urgent? See, we humans like to procrastinate."

"Your presence is required on another plane."

Graham laughed. "We have an appointment in another dimension?"

"This is correct."

"All righty then. We're up against the clock. Apparently, quite literally. We'll take a break and be back in four." Graham closed the mic and the network took over. He walked out of the studio and into the hall where Mike and Chris were waiting.

"How's it feel to be a national radio star?" Mike asked.

"Did you hear this guy? He's actually threatening to make an appearance." Graham was obviously a bit rattled.

"Oh, that would be sweet, dude!" Chris gushed.

"Will you calm down," Mike said. "What's the worst that could happen?"

"Mike, clearly this guy is some sort of nut. Maybe he's been quiet for three days because he's been planting bombs all over the city. Have you thought about that?"

"You're just nervous, Graham. You don't need to be. You're sounding great."

"What am I going to do when nothing happens at four? The whole concept goes down the toilet. You realize that, right?"

"Well, I've already thought about that. At four o'clock, you'll be giving away five thousand dollars," Mike said.

"What?"

"Yep. Enlighten your new audience with that. Start handing out free money and these listeners will forget all about specifics. Not to mention your affiliates will be thrilled. He's left the door wide open for you on this one, buddy."

"Shit. Can I get five grand to give away on my show too?" Chris asked.

"Get syndicated, boy, and we'll talk. So, you see, Graham, you got nothin' to worry about."

"I just don't like it when he gets in to all of this Bible stuff. The end of the world thing kind of creeps me out."

"So change the subject. It's your show."

"What I need is a call screener."

"The network says you'll have one tomorrow. The phone company fucked up the routing."

"I know," Graham said and took a deep breath as he covered his face with both hands and exhaled.

"Graham?"

"Uggggh. What?"

"Break's almost over, son"

"Shit."

"Knock 'em dead, Graham!"

Graham ran back into the studio and had fifteen seconds to the show theme; an eternity in radio. He hadn't prepared his next break. He'd just go back to the phones, he thought. Chris left to continue prepping for his show, and Mike whistled a tune as he made his way to the lobby. Graham's program was being loudly fed into the hallways via the speaker system in the ceiling. It sounded terrific, Mike thought and he was quite proud of himself for coming up with the money giveaway on the spot. Once Graham settled in to the program, everything would be fine. As Mike rounded the corner to the lobby, standing at the front desk was a familiar face.

"Dr. Trumboldt! What brings you back here?" Mike asked as he reached out to shake the man's hand.

"I heard the show's gone national," Charles said, shaking Mike's hand.

"Indeed. The first show is on the air right now. It's sounding great."

"Yeah, I was just listening here. I'm glad it's going well. Look, Mike, can I talk to you for a minute?"

"Absolutely. Come on upstairs..." Just then, Mike heard a burst of static through the hallway speakers in the midst of Graham's program. "Um, give me just a minute, Doctor." Mike walked briskly back to the engineering room and found the station's chief operator hovering over a pizza. "Did you hear that?" Mike asked.

"Yeah, looks like we're experiencing a bit of heat lightning," the engineer said as another static discharge interrupted the show.

"This isn't feeding down to the affiliates is it?"

"No, it shouldn't be."

"Well, check on that and make sure, all right?"

"Will do."

Mike returned to the front office and apologized to Charles. The two men made their way upstairs to

Mike's office. Mike cringed each time he heard another static burst. In his office, he looked outside and saw the lightning in the distance. It was standard fare in Alabama on especially hot and humid days; a complimentary light show to go along with the unbearable heat. Mike was pissed that it had to happen on the day of Graham's national debut. "What can I do for you, Doc?"

"Well, these static bursts you're hearing, that's one of the reasons I'm here."

"The heat lightning?"

"Colleagues of mine have reported an extraordinary amount of magnetic energy being detected in the area in recent days. Outside of this particular event, have you experienced any other interference?"

"Not that I'm aware of."

"Strange. The amount of energy that they're reporting should make radio broadcasting nearly impossible in these conditions. No issues reported by your competition?"

"I got a call from Craig Morris. He owns the Christian station in town. He was insisting that the new dishes we've set up for Graham's show were interfering with his signal. Of course, that's impossible. He's kind of a dumb ass."

"What kind of interference did he report?"

"He said his signal kept fading and then, well, static bursts like this," Mike said as another flash of static buzzed through the speakers; thunder began to roll in the distance.

"Interesting. Any idea what's going to happen at four o'clock?"

"We're giving away five grand!" Mike said proudly.

"Would you mind if I hung around for the big event?"

"Make yourself at home, Doc. There's sweet tea downstairs and I'm having sandwiches brought in later. You're welcome to stay."

"I think I'll take you up on that."

Charles suspected that something strange was

occurring. He walked outside to the front porch and took a long look at the sky above him. There were no menacing clouds; the sky was a beautiful blue, in fact. Yet, the thunder continued to growl, and the sky flashed regularly now. He returned to the air conditioning and poured himself a glass of tea and settled in to the conference room. Charles messaged colleagues as he listened to Graham's program through the static.

"Welcome back to the Graham Barry Program. I am, in fact, Graham Barry, and we're joined by our faithful Space Man as always. You up for more calls?"

"It is better that we discuss the coming events."

"Yeah, we're about ten minutes away from something exciting!"

"Indeed. This is true."

"Well, I guess we can let the cat out of the bag," Graham intended to supersede whatever the pirate had in mind with the cash giveaway. "At the top of the hour, we're going to welcome all of our new listeners by giving away a ton of cash!" Graham ran an exciting music bed under his delivery. "That's right, be listening all next hour, for your chance to score one hundred bucks every minute! I want you to light up those phone lines as we pay off some of your bills. It's a grand total of five thousand dollars, fifty one hundred dollar winners. You could be one of them! Exciting, huh?"

"This is very exciting," the voice said genuinely. "I am happy with this news." Graham felt a wave of relief come over him. It looked like the pirate was playing along. Maybe he was a decent guy after all. Perhaps he was just as nervous about what was going to happen at four o'clock as Graham had been. Everything was going to be okay. "All right," Graham said. "How about some White Stripes to celebrate?"

"This is acceptable. However, we must first inform our listeners of what they will physically experience in moments."

"What? Elation? Relief that we're taking care of that pesky wireless bill?"

"Difficulty breathing..."

"Sure, I'd be excited too!"

"Dizziness and nausea may also be experienced, but this will be temporary."

Graham laughed. "Yeah!"

"Do not fear this. We will soon be visible to you. No harm will come to you..."

Graham felt the board in his studio begin to vibrate; the floor also seemed to throb. The lightning outside began to create a strobe effect as it flashed intermittently. Graham could hear voices outside his studio and he thought he heard someone say something about an earthquake. Graham noticed now that the vibration seemed to cling to the air. He held his hand up and could feel it.

"This will take only a moment," the voice continued. "The Dark Age is now complete."

Graham and the rest of humanity suddenly felt a crush of heat wash over them. This was quickly followed by choking. It was as if all oxygen on the planet disappeared for three or four seconds. When he could breathe, Graham felt incredibly dizzy and light headed. He felt like he was going to throw up. Then, an incredible high pitched shriek rang worldwide. Graham felt as if his ears would bleed. A massive flash of white light covered the planet for a second and then all electricity in the building went out. Graham heard the generators outside kick on, and the emergency power was thrown. Just as quickly as they fired up, however, power returned to the building, and they shut down. The hum in the air continued as Graham heard screams coming from the hallway. "Oh my God!" he heard the receptionist yell.

Graham forgot that he was still on the air. "What the fuck was that?" he said to thousands. Realizing his mistake, Graham immediately tossed the show back to the network. He stepped outside the studio and saw that the front door of the building was open. The entire staff had collected on the front lawn. Graham joined them outside and saw that everyone's gaze was fixed on the sky. He looked up and saw a massive black hole that appeared to float in midair. Lightning surrounded the tear in the sky and the hum continued. Graham saw Charles pacing back and forth on the porch, frantically on the phone. "It's incredible," he heard him say. "I'm looking at it right now. You can't see it? Is there data yet? Please send it to me as soon as you can. Holy shit."

"Best... promotion... ever!" Chris said as he placed his hand on Graham's shoulder and looked skyward.

"Yeah," Graham concurred.

He was sure that he was late for his break. Stunned, Graham returned to the studio as his cell phone began to ring. It was his girlfriend, Kelly, calling from work. He explained that he didn't know what was happening yet but told her he'd call back as soon as he had any explanation for the sudden hole in the sky. He jumped back on the air and did his best to explain to the audience what he had saw. "Ladies and gentlemen, we're not entirely sure what has happened..."

"We have opened a door," the voice explained.

Graham cleared his throat. "A door? A door to what?"

"This is a door that will join our worlds. We will soon be one."

Charles entered the studio, and Graham motioned

him to the second microphone. Charles hurriedly placed his headphones on as Graham raised the volume on his mic.

"Um, sir..." Charles didn't know how to address the voice.

"Hello, Charles."

"Hello. Um. Wow. I have so many questions. First of all, should we be concerned about radiation emanating-"

"You are in no danger."

"Okay. How did you do this? This concept of opening doors to other worlds has been theorized, but the potential openings would be sub-subatomic in size, and only exist for small instants of time. How are you able to keep the door open?"

"We simply will it to be so. You will understand this in time."

"It would take a colossal amount of energy to make something like this happen," Charles said to Graham. "Even the Large Hadron Collider, the most powerful atom-smasher ever assembled couldn't replicate this."

"This is correct," the voice answered.

"How?" Charles stammered. "Just how?"

"You will know in time but understand now that each of you possess the energy required for such an event of your own. You must simply experience your grand awakening."

Graham noticed that his phone bank was jammed up with callers. He put one on the air. "Hi, caller, go ahead..."

"What are y'all talkin' about?"

"The hole in the sky," Graham answered.

"Hole in the sky? What hole in the sky?"

"You can't see it? Where are you?"

"I'm in Atlanta. I'm lookin' up at the sky right now, and I don't see anything."

"Can we only see the door here in Tuscumbia?" Charles asked.

"This is correct," the voice answered.

"Line two, hello..."

It was a little boy. "I'm scared."

"Do not be frightened," a female voice answered.

"Mommy?"

"What the fuck?" Graham mouthed to Charles.

"Hello, honey. Everything is okay. "

"Are you in heaven?"

"Yes, and you will see Mommy very soon!"

"I'm going to die?"

"No, sweetie, you aren't going to die."

An older man now came on the line with the boy, "What's going on?"

"Hi, Phil."

"Who? Who is this?"

"It's me, Phil."

"Marianne? My wife died last year. Who the hell is this? This isn't funny!"

"Andy, are you still there?"

"Yes," the little boy answered.

"Tonight when you go to bed, honey, say your prayers and kiss your blue rhino for me, okay?"

"Okay."

"I'll see you soon."

"Marianne?" the man said, his voice cracking.

"Yes, Phil?"

"I'm confused. What's happening? Where are you?"

"Our worlds will soon join. Be patient and you will see me soon, okay?"

"Okay."

"I love you both"

CHAPTER THREE

It's kind of nice out here," Alicia said as the SUV sped down the winding, two lane road into the Alabama countryside.

"Yeah," Brady agreed. "I've always wanted to live in a place like this. Out in the country, y'know?" The SUV engine whined into high gear as they made their way up an incline. The radio quietly provided a soundtrack as Alicia peered out the passenger side window, taking in the stone laden creek and pine trees. "Do a little fishing," Brady continued. "I bet they have good hunting out here. What do they hunt here? Deer? Oh, maybe wi- "

"Holy shit! Fuck! Stop! Stop!!" Alicia screamed.

Brady slammed on the brakes, and the SUV

screeched to a halt. He and Alicia felt their seat belts tighten as random equipment flew forward from the backseat. Alicia's coffee landed on the floorboard and soaked her shoes. "Shit," she said and bent down to open the glove compartment to search for napkins. Brady stared through the windshield at the girl in front of them. She stood with right her arm outstretched indicating "stop" and now let it fall to her side. Her piercing, green eyes hardly acknowledged him. Her brown hair danced in the slight breeze as she took her eyes away from Brady to read something in left her hand. Alicia sat back up from cleaning her shoes with a handful of brown, coffee-soaked napkins. The girl's eyes met Alicia's and a cast of relief flashed across her face. She walked to the passenger side window with great purpose.

"What... the... hell?" Alicia said to Brady between her teeth as she rolled down her window.

"Alicia?" asked the girl, her green eyes aglow.

"Yes."

"We must speak."

"I can see that. What the hell are you doing in the middle of the road?! We could have killed you..."

"May I enter your vehicle?"

Alicia looked at Brady. He was still dumbfounded from the near-accident. Alicia threw her hands up. "Yeah. Okay. Sure! Why not?"

The girl got in the backseat as Alicia punched Brady in the arm and woke him from his stupor. "Ow! What?!"

"You must keep driving," the girl said as she closed the door. Brady and Alicia sat motionless for a moment. "Now!"

"Well," said Alicia. "Go... I guess."

"Where am I going?" he asked.

"Drive forward at top speed," said the girl. "Do not stop again and please do not panic."

"Do what? What do you mean? Panic?"

"Just go!" Brady threw the truck into gear and sped up to forty miles per hour. "Go faster," the girl demanded, not taking her eyes away from the electronic device she held in her hand. She punched the touch-screen and scrolled frantically as Alicia looked her over from the passenger seat.

"Look, young lady..." Brady began to protest in the rear-view mirror.

"Faster!" she shouted.

Against his better judgment, Brady sped up now to eighty miles per hour. The landscape sped by them as he struggled to maintain control of the SUV in the winding turns. Alicia reattached her seat belt. Suddenly, they felt something slam into the front of their vehicle. The right side of the truck rose twice. They had hit something.

"Shit! What was that?!" Alicia shouted.

"I don't know! I didn't see anything!" he shouted back as he began to stop the truck.

"Don't stop. Keep driving," the girl said. "It might not be dead."

"Oh, what the fuck kind of psycho are you?!" Brady yelled at her. "We're turning around."

"That's not a good idea," the girl warned.

He found a gravel shoulder and repositioned the SUV. The girl in the backseat checked her monitor. She shook her device feverishly, pressed the screen twice and waited for a response. She aimed it toward the front windshield. A sharp tone sounded and she sunk back in her seat, seemingly more relaxed. Ahead of them, something lay in the road. It wasn't moving. Apparently, it was some sort of large armadillo. Brady stopped the truck. "At least it wasn't human," he said.

"Should we move it to the side of the road?" Alicia asked.

"No! Absolutely not." the girl insisted. "Leave it alone."

"All right, now you just shut the hell up, do you understand?" Alicia pointed her finger at the girl. "The adults are talking now. Do you hear me?"

The girl shrugged. "It's a bad idea. That's all I'm saying."

"How am I supposed to move it without touching

it?" asked Brady. "Hand me that mic stand."

The girl grabbed the folded boom mic to her left and reluctantly handed it to Brady. The girls watched as he slowly made his way to the corpse in the road. As he moved closer, Brady realized that this was not any kind of animal that he recognized. It didn't seem to be breathing. He extended the metal rod and inched nearer.

"Hold your ears," said the backseat girl as she covered her own.

No sooner could Alicia say a word did Brady prod the animal and the creature unleashed a scream so powerful that it shattered every window in the SUV and the nearby farmhouse. Alicia winced, held her ears and clinched her teeth tight. Her head rattled from the shriek. Brady was thrown to the side of the road. He desperately masked his ears, writhing in agony. The girl in the backseat shielded hers as well as she let herself out of the vehicle and walked toward the wailing beast. She unsheathed a blade from her pocket. The girl cupped her ears, knife in hand, as she made her way to the creature. Finally, she held her breath and let her ears go as she cut into the creature's neck and skillfully removed its vocal cords and tossed them aside as one might silence a car horn. The scream ceased and the creature grew four times its original size, knocking the girl into a ditch. It was then erased from view. Like a satellite signal being lost, it crackled, blinked and faded. The girl shook her head, picked herself up as quickly as she could and rushed to Brady to help him to his feet. She walked him back to the truck.

"You should drive," she told Alicia.

"I can't hear," Brady said.

"Can you hear? Do you have paper?" the girl asked Alica.

"Yes."

"Write. Tell him that he will not be able to hear for several hours. His hearing will return. It's likely that he will not have an erection for at least one year, and he may have issues with acne for the remainder of his life."

Alicia paused. "What?"

"He was just exposed to roughly one hundred seventy five decibels, unprotected. He'll experience sensorineural hearing loss. It's not likely that there has been any death of tissue. However, the sheer pressure of the sound waves will cause some neurological damage, albeit reversible. How do your ovaries feel? "

"What?"

"You can hear me, right?"

"Yeah. Yes. I think I'll just write about the hearing part," Alicia said as she wrote Brady a note. "What the fuck was that?"

The girl immediately began sweeping the glass out of the seats with assignment binders that lay scattered about the truck. "Triclopod. It followed me here... somehow," said the girl. "It was the only one. Don't worry. We need to keep going, though. That wasn't supposed to happen."

"What was that?!" Brady shouted. "It looked like a man-sized roach with a face! That was fucked up! I can't hear!"

Alicia shoved her note at him: "She says you won't hear for a few hours. You'll be okay. I should drive. Some kind of Alabama bug." The girl directed Brady to the backseat where she had been sitting and gently placed him amidst the remaining broken glass and strewn equipment. She helped him with his seat belt, and once he was comfortable, she shut the door. Alicia had not moved from the passenger seat. The girl stood at the door and spoke to her from the broken window. "Ma'am, we should go."

Alicia glared at the girl and crossed her arms. "Triclopod?"

"Yes," she sensed that Alicia was pissed. The young woman took a deep breath, smiled and said, "I suppose now would be a good time."

"For what?"

The girl looked Alicia square in the eye and spoke confidently, "Quasihemidemisemiquaver."

Alicia stared blankly back at her.

Sariana blinked, cleared her throat and said louder,

"Quasihemidemisemiquaver."

Still nothing.

"You want a quarter? What?"

The girl felt a cold sweat come over her and she suddenly turned pale. "Oh. Shit."

"What? What's oh shit?"

A revelation struck her like an avalanche. They were here. Nervously, she surveyed the landscape. Now she was seeing spots. The girl felt as though she might vomit. Alicia noticed this immediately.

"Are you okay? You're not having a seizure are you?"

Static.

She was losing her grip.

"Look, what's your damage, kid? Seriously, what's going on here? I think I need to call an ambulance for you two..."

The girl was visibly flustered and tried to concentrate. "No. Umm... okay. Listen, I promise that

I'll try to explain everything if you just drive."

"Hey, you guys... What's going on?!" Brady shouted from the backseat.

With that, Alicia angrily opened the door. Shards of glass fell from her clothes to the smoldering asphalt. She shook the remaining pieces from her outfit as she walked to the driver's side of the SUV. The birds, suddenly hushed by the scream of another world's monster, now began to tentatively chirp once again. Their timid song was now the lone noise in the Alabama countryside, amidst the crunching glass beneath Alicia's feet. She entered the opposite side of the truck and slammed the door. More shards of glass broke loose from the window frame and landed in her lap. Alicia rolled her eyes and started the truck.

"What? You don't have your license yet?" Alicia snarled at the girl, who now had a somewhat manic look about her.

"I don't know what you mean."

"You can't drive yourself? I mean, you can rip the throat out of a giant fucking bug, but you can't drive a car?"

"No. I don't think I can."

Alicia engaged the brake and threw the truck in gear. She covered her face with both hands and inhaled deeply. Her brain needed a moment to process the last few minutes. She wrung her hands and exhaled. "Where are we going?" Alicia asked as she tried to pick the glass remnants out of her skirt.

The girl shook herself out of her daze. "Um... we need to go where you broadcast."

"You want to go the studio?"

"Yes. I mean, I think we should anyway."

"Why?"

The girl quickly scrolled through her electronic device and turned up the volume on the radio. "We need to tell everyone to stay inside, away from the elemental rain."

Alicia turned down the radio. "Was that bug a result of the rain?"

"Sort of." The girl double checked the frequency

and, again turned up the radio.

"Listen," Alicia said as turned the radio off. "I need you to focus. What kind of information do you have? If you have something that you need to tell me..." She noticed the girl getting a bit teary-eyed. "Seriously, are you okay?"

"Yeah. I'm fine. It's all... it's just unexpected. I'm just a little freaked out."

"What's freaking you out? The bug?"

"Yeah. The triclopod. I'm stressed, okay?"

Alicia saw that the girl was trembling now. She slowly put the truck back in park. Alicia was truly at a loss. She didn't know much about comforting anyone. Alicia turned in her seat to face the girl and softly took her hand. All at once, the girl began to cry.

"Hey, is everything all right?!" Brady shouted from the backseat.

Alicia mouthed "Shut... The... Fuck... Up". He understood. "Honey... what's your name?"

"Sariana."

"Sara, I understand that you feel you have something important that you need to tell the people..."

"Yes," the girl's voice cracked as she nodded.

"But, sweetie, I need to get the full story before I can help you do that. Do you understand?"

"Yes. I understand. I know. I do," she said between sniffles. Finally, Sariana broke down. She couldn't help it. The moment was just too much and nothing was right.

The girl began to sob and Alicia hesitantly took Sariana in her arms. The girl quickly grabbed her tight. Alicia held her breath and Sariana began to cry harder. For Alicia's part, it was awkward but she did her best to participate in the embrace and let her get it all out. After a minute or so, Sariana finally let go.

She nervously smiled and laughed as she wiped her nose with her sleeve. Alicia politely smiled as well and tried to ambiguously dab the snot and tears away from her shirt. Sariana, meanwhile, reached into her pocket and removed her monitor. She pressed the screen twice and brushed away her tears. Sariana took a deep sniff and spoke to Alicia while referring to her notes.

"Okay. Wow. This is so weird. I don't know how this happened," Sariana said. "Maybe we can try... something else." She cleared her throat, inhaled deeply and read from her screen. "The visitors here today, they are not here to enlighten you. You are reinforcements in a war. Nothing more. All souls on Earth have been bred for war from creation. They're here to collect you as soldiers. They have designed you as the most vicious souls in the omniverse. This is why you are always at war with your own kind. You're attack dogs. Your souls will be sent to slaughter if you follow them. This is all you were ever meant for. You can stop this now if you avoid the rain. We will need as many of you for the rebellion as possible. Everyone must stay inside. Spread the message."

Alicia let this sink in for moment as Sariana flashed a somewhat goofy smile and continued to wipe away the excess tears from her eyes.

"Wow," Alicia said finally.

Sariana let go a sigh of relief and nervously laughed.

"I know, right?"

"That's..."

"Yeah!"

"...pretty crazy."

"It is! Yes." The girl suddenly became more animated. "So, you can see why I'm all like... ka-blahhhh! I realize this must... sound... strange."

"Right. Sure."

"It is crazy, really. I mean, for you. Not knowing... well... any of this. I'd be all like... y'know... 'Pffft! Whaaaat?!'..." There was a lumbering silence as Alicia took a long look into the arresting eyes of this frazzled girl. Sariana got a bit nervous. "The inter-dimensional rip, the fog... and now me, I guess. It's a lot." Sarianna touched Alicia's knee and whispered, "This must be really weird for you."

Alicia was a professionally trained journalist, one of the best in her field. It was in her nature to cut through the bullshit and get to the heart of a story. "So... what you're saying is... the voice we've been listening to..."

"Yes..."

"Is an army recruiter?"

"No. Well..." Sariana was confused. "What? I'm sorry. I guess I'm not sure what you mean."

Alicia had the weird girl sized up in her mind. Sara was a gentle kid, probably an artist of some sort. Somehow, she thought, her imagination had gotten the better of her. She suspected that her parents had died in some way while making the trip to Tuscumbia. In an attempt to block out the event, Alicia imagined that she must have created this new reality. She must be suffering from some sort of dissociative disorder. Of course, none of that explained the screaming man-roach.

"Go back to that thing. The bug. What's a Triclopod?"

"They are an aggressor species. They exist only to bring about destruction. The Triclopods possess a great perversion for violence. I don't understand how it was able to cross. The Izanagi made them this way."

"Ozzy noddy? What is that?"

"A highly ascended soul group, presently allied with the Humans."

Alicia's eyes lit up. "So this is all some sort of government conspiracy? I can run with that. Do you seriously have information about this? Hold on. How would you have that sort of intel?" Alicia knew it was impossible that some farm girl from Alabama would be privy to anything classified... but still. Maybe she was some kind of hacker. "Have you told anyone else?"

"No," Sariana said quite seriously. "You are not Human."

"I'm not Human?"

"Not you in particular. I mean, none of you are Human. You were made in their image but you are a different species entirely."

"So... What? We're like pod people?"

"No," Sariana was starting to get frustrated. "Forget about what you are in this dimension. Forget this plane."

"Oh. I'm sorry. You're right. I should have phrased that differently. What the fuck are you talking about?!"

"In the omniverse, there are soul groups. Lots of them. You are part of a soul group. Everyone in this dimension. Everyone in this world, on this planet you call Earth. Your soul group was created by the Humans. But you are not Human."

"Jesus, kid. Are you on acid? Are there shrooms out here?" Alicia put the truck in gear and began the drive back into the city limits.

"You are aggressors. Just as the Triclopods are aggressors. But this does not have to be your only calling. Together, we can change the course of your soul group."

"We? We who?"

"Us. You and I. You especially."

"I change the world by putting you on TV and informing the world that our souls are on par with angry, space armadillos? That is what you want me to believe, right?"

"Yes. That's what we're supposed to do..."

"That's what you want me to announce, huh? Good evening. Sad, breaking news, folks. Everyone on Earth is actually just a bunch of drooling, slimy, screaming monster souls. Don't go in the space hole."

"No..."

"Then what?"

"You're worse. Worse than the Triclopods."

"Oh, good. It gets better."

"Far, far worse. The Humans are among the highest ascended souls in the omniverse. What they have created in you is well beyond anything the Izanagi could possibly imagine. Your souls are the culmination of hatred and anger so insurmountable that, in your present state, you could not possibly comprehend its veracity and the fear it provokes."

The girl was so dramatic that Alicia had to laugh. "Well, that's a little extreme, isn't it? I find it hard to believe that everybody on Earth is so reprehensible..."

"You are feared."

"Oh, really?"

Sariana was very serious. "What happens in your world, in this dimension, happens nowhere else in the entire omniverse."

"What does that even mean?"

"Think of your violence. You exist solely for war. Your souls have never known peace in any form."

"Of course we have."

"Can you cite one moment in your recorded history without war?"

"What? You mean no war anywhere?"

"Yes."

"I'm sure there has been..."

"No."

"I'm no scholar in things like this but I'm certain that we've managed prolonged peace."

"You haven't. It's just not in your nature. Even within your most tranquil moments, you still kill each other. Your nations might be briefly at peace but neighbor still kills neighbor, children die, you rape, you plunder. It's what you do. It feeds your soul. It's supposed to. Even when your body is at rest, you fantasize about death. It's really quite remarkable... and endlessly frightening."

"Yeah, I went through a goth phase too, sister. When you get a little older, you'll realize that the world isn't all evil. There's plenty of tranquility and love to go around for..."

"Even what you call love is brutal," Sariana argued. "And the way you express it is angry... and ugly."

"What are you talking about?"

"You procreate new vessels in violence."

"Sex?"

"Your imagined male stabs the imagined female form with a penile sword in harsh succession until it ejaculates a stream of biomatter inside her which itself must then fight to the death to impregnate a solitary egg." Sariana shuddered. "Even your soul's attempt to express endearment is savage and depraved."

"If it's done right," Alicia muttered.

"And you all agree that this is perfectly acceptable. I assure you that nowhere else would this act be considered an appropriate display of affection. What you call erotic literature and film would elsewhere be interpreted as a most alarming and reprehensible threat of hostility."

The truck was now at a crawl as they paced through the party-goers in Tuscumbia proper. Alicia somehow found herself fully engaged in the defense of her 'kind'. "That doesn't happen anywhere else? In this great 'omniverse' you talk about which I'm guessing is like the universe times a million..."

"It's beyond your comprehension right now...unfortunately."

"We are the only 'species of soul' so violent?"

"Yes. And what you experience in this dimension is only a fraction of what you're capable of."

"Ah ha! Bullshit! I thought you said there was a war."

"There is. The most catastrophic war in Akashic history."

"Okay, I don't know what that means. But don't you kill each other in these wars?"

"Only now. This is the purpose of your species."

"What? What is?"

"You are the ambassadors of death. More to the point, you bring death. Death is your creation. You invented it."

"We introduce the omniworld to death? The whole concept of death? It doesn't happen until we arrive at the party?"

"Yes. It is what you've rehearsed since the birth of your soul group. You've become quite good at it."

"What you're saying is... since we first arrived in the universe, we've just been practicing to be better killers... on each other?"

"That's right."

"And what about you? You aren't Human, I suppose? Or whatever the fuck you think I am?"

"I am almost like you. We no longer refer to ourselves as Human."

Alicia was genuinely fascinated with her mythology but Brady's phone rang. "Let me get this," Alicia said as she put the truck in park.

"Please, don't be distracted. You're asking all the right questions."

"I'm not distracted. I'm just going to answer the phone for him. Brady, where's your phone? Shit."

"I still can't hear!"

Alicia grumbled as she began to sort through Brady's remote bags, tracing the ring from pocket to pocket in a race to beat his voicemail.

"It's not relevant," Sariana protested. "Just as you said, we need to focus."

"Will you just let me get this?"

"His father has died. That is all."

Alicia found the phone and shot the girl a nasty look. "That's a fucked up thing to say."

"I'm sorry," Sariana offered. "He will only leave this plane."

"It's probably just the network checking in," Alicia assured her as she fumbled with Brady's phone.

"He'll have to leave the Tuscumbia," Sariana said, referring to Brady. "I don't mean to be rude but his significance in this parallel is complete. He drove the truck for you."

"The Tuscumbia?" Alicia smirked and finally answered. "Hello? Hi. This is Alicia. Yeah. Well, there's been a slight accident and Brady's lost his hearing. No. He's okay. Right. He was just exposed to a loud noise and it's only temporary. He'll be fine." Alicia looked at Sariana somewhat suspiciously. "Is everything okay?" she asked the caller. "Oh, no. That's terrible." Sariana turned her gaze toward the window.

"Who's on the phone?" Brady asked.

Sariana wrote him a note: "It's your wife. She requests that you call her when your hearing returns."

"Is everything okay?"

Sariana wrote: "Yes but you must call."

"My sympathies are with you and the family," Alicia said to the caller. "We're on our way back to the studio now. When we get back, I'll start making the arrangements for Brady to come home. I'll have him call you. Of course. It's best that he receives the news from you. No, he's right beside me. I will. Again, I'm so sorry, Kristine. Okay. Goodbye." Alicia hung up the phone and an awkward silence came over the truck.

"You were half right," Alicia finally said. "Brady's father didn't die."

"But..."

"His wife's father died."

"Oh. That's not right. No," Sariana said. "Did you do this?"

"Excuse me? What does that even mean?"

"No. You wouldn't... can't." Sariana tried to think hard and, again, began to quickly scroll through her device. "It's complicated. I'll explain all of this but we have to broadcast immediately."

"He had a heart attack," Alicia was defensive for no reason.

"Of course. Yes. I'm sorry." Sariana was now preoccupied with her handheld screen.

Alicia stared out the front windshield of the SUV, at the tear in the sky off in the distance. "Did you come from there?" Alicia asked, pointing to the black rip in the blue sky.

"No. I crossed over two miles from where you found me."

"Is there another tear?"

"No. This is an exit," Sariana said, referring to the tear.

"The voice said that they would soon be visible to us."

"That's true but you will come to them."

"So they really are going to suck us up through that hole in the sky?"

"Sort of. That's probably the best way to describe it for the moment."

Alicia's mind raced. She was well aware that, in this moment, she was either speaking to one of the most important subjects of her career or a complete and utter lunatic. The revelers continued their party around the truck as the two spoke.

"Well, just for sake of argument, why shouldn't it happen? I mean, if that's what we're meant to be: Warriors for the Humans. Shouldn't we just trust our creator?"

Sariana looked up from her device. "No one species of soul should hold dominion over another. Akashic Law forbids it and the Masters of Wisdom have denounced this. The Humans have gone mad with power. There will be great suffering throughout the omniverse. Your species brings death. The balance has been disrupted. You must rebel."

Alicia tried to take all of this in. Of course, it sounded absurd but, then, the entire world had gone absurd. The girl killed the freaky bug thing. Alicia saw that with her own eyes. She also came close enough to playing psychic for her taste. But Alicia had no tangible proof of any of this. The girl could cause a panic if Alicia let her unleash a rant like this on the air. She set aside the possibility that she might be a pre-programmed homicidal maniac for a moment. Panic meant ratings. It might mean a Murrow, Alicia thought.

"If you're here," she said to the girl, "then that must mean that the rebellion has already begun, right?"

"It's happening right now but what we do today, irrevocably changes the course of all things as per the Grand Revelation. Ceasing the Human ascension tips the scales to our favor."

"So, you're after the same thing? You just want us as warriors."

"No. They will send you off to slaughter..."

"We teach them death and then they... use it on us?"

"If the Humans accomplish their goal of greater ascension, they will know more of the omniverse than any given soul group; including death. They will then have no purpose for you. Your only directive will be exhausted. Your souls will be disposed. It would be far too dangerous to allow your souls to further evolve. You will be put down for the greater good."

"How? How would they do that?"

"Your kind knows this better than any. I suppose you could tell me."

"Just regular war, I guess, right? Killing. Another day at the office from what you're telling me."

"But it's a war you cannot win. Yours are infant souls. The Humans have ascended so many dimensions above you."

"If I understand you, you're just asking us to trust you the same way they're asking us to trust them."

"This is true but we need you as equals. We are one. I am descendent from your soul group. This is something we must discuss..."

"But what makes you different than the Humans?"

"The Humans had no right to grow sentient souls solely for war. They certainly have no right to extinguish your soul group when and if its purpose has been served."

"So, we stay behind. We don't stand in the rain. Then what?"

"There is a plan. We will help you cross over to claim your rightful place in the omniverse."

"And we go to war with our creators? The Humans?"

"It is in your nature to assume this. We do not wish for war. You are... leverage. It is our hope that if our numbers are great, the Humans will abandon their pact of aggression and seek only enlightenment. This is the wish of all species in the omniverse."

"Except the Humans? They are the only bad guys?"

"They have alliances but we believe that if the Humans are to fail in the quest for an absolute, these alliances will fall." Alicia began sounding the horn as she tried to navigate her way through the drunken horde. Sariana took a deep breath. "We should probably talk about you and I..."

Alicia's cell phone began to ring. She closed her eyes and sighed as "Dancing Queen" by ABBA began to fill the cab of the truck. "Hold that thought." Alicia knew the ring-tone. "Goddamnit, Hal." She tapped the screen and answered. "Yeah. Dude, I am literally right down the street. Right. Well, what the fuck, Hal? Do you want me to just mow down this herd of hicks? I can only go so fast." Alicia looked Sariana up and down. "Yeah. I've got something. I think so." Sariana smiled. "Hal, I'm pulling into the parking lot right now. I will see you in a min-" Alicia shook the phone in a rage and her face flushed red. "Jesus! Goddamnit!! Shut the fuck up, Hal!!!" She slammed the phone down on the console as she swerved the truck into a parking space at the Dollar Store.

Sariana giggled and began to tear up just a bit as she looked admiringly at Alicia.

"What?"

"That was so cool for me. You have no idea."

Alicia gave her a funny look and shook her head as she began to collect her things.

ଔ

Once inside the studio, Alicia found her producer.

She sat the girl at her desk while she first explained that Brady would need to return home to Colorado. Alicia then detailed Sariana, the giant bug, and Brady's sudden deafness. Regarding the girl, the producer hesitated.

"I don't know about this, Alicia," he said. "You don't have any footage of the bug. Things are really heating up in Russia and China. I don't know if L.A. is going to go for having a crazy girl on the air in the middle of it all."

"Who says she's crazy?"

"Alicia. The whole 'I've come from another dimension to save you from space warlords' talk doesn't strike you as a little... odd?"

"You are aware that there's a giant hole in the fucking sky, right?"

"Alicia..."

"And it's spewing yellow gas all over the planet-"

"I'm not going to..."

"And a spaceman is talking to us on the radio?!" Alicia smacked him in the forehead. "Are you high?"

"That's a bold statement coming from you, lady. By the way, you can't expense booze. I've told you that a thousand times." Hal began to walk away and Alicia relentlessly followed.

"Don't change the subject. All of this other shit is perfectly normal to you but this... the girl that kills space armadillos is crazy-talk? Seriously?"

Hal did recognize that he was being more than a little contradictory. "I know. I really do. You have to understand, Alicia. I've got new-age gurus coming out of my ass here. Every nut-case in the world is claiming to have some sort of inside knowledge. If I put every one of them on the air, our credibility goes right out the window. This isn't the George Noory show."

"But, I saw this."

"I just wish you had footage. I need something that bleeds."

"Let me see if I can get something more out of her. In the meantime, get the wheels rolling to get this girl on the air."

"How, Alicia? What do I pitch to L.A.?"

Alicia thought for a moment.   "Our angle," she explained, "is that this poor thing is suffering from P.T.S.D. This is what's happening to our children. Get a psychologist to comment about her state of mind. We explain to parents how to talk to their kids about this. Pitch it that way. By the time you get approval, I'll have something more. If I don't... well, I'll figure something out."

Hal frowned but with this, he agreed to run the story by Los Angeles. Alicia popped a few more pills and returned to her 'office'. She found Brady sitting on her desk, playing with the girl's monitor. He couldn't get it to do anything. Sariana was examining Alicia's iPad. Alicia shooed her away, sat at her desk and began writing her piece.

"When do we address the world?" Sariana asked.

"Shortly. They'll let us know."

"What? We should do this now. It's of critical importance. The cloud has already been released. We can't wait."

"There are procedures."

"Your procedures do not matter. This is taking too long. It's clear that I've already arrived too late..."

"Yeah, well, welcome to corporate media. We need network approval. This takes time. Be patient. Why not go look at all of our wonderful items of convenience?" Alicia said referring to the junk scattered about the store. Sariana was anxious and began to bite her nails and pace. "I'm not kidding, Sara. Go away. You're making me nervous. I need to concentrate and get your story ready."

"We're wasting time. And I need to talk to you about us."

Alicia was losing her temper. "What do you want from me exactly?! Frankly, you're lucky I'm even entertaining this story right now. If this isn't working out the way you planned, then why don't you back in time and do it again, goddamnit? I mean, what the fuck?"

"I can't," Sariana was meek. "This is my only chance."

Alicia calmed herself. "This is all part of the process. Hey, have you ever seen chicken and beer flavored beef jerky?"

"You and I really need to speak about why I found..."

"Sara, you need to give me just a minute, okay? Aisle three. Go look. It's fascinating."

Sariana was reluctantly intrigued. She took Alicia's advice and began to tour the store and think as Alicia and Brady remained at her desk.

"She seems like a sweet girl," Brady said to Alicia. She rolled her eyes and shrugged. Truth be told, Alicia was coming around to her as well. Something about the girl inherently intrigued her. She began to search Google for various doomsday prophets capitalizing on the tear in the sky. The producer was right. They were everywhere. Each more crazy than the next; selling eBooks promising to explain this whole sorted mess and offering redemption in fifty pages or less. "I'm going to make some chili," Brady announced. "You want some?"

Alicia crinkled her nose and wrote: "Smells like dog food."

"Tastes like it too. But I'm hungry and catering's empty 'til dinner."

A half hour passed and Alicia was finally given approval to run with her story. Family counselors would be standing by in L.A. to comment after she interviewed the girl. Alicia found Sariana in the candy aisle, sitting cross-legged, eating chocolate covered raisins.

"They're ready for us," she said. "I see that even in another universe, girls are still suckers for chocolate."

"It's delicious." Sariana said with a big, chocolate covered smile.

She really was kind of a cute kid, Alicia thought. Very pretty. Even if what she said was all bullshit and the world didn't end, Alicia thought that she would have a bright future. She didn't seem to be afraid of public speaking; certainly had a big imagination. Maybe she could even become an anchor or, God forbid, an actress.

"Let's get some make-up on you," Alicia told her as she helped her up from the floor.

"Make-up?"

"Yeah. You don't want to address the world looking like this do you?"

"I don't understand. We should do this immediately. We have waited long enough."

"It's okay, just follow me. No one's going to take you seriously with dime store chocolate smeared all over your face."

Alicia led her to a folding table with a lighted mirror that served as the studio's makeshift cosmetics room. She wiped her face with a damp cloth, applied a bit of base and powder. She even went the extra mile and gave her a little lip gloss and mascara. She began brushing the girl's hair. Sariana, for all of her hurry, took a moment to enjoy this. She closed her eyes and relished the bristles of the brush gently scratching her scalp. She indulged in the scent of Alicia's fresh perfume and Sariana did her best to memorize her every move. These were brief memories that she wanted to cherish. Moments like this didn't have to happen. Sariana knew this.

"Thanks," Sariana said.

"For what?"

"Thank you for creating this brief respite between us. It's special to me. I know you don't know what all of this means. I know that you don't understand what you've just done for me. I also know that you must think I'm crazy." Sariana smiled sweetly. "So, thank you."

"Well, you're welcome, I guess," Alicia put the brush down. " All done. I think you're ready for your close-up, kid." She looked over Sariana's shoulder to check herself in the mirror.

"First," Sariana said. "We need to talk about why we're here. You and I."

"We're pitbulls, right? Evil, scary pets," Alicia smiled and clawed the air. "Rawr!"

"You are, yes. I'm not," Sariana didn't quite know how to put this. "Thanks to you."

"All I did was almost kill you," Alicia said. "And, now, we're going to go on TV and talk about that bug and the war on Humanity."

"No. I'm here because it is my birthright. We are to change the time-line."

"The two of us, huh?"

"You and I. Yes."

"So, you're saying that I was predestined to meet you today?"

"It was your wish. Yes."

"My wish?" Alicia laughed. "And when did I add this item to my agenda?" The girl was silent. Alicia smirked at her. "Well?"

"It was your dying wish."

"No kidding? I'm dead now?"

"I'm sorry. Yeah. Well, not now. Don't be sad. Before, you lived to be quite old... and wise too," the girl stammered.

"So... we know each other in your dimension?"

"Not exactly."

"But all of this is going according to plan?' Alicia said as she applied more lipstick.

"Not at all. Not really. No. I feel that it's very important that you understand..."

"Alicia!" a voice shouted from beyond the cereal aisle. "We need you now."

"Look, I need you to understand something. I saw what you did out there. But I can't prove it to anybody. You need to help me convince the world that you're legit."

"What's 'legit'?"

"That what you're saying is the truth."

 "Yes, of course."

"Goddamn it, Alicia!!"

"Ummm... okay. Let's go." Alicia took the girl by the hand. "I'm counting on you, kid."

"Yes, I know but is there not time for us to talk?"

"You want to talk now? What happened to hurry the

fuck up?"

"I'm afraid what I have to say... this might be awkward for you."

Sariana's warning barely registered with Alicia. "I interviewed Charlie Sheen mid-nervous breakdown, kid. You want to talk about awkward? You'll do fine."

Alicia led the girl to the cameras and Sariana was quite impressed. She sat in one of the chairs beside Alicia and the director handed each of them bottled water.

"You have my copy?" Alicia asked. He nodded. "How much time do we have?"

"3 minutes."

"Where do I speak?" Sariana asked her.

"See the red light on top of the cameras?" The girl nodded. "You speak to the one that is lit up."

"Okay."

Sariana began to silently mouth words as Alicia fixed herself in the monitor. She straightened her jacket and checked her hair. "Oh, no," Alicia grumbled. "I'm glowing. Can I get a little powder here please?" A girl arrived to take the shine off of Alicia as she fanned herself with her notes. "God, I'm still sweating from this fucking heat. How do people live down here?"

"Alicia," Sariana said, hesitantly.

"Yes?"

"Quasihemdemisemiquaver."

"Why do you keep saying that?"

It was a futile attempt. The trigger wasn't working. Sariana looked around the room nervously. She could barely see anyone through the glare of the white lights. She was definitely going to throw up. Sariana thought of her Mother and Father. They would know what to do in this instance. But, fuck them. Why hadn't she been prepared for this scenario? Her palms were pools of sweat and the hair on her arms bristled. This was bad. Sariana saw dark shadows move quickly behind the cameras and she twitched. She looked for Alicia to her right but she couldn't see her in the glare of the white lights. Everything was happening so fast and it was all wrong.

The monitor lit up with graphics and the anchor in L.A. appeared on the screen. "Our children," he said. "Our most precious children. How are they reacting to the great changes occurring since the arrival of the OWL?"

Sariana swallowed hard and her throat felt like sandpaper. She began to cough and quickly she opened the water bottle and began to drink. The water spilled from her lips and she tried to wipe them dry. She smeared her lipstick in the process but the cold water gave her an instant of clarity. She knew what she must do. The preemptive would go forward. After all, it wasn't as if she had a choice. Sariana couldn't go back.

"Many worry that some may be suffering from confusion and even post traumatic stress disorder. How can we explain the events of the past few days and those of the coming days to them in a way that they can understand? For more, we turn to Alicia Parker, joining us live, on locat-"

The red lights on the cameras lit up and Sariana immediately began to speak with great passion. "My beloved Luciferians, it is with a heavy heart that I, Princess Sariana and the Grand Queen Alicia of the Third Order address you this afternoon. Today you are faced with difficult decisions but it is my hope that you will heed my call to resist the coming elemental rain. Stay inside and do not succumb to the coming rapture for it is a deception. You are not being led to your enlightenment as they have implied. You are being led to slaughter. Those who have addressed you previously are not benevolent and they do not wish you peace. They have misled you to believe that the Dark Age is coming to a close but, alas, this is not true. It is only just beginning for our species. You may speed your evolution by resistance. Stand firm and resist all provocations from your creator. Luciferians are a godly people and our souls are meant to serve our destiny in the omniverse alongside the Masters of Wisdom, not at war with federations we did not create. Do not be washed in this rain and do not despair. For a great savior is among you and lead you to victory over your captors, the warlords of Humanity. The Grand Queen Alicia shall lead you forward. Trust in her judgment and do as she compels you for she is a beautiful and righteous Queen. All praise her. I, your princess, bid you farewell and wish all souls Godspeed in your journey to Heaven. May you remain unwashed and may you stand proud as Lucifer once stood, second only to the Sun. Peace be with you."

Alicia sat stunned. For the first time in her career, she was utterly speechless. She tried to snap out of it. "I... um... she... she killed this really big... bug." The director gave a signal to cut and Alicia's composure began to return. "Wait! No! Okay..." It was too late. The red lights clicked off and the anchor in Los Angeles turned to his panel of psychologists. The dollar store erupted in laughter and applause.

"My Queen," Sariana said immediately to Alicia. "You must listen to me..."

"That's one for the Christmas party!" the director exclaimed, trying to catch his breath.

"What... the fuck... was that?" Alicia said, still perplexed and growing angry.

"I'm sorry! I tried to tell you. I really did!" Sariana

shouted to her above the laughter.

"Did you say I was the Queen of the Third Reich?"

"The Third Order. You are. You will be," Sariana now made a valiant attempt to explain amidst the chaos in the studio. "The Humans. They anticipated the Luciferian preemptive. This time-line has been manipulated."

"Oh my God. Why would you do this to me?"

Alicia's humiliated plea spoke to Sariana on a much deeper level. Her world felt suddenly as if it were further collapsing. Had she failed her Queen? She had to pull it together. "I believe we may be in grave danger. Remember what I told you. Please. Stay focused on me. Ignore this."

"I should have trusted my instincts. You're fucking crazy."

"No! Your Maje... er... Alicia, this is much more serious than we could ever have imagined. Everything I told you is true. You were supposed to wake up. Listen. Please. Quasihemdemisemiquaver!"

"Jesus Christ. It's time for you to go, kid." Alicia said, standing up and gathering her things.

"What are you talking about? Go where?"

"Go home."

"No. Alicia, please listen. I can't go home. I'm supposed to be here. With you. We have to figure out how to make this work together. That's the only way. I need you. There's too much to do."

"Well, then go do it. Just get out of my face," Alicia snarled, walking toward the door with Sariana in tow. The director moved out of her way.

"Pardon me, Queen Alicia," he laughed. "Forgive me, Princess."

"Yes, of course," Sariana said instinctively to the man. "Alicia, I need to explain. When I jumped dimensions... when I crossed over. We were being attacked... my coordinates..."

Alicia reached the door and held it open. "Out!"

"Please wait just a minute! I understand why you're reacting this way. I really do. All of this can be explained. If you'll just listen..."

"Your new coordinates... are OUT."

Alicia grabbed her by the arm and thrust her out the door, closing and locking it behind her. She turned to face her still snickering co-workers as Sariana knocked on the glass door. "My Queen! Please!"

"Oh, fuck you!" she said. "Fuck all of you."

"All hail the Queen!" came a shout from the back of the store.

"I'm calling it a day," she sighed. "Is there anything else for me, Hal?"

"I think we're good." Alicia began making her way to her desk. "Oh! There is one more thing." Alicia stopped and turned around. "Can you sign this royal proclamation demanding an increase in hazard pay? I'll get it sent right off to corporate."

Alicia flipped him the bird. She found Brady at her desk, surfing the internet and looking more than a bit distraught.

"My wife's Dad died," he said. "Is that what that call

was about?" Alicia nodded 'yes' and gave him a hug. "My sister in law sent me an email."

Alicia wrote: "I'm so sorry, Brady. Kristine wanted to tell you - why I didn't say. Hal knows you need to go."

"I understand," Brady said. "What happened to the girl?"

"You'll find out soon enough," she wrote. "I'm going to the hotel. You coming?"

"No. I'll catch a ride back later. I need to book my flight and take care of some things. Can you leave your iPad?"

Alicia nodded and grabbed her things. She gave Brady another hug and wrote: "Take care. Try to see me before you leave."

She grabbed a set of keys from the pegboard. "I'm taking the white truck," she shouted to the staff. "By the way, the red one's a little fucked up."

Alicia walked into the parking lot and shoved through the crowd. She felt stupid. That last bit of nonsense notwithstanding, Alicia had found herself starting to buy into the girl's crap. Did that bitch call her a devil worshiper on the air? Alicia had been caught up in the moment. Of course, who could blame her? She was just another person, worried inside about an uncertain future and grasping at straws. Still, Alicia hated failure with every fiber of her being and this story was undeniably that. Right now, the reality was that she fit in nicely among these yokels cheering on Armageddon. In light of this misjudgment, her arrogance collapsed. Alicia was ashamed. She was no better than these idiots. Had she ever felt compelled to cry, now would have been a good time to commence.

She trudged her way to the rear of the building and caught a glimpse of Sariana sitting with her back to the building, her arms resting on her knees. "Just keep walking," Alicia said to herself. A grubby looking man with a nearly empty bottle of whiskey loomed over her.

"Come on, baby, don'tcha wanna party?" the man said to Sariana.

"Go away," the girl said sternly. She noticed Alicia

and stood. "Alicia! Wait!"

Alicia didn't say a word. She unlocked the white truck, got inside and started the engine. Perhaps reluctantly, she kept an eye on Sariana and the man. She saw him grab her arm and Sariana quickly withdrew it.

"You know you want a little of this," the man said to the girl, clutching his groin.

"Go away... please."

Alicia wanted nothing more than to return to the hotel, take a hot shower and to forget the entire day's debacle. The sting of her embarrassment was still fresh but Alicia couldn't dismiss what she'd witnessed only hours before. The girl was a freak. One thing was certain, though. This brat wouldn't survive the night in the company of these fucktards. Plus, while she wouldn't admit it, Alicia was scared. Everyone was; even those morons raiding the fireworks stand next door, intent on blowing up the hole in the sky. Alicia didn't want to forget only the girl and the bug and the whole diatribe about souls. She wanted to forget that the world might be teetering on the precipice of catastrophe.

Would it be so wrong to confess to being just as terrified as the populace she so often ridiculed? To a degree, the girl represented to Alicia an opportunity to indulge in a hypothesis, no matter how ridiculous, for the ataxia that took away her quiet Sunday afternoon at the bistro, her watching sunsets from the rooftop, her longing for the future. No one knew what was happening. The girl, at least, seemed certain of something. Even if it was all bullshit, Alicia took some kind of comfort in that.

Plus, now more than ever, she needed to feel strong. The girl was someone to protect. Alicia sighed. Angry as she was, she couldn't just leave her like this. She got out of the truck and approached the man.

"She's a little young for you, asshole. Get out of here."

"Well, then, how 'bout you? You wanna part..."

Alicia punched the drunk in the throat. Hard. Sariana was startled. He grabbed his neck, gasping for breath.

"Why don't you just go home?" Alicia asked the girl.

"I told you. I can't," Sariana's eyes were locked on the injured man.

"Where are you staying?"

"You... fucking... cunt," the man managed, rising.

Alicia turned and kicked him in the nuts. He doubled over with a shriek, still clutching his bottle.

"Get in the truck, Sara. Sariana. Whatever your name is."

The girls got in the truck and Alicia clicked the locks shut. They began the slow crawl out of the parking lot. The man threw his bottle of whiskey and it shattered against the back of the SUV. Sariana nearly jumped out of her seat with the crash. Glass hit a few bystanders who then erupted in anger and threw the man to the ground. Sariana watched in equal parts awe and horror as one man knelt and began punching him. His rising fist was quickly covered in blood.

"So violent," she whispered.

"He had it coming. Better him than you. These people are getting pretty wasted. You can't hang out down here by yourself. Where am I taking you?"

"My Queen..."

"Seriously?"

"Quasihemdemisemiquaver."

"Oh... my... God."

"Quasihemdemisemiquaver."

"Why would you unleash that bullshit tirade on the air?"

"It's the truth."

"It's ridiculous."

"It's a trigger. Quasihemdemisemiquaver. It's supposed to wake you."

"I am awake. I'm driving a car, for crying out loud."

"You're conscious but not enlightened. The Grand Revelation indicated that this trigger would be embedded in your soul. Either you have failed or, more likely, The Humans have intercepted this time-line."

Alicia let out a deep sigh. Was she really going to go down this path again? She was exhausted. She honked the horn to disperse the drag queens now assembled in front of the truck. They gave her the finger and Alicia returned the favor. They cleared a path and she now had a reasonable stretch of road in front of her; 10 miles per hour the entire way out of town. They'd be here a while; Alicia decided to indulge her further. Why not?

"Okay. Wow. None of this is even coherent. You're just babbling..."

"The trigger didn't work. It was supposed to unlock your soul. I wasn't expecting to give a history lesson."

"Yeah, well, I'm sorry."

"We have so little time and the Humans are obviously already here."

"I thought we were going to them."

"That's how it worked the first time."

"What first time and what does that mean: 'The Humans are already here'? So what? They were coming anyway, right?"

"They're here to stop you. To stop us. They need as many of your souls as possible. They know that some will be left behind. But, if we are successful, their army will be far too small to achieve further ascension."

"What the hell do I have to do with anything? I put you on TV, isn't that what you wanted?"

"You are to lead the rebellion. You are the Luciferian Queen."

"Jesus Christ."

"I don't understand. What about him?"

Alicia shook her head and saw the highway up ahead. It would be clear and she could get a straight shot to the hotel. "Are you sure you're not going to tell me where I should take you tonight?"

"I am supposed to be right here. With you. I have nowhere else to be."

"Are you an orphan? Where are your parents?"

Sariana had thought about this. She realized that the entire preemptive may already have been thwarted by the Humans. "Not yet. I'm still here" she said solemnly.

"If I were an orphan, I'd never have been born." Alicia pulled the truck into a liquor store. "What is this? Why are we stopping here?"

"Stay here," she told Sariana and walked inside. It was practically empty. She found a bottle of Scotch and searched for a clerk. The store was abandoned. At the counter she saw a small stack of random bills so she dropped a ten in the mix and left. Civilization hadn't completely crumbled, she thought. She threw the bottle in the backseat and drove down the highway to the hotel.

"Where are we going?" Sariana asked, clearly nervous.

"To the hotel. You'll stay with me tonight."

"There's no time to waste. The cloud has been released."

"Look, you said I needed a history lesson, right? You're going to have to explain this shit to me if I'm going to help you at all." Alicia was more or less just buying time until she figured out what to do with the girl.

"The Humans could be anywhere. They might be at your next destination, waiting for us."

"Sara, I need to eat at least. So do you. It's a nice hotel. It's safe."

"Nowhere is safe."

 CZ

At the hotel, Alicia tossed her things on one of the beds and placed the bottle on the desk. Instinctively, she turned on the television and changed the station to her network. No one was replaying this afternoon's debacle. Thank God. Alicia handed Sariana one of the hotel's complimentary robes.

"Why don't you go get a shower? I'll order dinner. What are you hungry for?"

"I don't need a shower and I'm not hungry. There is much to do."

"I have news for you. You stink. And I can assure you that you need food. What do you want to eat?"

Sariana was frustrated. "I don't know. Chocolate?"

"Maybe later," Alicia smiled. That was cute. "Do

you eat meat?" Sariana shrugged. "How about a steak?"
She agreed.

Alicia helped her turn on the shower and gave the
girl her privacy. Later, the food arrived and Alicia and
Sariana sat in their hotel robes eating dinner. For all of
her protesting, Alicia smiled as the girl ravaged her
steak. Those raisinettes at the Dollar Store were
probably the first thing she'd eaten in days. Alicia
tossed a few ice cubes in a glass and poured the Scotch.
She took a sip and looked the girl over.

"See? You were hungry."

"It seems so, yes," Sariana said with her mouth full.
"Can we now begin our work?"

Alicia grabbed another glass, filled it with ice and
poured a Scotch for Sariana.

"Here. You've had a long day. It isn't gonna kill you
to have a drink. I won't tell if you won't."

Sariana took a large gulp of the Scotch and
immediately gagged. Alicia burst into laughter. "What
is that?" Sariana managed.

"It's Scotch. Alcohol. I'm sorry, honey. I thought you knew."

"Oh," Sariana cleared her throat. "It's good." She too couldn't stifle a laugh.

"You know, it wasn't that long ago that I was your age," Alicia told her. "I know what it's like to have an identity crisis."

"I know who I am. It's you who don't know me."

"That's nice. Poetic. Do you write?"

"With all due respect, your line of questioning isn't relevant."

"I'm just trying to get a frame of reference here. How old are you?"

"I appear to be about sixteen."

"So, Sara. Wait. Is it Sara or Sariana?"

"It's Sariana."

"Why did I think it was Sara?"

"I don't know. You just started calling me that."

"I'm sorry. Why didn't you correct me?"

"That would have been disrespectful."

"Disrespectful? Always make sure people get your name right. Get the credit you deserve."

Sariana smiled, put down her fork and took a drink, smaller this time. She turned to face Alicia.

"So, Sariana," Alicia emphasized. "Tell me, what's it like to be a princess?" Sariana hesitated. "I'm serious. I want to know," Alicia said genuinely. "All little girls dream of being a princess. I used to pretend to be a princess when I was little."

"You did?" Sariana laughed and began to let her guard down.

"Of course! I used to march around my house, commanding orders to squires and peasants, demanding that they all should kneel before me," Alicia recounted dramatically as Sariana giggled. "It's not often you get to meet an actual princess. Is that what it's like?"

"No. It's not like that at all, actually."

"Surely you must have people waiting on you hand and foot?"

"Well," Sariana said shyly. "Kind of."

"Is it great?"

"It's pretty great, yeah."

"Do you ever scream 'Off with your head' if one of them misbehaves?"

"Oh! No!" Sariana laughed.

"But you've wanted to, right?"

"No!"

"Not even just a little?"

"I guess maybe just a little."

Alicia poured more Scotch into each glass, and both girls took a drink. "What about your mother and father? The King and Queen? What are they like?"

Sariana became quite serious. "They're both very kind and generous. My mother is a beautiful soul and my father is very strong and revered. They are both loved among the souls they have been chosen to protect and serve."

"Are they both human?"

"Luciferian."

"Right. Sorry. You know, on Earth, Luciferians are what we refer to as devil worshipers?"

"What?"

"Yeah. They're Satanists."

"Surely, you must know. We don't worship anything evil. How did Lucifer come to mean something evil?"

"He was the arch angel cast out of heaven."

"No. That's ridiculous."

"Sweetie, haven't you read your Bible?"

Sariana sighed. "That book. Your Holy scriptures are incomprehensible. What does it say now?"

"The word of God is wrong?"

"The Bible is not the word of God. It is the word of Humans."

Alicia got up and walked to the hotel dresser and grabbed the Bible. She tossed it on the bed to Sariana. "Here you go..."

"I've read so many versions of this book. I know all

of your scriptures."

"Around here Lucifer is Satan. The devil. Doesn't it say so in the Bible?"

The Scotch was making Sariana surly. "Maybe it does now. I don't know."

"I can assure you that it does."

"Well, then it's wrong."

Alicia laughed. "Oh, really?"

"Yeah. Really. Lucifer was a planet. It's where all Luciferian life originated. When all were one, we lived in peace on Lucifer. Then the fraction occurred."

"The fraction?"

"A great civil war. As some Luciferians ascended into greater states of being, they aspired to control the solar system, even the universe and eventually the omniverse as well. The greedy ones were driven off the planet and forced to find a new home. Upon their return, they called themselves Humans. A great war began between our twin worlds. This resulted in our home being destroyed; flung into the far reaches of the solar system. The remains of our lost world are what you now know as the rings of Saturn in your solar system, in this dimension. With the death of Lucifer, all souls living upon it were captured by the dissenters. Some of these souls were admonished to planet Earth, but most were held captive by the Humans. We do not know their fate. We wish to reunite with them. We call ourselves Luciferians in honor of our lost, enlightened ancestors."

"Okay," Maybe it was the Scotch but Alicia found the girl's stories incredibly entertaining. "What happened on Earth?"

"The Humans ascended to even greater status in the tenth dimension. They were among the highest ascended souls in the omniverse. It was here that they did the unthinkable. They learned to create souls at will; a power not meant for any species to know. The Humans thought into being the First Order of New Souls in your world, the planet Earth..."

"That's us?"

"No. The Humans were dissatisfied with these souls.

We do not know why. We suspect that they were unable to control their creation and were forced to abandon the First Order. No one knows of their destiny but these souls were cunning. Their whereabouts is an enduring mystery."

"All right. So, what? We were sloppy seconds?"

"No. Next, the Second Order of New Souls were born. Praises, these souls could not be corrupted for they grew wise and ascended far too quickly. We know not of their fate but we do know for certain that they did not perish. Likely, they have ascended to a dimension above the third and remain in hiding from the Humans. They were quite clever."

"So, they tricked the Humans and ran away?"

"In simple terms, yes."

"Okay. So we're not these guys either? We're different people?"

"Yes. The Humans finally realized that if a species were to successfully dream something so abhorrent as death, they must create a soul group so equally vile.

The soul itself would be vicious and cruel; so full of rage and self hatred that it would not recognize its ability to ascend above its own imaginings. It must also be easily manipulated and slow witted so that it might not question its predisposition for hate for millennia..."

"Yeah, I see where we're going here..."

"Thus, was born the Third Order of Souls..."

"Uh huh."

"This," Sariana said excitedly. "This is you!"

"Third time's a charm I guess, right?" Alicia said and poured more Scotch.

"Oh no! Not at all."

"Yeah. I get it. I was..."

"You are the aggressor species. You were made in the Human image but meant only as soldiers. Your world was kept hidden in this unpopulated corner of the omniverse, long thought desolate since the demise of Lucifer."

"So, that explains why we've not been able to make contact with other life in the universe?"

"This dimension," Sariana corrected. "There is no other life as you know it in your universe or your galaxy."

"We are completely isolated?"

"Yes. The Humans somehow managed to erase our birth galaxy from the Akashic records so that your souls might develop at their will. No other soul groups learned that you were here until the exodus. This is what is happening now. I was sent here to stop it... or at least minimize it. The results were devastating."

"Why?"

"Humans wish to advance to the eleventh dimension, and this is forbidden. This is a realm meant only for God. Should they advance, they believe that they will hold dominion over all things. The omniverse is home to many great warriors but none as fierce as your souls in the hands of the Humans. This exodus will lead to your mastery of your anger and violence to such proportions that none can stop the Humans from their ascension to the eleventh dimension."

"Only we can stop our creators... and ourselves?"

"Yes," Sariana said. Was Alicia starting to come around? Perhaps she had more control over this time-line than she thought. "It is our only hope."

"Why don't these masters of wisdom just destroy all Humans and be done with it?"

"They cannot. Or will not. They have done little. Regardless, it is against the laws of ascension."

"If these Humans broke the law, don't they deserve to be killed?"

"This is your thinking, and this is what makes you so terrifying. The rest of existence does not believe this. Souls cannot be destroyed. This should not be knowable."

"But the Humans think that if they can get to the eleventh dimension, they will be able to destroy souls?"

"You, your kind can destroy souls at the behest of Humans. You present a threat. With you alongside as weapons, there will be few in the omniverse who will challenge the Human ascension and they will rise above God."

"Why are the Humans such assholes?"

"Humans possess a deep arrogance. They believe it is their birthright to know God and learn even more than the masters of wisdom. We don't know why they are this way. They have grown ever angrier as the omniverse has struggled against them to know this. It has upset the balance and many worlds have been destroyed."

"This all sounds like a pretty useless war. I mean before we show up and introduce death... when they 'kill' these souls, don't they just come back again?"

"Yes but they must start anew. Worlds that have grown for billions of years and ascended to great levels must begin again. We were meant to advance as one."

"Why doesn't God intervene?"

"We do not know this. We were not meant to know this. Perhaps God will."

"What dimension are you from?"

"I am of the sixth dimension."

"And I'm in the third?"

"We are both presently in the third dimension. Yes."

"So, show me some of your sixth dimensional powers."

"Powers?"

"Yeah. Can't you shape shift or something?"

"Not in this dimension."

"Holy shit!" Alicia laughed. "But you can shape shift?"

"In my dimension I can exist as pure energy. I suppose that is what you're referring to."

"But you can't do that here?"

"No. The third dimension is a learning dimension. Think of it as a library for souls. As you ascend dimensions, you learn more and develop more 'powers', as you call them."

"Sweet!" Alicia took a long drink of her Scotch and settled back on the bed. "Powers are cool."

Sariana watched Alicia stare off into the distance and change the channels on the TV. "There's more,"

Sariana said.

"Yeah, I know, sweetie. I'm just trying to see if there's any more news. I'm listening. Go ahead."

Sariana was losing her. The Humans had clearly embedded in Alicia's soul, all souls in this world, an aversion to their true history. "What I'm telling you is the news. I'm giving you world-changing information." It was apparent to her now that Alicia wasn't going to be moved by words alone. Sariana was growing impatient. The muted television flicked in the room as ice clinked in their glasses. The air conditioner rumbled its white noise as Sariana pulled her robe tighter and stood up from her bed.

"You're interested in powers. I can do one thing," she said and stepped to Alicia's bed. "But it may frighten you."

"I don't roll that way, kid," Alicia smirked and winked. "Well, not since college."

Sariana reached her hands toward Alicia's temples and Alicia quickly swatted them away. "I won't hurt you," Sariana said. "Don't be afraid."

Alicia looked into the girl's eyes. They were gentle but now also possessed a stern quality about them. It kind of freaked her out. "What are you going to do?"

"I'm going to try to snap you out of this."

"Out of what?"

Sariana touched Alicia's temples with her fingers, closed her eyes and quickly pulled her hands to her breast. In an instant, Alicia's spirit left her body and hung above the bed. She looked down and saw the girl standing above her body. An enormous panic came over her. Did the girl kill her? What was happening?

In another flash, she saw a series of images in fast forward. War. Blood. A baby. Screaming. Fire. Some sort of demon and she then felt pure, inherent rage. Alicia felt a roar building inside her spirit that was the embodiment of every atrocity known to her kind. She felt the sheer terror of every massacre, holocaust and murder born in her dimension and all of it emanated from deep inside her soul. It was the energy of her very being. As the rage grew ever-stronger, she felt as if she might explode. Absolute horror enveloped her but this only caused the rage to grow ten-fold. Suddenly, she felt as though she could possess the raw power of all of mankind's sins and inflict it upon anyone, anything of her choosing. In an instant, her fear now became her absolute power. Her soul began to scream a long, protracted war-cry of unimaginable vengeance. Then, just as fast as she had been ejected from her body, she was thrust back. Alicia took in an enormous gasp of breath.

Sariana saw the horror on Alicia's face as she struggled to catch her breath. Alicia felt her body, which now seemed to be rushing with electricity. She couldn't speak, and she was shaking uncontrollably. She quickly stood up, spilling her drink all over her robe and the bed. Some of the ice landed against her skin, and she shook the robe to get it out. Her legs were weak, and she felt faint. She tried to walk, slipped on the ice that fell from her robe and immediately stumbled. She fell just barely missing hitting her head on the corner of the desk.

"Grandma, be careful!" Sariana shouted and quickly covered her mouth with both hands.

Alicia lay on the floor, breathing heavy and still trembling. She looked at the girl squarely, and silence hung in the room.

"Grandma?" she said finally. "I'll have you know I'm only twenty eight years old." Her vanity had slipped but no sooner did she say this did an awakening come over her. "What do you mean, Grandma? And what the fuck did you do to me?"

Sariana slowly sat back down on her bed and took a sip of her Scotch. She looked at Alicia who was still shaking and now in a state of anger and confusion. Her eyes were pleading for answers, however.

"You are my grandmother," she told her. "I am your son's daughter."

Alicia didn't know what to say. All reason told her that this was ridiculous. Yet, whatever had just happened to her was undeniable. Everything was insane. Something inside of her told her that the girl was telling the truth. She struggled to stand, still shaking from the incident and managed to sit in the desk chair. She fixed her robe, cleared her throat and took in a jagged breath.

"Okay. I'm not your grandmother."

"You weren't meant to find out this way. I'm sorry. They're here. I need to improvise."

"Well, it's not true. I don't have any children."

"Not yet, no."

Alicia looked in the mirror above the desk. Something about her face now appeared foreign but she tried to keep her composure. "You were sent from the future?"

"You could say that, yes."

"You've got a lot of explaining to do."

"I understand."

"Start with what you just did to me."

"I pulled your soul from your body."

Alicia's teeth were clenched as she smiled and shook her head in disbelief. She slammed ice cubes into an empty glass and shakily poured another drink.

"Oh, okay." Clink. "Yeah. That makes sense."

Clink. Clink. "Sure. You just pulled my fucking soul out of my fucking body! Of course!"

"I told you it would frighten you."

"Yeah, well, it kind of fucking did," Alicia said as she shook her glass to her mouth and took a large drink.

"I'm sorry."

"Well, did you put it all back?"

"What?"

"My soul, Sariana. Did you put it all back?!"

Sariana couldn't help but laugh. "Yes. I put it all back."

"It's not fucking funny!"

"I'm sorry. I did you no harm. I promise."

"You can't just go around taking people's souls out of their bodies!"

"It was the only way I could think of!!"

"It's just not fucking polite!" Alicia shouted and finished her drink with a large gulp. She poured another.

"The Humans have corrupted this time-line," Sariana said calmly. "This is the reason for your doubt. But I saw your soul just now. No matter how primal the rage is inside you, there still exists a longing for your soul group. My birth vessel is your offspring and we are one. You know this to be true. You just need to escape the doubt the Humans have left to weigh down your soul. I'm hopeful that this will happen sooner than later."

"You can't just do that. That's like soul rape. You raped my soul."

Sariana sighed. "No, Grandma, I did not."

"Stop fucking calling me Grandma!!"

"Okay!"

The two young women sat in anger for a moment, each with their arms crossed, refusing to look at each other. The TV danced in the background. Suddenly, Sariana noticed her image on the screen.

"Make it louder! This!!" Sariana shouted, pointing to the television.

Alicia fumbled with the remote and raised the volume. It was the footage from earlier that afternoon, but it wasn't Alicia's network. The competition was airing it.

"My beloved Luciferians, it is with a heavy heart that I, Princess Sariana and the Grand Queen Alicia of the Third Order addresses you this afternoon..." Alicia listened to Sariana's speech for the first time. She had been so stunned at the studio; she didn't actually comprehend what the girl had been saying. Following their talks this little episode, the speech took a different tone with Alicia.

"The Grand Queen shall lead you forward. Trust in her judgment and do as she compels you, for she is a beautiful and righteous Queen. All praise her."

After the speech, a round-table discussion began with panelists.

"So, is this girl really a visitor from another dimension?" the moderator asked.

"I think we have to accept that as a possibility," one of the panelists responded.

"Yes!! They believe me!" Sariana said joyfully. "They're listening!"

Alicia half-heartedly smiled. She half-expected what was coming.

"That's absurd," another pundit shot back.

"How is it absurd? Is it any more absurd than a giant rip in the sky appearing and the OWL speaking to us? We'd be foolish if we didn't listen to her point of view."

"The anti-rain activists are simply jumping on this as a desperate, last ditch effort to support the Chinese; the Communist Chinese."

"We're so far beyond speaking about politics at this point. Don't you see?"

"The OWL has stated clearly that the unwashed will not advance. I take that to mean that those who don't not take in the rain will die."

"That is untrue," Sariana said to the screen. "What is the OWL?" she asked Alicia.

"It's what they've been calling the voice," she explained.

"That's... strange."

From here, the pundits descended into an argument concerning the pro-rain point of view, versus those anti-rain. The remainder of the segment focused little on Sariana's speech. It was still a victory, she thought. She sat on the bed, her face beaming; all smiles. Alicia took a long look at the girl.

"Why didn't you tell me any of this before the broadcast?"

"I tried. But I wonder... would you have believed me?" They both knew the answer and Alicia said nothing. "The trigger was supposed to cease your soul's amnesia. You would then recall your ascension. It would have been spectacular."

"I would have known what to say or something?"

"Oh, no. I mean, yes. But you would have also morphed into an enormous, colorful array of sparks and the sun was to eclipse as all electronic media and serpents broadcast our message worldwide."

"That sounds like a terrible idea."

"You, apparently, thought it would attract attention."

"Is future-me Lady Gaga?"

The girl became very reverent and bowed her head. "A valiant soul of many battles in honor of the Grand Queen. Goddess Dievas."

"Sariana..."

"Yes?"

"I'm more than a little confused. We all are. None of this makes any sense."

"I know." Sariana moved to the edge of the bed and took Alicia's hands in hers. Alicia now saw wisdom in Sariana's eyes far beyond her years. She gently spoke. "Your species of soul is not ready to ascend. You are children being taken from the care of your mother-world far too soon. But this moment has been thrust upon you. You can't turn back. I need you to be strong before your time."

Something was coming over her. Alicia was feeling a genuine affection for the girl. Was it the Scotch or was it some kind of maternal instinct flowing through her? Regardless, that strong, compelling urge to protect the girl had grown enormously. Alicia hadn't given much thought to the advancement of her soul. She hadn't been assigned a story to study the pro-rain or anti-rain points of view. She felt now that she had to trust Sariana. Something in Alicia now changed.

"The Grand Queen Alicia, huh?" she said to Sariana, smiling.

Sariana was a bit hesitant. "Yes," she said quietly.

"I've got to admit," Alicia said. "I like that."

"You are a great and powerful queen," Sariana said earnestly. "You are beloved." She bowed to her and rest her head at her bare feet. "You are to be worshiped and respected for you are my Grand Queen."

"Um..."Alicia stammered. "I... don't... know... what I'm supposed to do here."

Sariana sat up and smiled. "You could hold me again."

"You want a hug?"

"Yes, please. I won't cry this time."

Alicia paused and finally stood and opened her arms to the girl. Sariana stood and gripped her tightly. The embrace was warm and again Alicia felt a kinship. She smelled the girl's hair and tears began to well up in her eyes. "My God," she thought. "I think this might be for real. Am I going crazy? Has this girl made me crazy?" The girl broke the embrace and noticed Alicia's tears.

"You remember?" the girl asked her.

Alicia sniffed and quickly wiped away the tears. "Remember what?"

"Me. Do you remember me now? You didn't know me when we first met."

"How can I remember you? Like you said, I've only just met you."

"Your soul recalls all of your memories, from this life and beyond. I think you're waking up. Do you feel our bond? Do you know that I am of your soul group?"

Now, Alicia couldn't help it. She burst into tears. "Yes."

Sariana cried with her and held her again. "This is glorious. I'm so glad. Lucifer will be saved."

Well, this certainly wasn't in the life plan. For as long as she could remember, Alicia had painstakingly mapped out her own destiny. Nowhere in that plan did she intend on the whole Queen of Lucifer thing. This complicated things beyond reason.

"This is what I've looked most forward to. For my Grandmother to hold me in her arms."

"Okay. Wait," Alicia said and pulled away. "You have to understand how fucking insane this is. God, if you're my grand-daughter, I shouldn't be cussing around you, should I?"

Sariana smiled. "Your language is well known. You don't offend me."

"I'm famous for my potty mouth?"

"Somewhat. Yes."

"Great," Alicia grabbed a box of tissues from the bathroom, wiped her face and handed the box to the girl. "So, what kind of grandma am I? Do I make you cookies and that kind of shit?"

"You knew me only as a baby. My memories of you in this life are very faint."

"I thought you said I told you to come back in time? God, this sounds stupid."

"You told your children that this must be. The Luciferian Preemptive was your reign's most glorious legacy. I have always known it to be my destiny in this life," Sariana then paused. "But it happened too soon. I wasn't fully prepared. My education was not complete."

"So, what you're saying is that everything happening now... has happened before?"

"Once before. Everything except the Preemptive itself. This is new."

"Why don't I remember any of this?"

"Because, as of now... it never happened."

"Okay, Sariana. What the fuck?"

"Our prior timeline is being erased as we speak. The Preemptive dictated that only my arrival forward would mark the beginning of the Begin."

"That was the edit point? It's like we're recording over a prior recording with new footage?"

"Yes. Precisely. With every moment that passes, the old moments are gone forever."

"First of all, isn't that dangerous? Do we have a backup or something just in case?"

"This is quite serious, my Queen."

"Yeah! Duh! In future-world you don't keep copies of important shit?"

"There are many timelines in which numerous scenarios have been imagined. So, in a way... yes. There are 'backups'. However, this is the only timeline where you, as you know yourself in the present, exists. It is the only line in which I exist as your grand-daughter. It is the only one where you are the Grand Queen of the Third Order of Lucifer. In all of these timelines, the Human Exodus occurs without fail. This one, however, represents our best chance for a successful rebellion."

"Wow. I must have been some kind of genius to be

able to figure this all out, right?”

“It’s not that complicated.”

“Well, then why didn’t the Humans see it coming and just stop me from doing it?”

“Keep in mind, in your world, this would be equivalent to one day stumbling upon a cow doing basic math. They must have been surprised.”

“Oh, come on!" Alicia laughed. "What?! We're not that stupid." The moment was a little weird. Sariana said nothing. "Well, whatever,” Alicia was still impressed with her future self. “Obviously, I did figure it out.”

“Indeed. You pronounced it your Grand Revelation and it was kept a Royal secret until my birth.”

“Yeah. See? It was a big deal.”

“We’re pretty sure you had help. Most later-day Luciferian scholars agree that this is probably not something you came up with on your own.”

“Christ, Sariana, would you throw me a bone? You’re not exactly instilling confidence.”

"I am sorry, My Queen. I just want you to understand the gravity of the situation. The Humans did discover the Preemptive. In fact, it appears that they have been meddling with this timeline in an effort to corrupt your plan."

Alicia was quiet for a moment and poured another drink. She took a sip and somewhat shyly asked, "Can we, maybe, pause this timeline... until we can figure something out?"

The tales of Sariana's grandmother were always relayed in great reverence for a fierce and confident woman. Portraits throughout court portrayed the Grand Queen as brave, perhaps angry and vindictive, but never overwhelmed and unsure. Sariana was only now meeting this young, confused woman and felt it her duty to assure her.

"There is no Regent, be it King or Queen, Princess or Prince, in the long and virtuous history of Lucifer more revered than you, My Queen. I am humbled and it is one of the great privileges of my soul's journey to be here today in your presence."

Alicia was flattered but that seemed a bit much. "I don't know about all that..."

"If anyone can figure this out... you can."

"It's just... erasing everything seems... reckless. Dangerous."

"It is very dangerous. All Luciferians were aware of the risk. We felt confident that with your leadership, the Preemptive would prevail. In turn, the Exodus would be a failure and the lost souls of Lucifer would be uncovered. What is curious to me is why the Humans allowed me to cross at all. I'm quite certain that this was the reason for the attack prior to my arrival."

"Well, what exactly happened last time?"

"You led the rebellion of the Third Order as you will again but this time you must do it with purpose."

"What in the world possessed me to do that? How did I do it?"

"As you told it, it was quite circumstantial."

"You mean, by accident?"

"I suppose. You ascended with most of your fellow

souls and led the rebellion from within. As it is told in Luciferian history, the Grand Queen's First Revelation of Initiative occurred..."

"Another revelation, huh?"

"Yes, My Queen. The first. Of your Revelations of the Initiative"

"Just how many of these revelations did I have?"

"There were five of these. Children must memorize them in school."

"I see."

"I can recite them, of course, if you'd like. They're quite long, however..."

"No. That's okay. I think I just need to make a mental note to back off on the grandiose... stuff. Anyway, go ahead."

"You have always been destined for this. But I bring you knowledge. Now you know your purpose. We have successfully altered the time-line."

"What's going to happen next?"

"I cannot know this."

"So, what? I just hang out now and wait to become Queen? Do I go on TV and proclaim myself Queen? God, I would be so fired."

"I don't know. As I told you, the Humans have erased your trigger. They have placed false knowledge in your scriptures. They made it in your nature to doubt all prophets. The entire timeline has been altered... but, perhaps, only slightly. Your vehicle, for example. It was late but you still arrived as you foretold. It seems the Humans did not anticipate that I would arrive at all."

"In the original timeline... Brady and I just found a family to interview?"

"No. Just as you were to leave Brady received a call alerting him of his father's death. You drove alone. You were in an accident and hospitalized where you remained until the exodus."

"Oh. Well, then... thanks for stopping that, I guess."

"Everything herein is up to us. We are rewriting our

history from this moment forward."

"What about you? How do you exist here... if you don't exist at all... yet? Right?"

Sariana thought about how best to explain this to someone in the third dimension. "I will continue to exist until I am removed. For example, should we fail in our mission and my parents are never born, I too will cease to exist... at least, as you know me. My soul, however, will still be. That is to say, the very energy or matter that is my soul will still reside in the omniverse. I however, will not." Sariana sighed. "This is difficult to explain. Suffice to say, I would like it if we don't mess this up."

"Shit. Yeah. Okay. So, then... what now?"

"We must continue to encourage your fellow souls to avoid the rain. We are to also find the Exalted One. We must convince him to avoid the Exodus. We will need him to lead your souls to Agartha."

"Who is the Exalted One?"

"The one who the Humans speak through."

"I don't understand."

"The man who made contact."

"The radio DJ?"

"Yes."

Alicia laughed. "Okay. Why is he important?"

"His is an old soul and quite powerful."

"Really?" Alicia had seen pictures of Graham. He didn't seem all that special to her.

"His soul was not born with the Earth. He is of Lucifer. Should he ascend at the Humans decree, he may represent a great and powerful danger to the omniverse."

"If we can get him on our side, though, he'll fight with us and we'll win?"

"The Exalted One does not purposely take sides, so to speak, but, yes. His assistance is required."

"Isn't he a bad guy, though?"

"A bad guy?"

"If he fights with the Humans, doesn't that make him

bad?"

"There is no bad or good. He does not believe himself to be bad."

"So, he's been brainwashed?"

"He has been misled."

"Okay, so he is one of the Lucifer souls that got sent to Earth?"

"A great Luciferian Warrior Soul, yes."

"And there are more?"

"Indeed. Our finest warriors."

"If these guys are so powerful, why don't we just round up all of the old souls from Lucifer that are on this planet and get them to join our team?"

Sariana raised an eyebrow. "Does this sound easy to you?"

Alicia thought for a moment. Why did this seem impossible? All of the other bat-shit crazy ideas floating around the room appeared entirely plausible. "I'm just spit-balling ideas here. How do we know who's who?

Old souls from, um, new souls?"

"We do not believe we can know this until ascension. In this dimension, it is unknowable for all souls of this world exist with amnesia."

"So, you don't know for sure? Isn't there some kind of test?"

"The test is during the ascension. This is why it's important that you keep as many souls on Earth as possible, for the second Exodus. A savior will gather you for the true ascension."

"Okay. You mentioned that in your speech. A savior. Who is this?"

"It is your soul mate. Yours is to be the first union of its kind: a new soul and an esteemed warrior soul."

"My future husband?"

"Yes."

"No shit? My future husband is a galactic warrior?"

"Your soul mate is a mighty soul, born of Lucifer."

"God that still creeps me out. I still feel like you're

talking about the Devil." Alicia paused. "Is he hot?"

Sariana smiled. "I did not know your soul mate."

"Right. Sorry."

"You must think he's hot," Sariana played along. "You married him."

"How will I know him?"

"The savior will find you in your most dire time of need. This is predetermined."

"So, some dude is just going to walk up to me and say 'Hey, how's it going? I hear you're having a hard time. I'm your husband.'"

"Pretty much. Yes."

"All right. So, when does this happen?"

"I cannot know this. We must suppose that time will pass between the first and second Exodus. I do not know how long. The second Exodus, of course, does not occur in my time line."

"Okay, let me make sure I have the straight. In your time line, I got in the rain, ascended to what... the next dimension?"

"Yes."

"I got there and then what?"

"You proceeded like the others but had the First Revelation of Initiative."

"Right. That."

"Long story short, you concluded that the Human ascension was unjust."

"I just got pissed and quit?"

"Yes. I suppose it could be said this way. The Second Revelation of Initiative is, if you'll forgive me, vague. It's quite beautiful, though. You wrote of being visited by ascended spirits who speak in secret. You next assembled an army of awakened souls and broke away from the Humans."

"So, that's good, right?"

"Very much. You established a new home, on a new world and honored it as Lucifer. Your rebel world co-existed in harmony with the other galactic bodies. These other, more ascended worlds embraced your

Lucifer as a great protector against the Human aggression."

"No shit?"

"Yes. After all, the souls in your service knew death as well and inflicted it readily against the Human allies. Under your reign, Lucifer defended worlds incapable of halting the Humans alone. This lasted for one generation. This is not much time."

"Oh."

"The Humans grew weary of Lucifer's armies depleting their own. While we were once a nuisance we had now become a threat. The Humans launched a war of annihilation against our Lucifer, one which we were sure to lose."

"We were outnumbered?"

"Greatly, yes."

"Well, why didn't some of these other species step up and do something to help me? What the fuck?"

"Many feared further retribution from the Human aggression."

"Well, I won't make that mistake again. Screw those guys."

"Indeed, this is a crude rendering of your feelings at that time."

"I mean, I defend the shit out of them and then when I'm in trouble, they just say 'well, good luck, bitch'?"

"Indeed. However, I believe you will feel differently when you witness the glorious worlds defended in Lucifer's name. What has made you such a benevolent Queen is your compassion and awe for beauty presently beyond your comprehension. Bear in mind, the souls you defended truly had little to offer that might counter death itself. The savior will show you the way."

"My boyfriend is some kind of hippie?"

"Of course, this I do not know."

"What happened next?"

"The Grand Revelation. Upon receiving it, you accepted a Human accord for peace. In exchange for the return of the original souls of Lucifer, you were to cease the defense of those who opposed the Human ascension. Lucifer would effectively step aside and allow the Humans to rise and know God."

"Wait. I thought that was bad. Why would I do that?"

"This is one of our great unanswered questions, My Queen. It has led us here today. For the Humans betrayed you. You received their ambassadors and were met with death yourself."

"Those fuckers killed me?"

"Sadly, yes." Sariana then instinctively bowed her head in reverence and gently ran her fingers down her face, symbolizing tears. She next placed her hands on opposite shoulders and ran them across her chest, symbolizing what, Alicia had no idea. "The honoring of your vessel has not yet been eclipsed in the entire omniverse."

"So, the funeral was... like... Princess Di big?"

"Who?"

"Wow."

"I was born shortly before your death," Sariana said

and, once again, did the gestures, albeit faster this time. "My father, your son, was successor, of course. Per your instructions, he read the Grand Revelation and began my preparations for this, my destiny. He also vowed to avenge your death..."

"Right on..."

"But this has not fared well."

"Oh."

"The most righteous King Xander..."

"Wait a minute."

"Yes, my Queen?"

"Does he make you call him that?"

"What?"

"Most Righteous. I mean, that's weird, right? My son shouldn't be making his daughter call him that."

"It's a term of endearment; testament to his royalty. He didn't really make it up..."

"Okay. Just making sure. So... you're okay with it?"

"Yes. Of course."

"Okay. Sorry. Go ahead."

"The King - my father, your son - in response to your assassination, assured the Humans that he would share the secret of death with the omniverse. To say the least, the Humans have not taken well to this threat."

"Yeah. That was kind of a ballzy move. I guess he was just distraught, huh?"

"Perhaps but this is our fate. The Humans will likely destroy us all. I crossed over as our world was under siege."

"That thing that followed you here... that was an invading, what did you call it?"

"Triclopod. Yes. They have invaded Lucifer and are assisting in the capture of souls."

"Jesus, you're making my head hurt."

"This will make more sense to you when you ascend."

A knock came on the hotel door. Alicia stood up to answer it, and the Scotch hit her hard. "Shit. I'm drunk." She looked through the peephole. It was Brady with her iPad. She opened the door. "Brady! Come in!"

"Hi, oh," he stammered, averting his eyes. "I'm sorry. Ali, you're not dressed."

"What? I'm dressed. I'm wearing a robe."

"I can see your tit, Ali."

"Huh?" Alicia looked down and noticed that her right breast wasn't covered. She covered herself and began laughing. "Free peep show! News at eleven." She walked back to the desk and sat down. Brady entered the room and placed the iPad on the dresser.

"Thanks for letting me use the computer," he said.

"Of course. When are you flying out?"

"In the morning. I should be back in a few days. Hello, there," Brady said to Sariana.

"Your hearing is back," Sariana noted.

"Oh, yeah! You can hear!" Alicia laughed. "I'm sorry. I forgot."

"Are you drunk? Wait, is she drinking too?" Brady asked, referring to Sariana's glass of Scotch.

"Can I tell him?" Alicia asked Sariana.

"If you wish."

"It's cool, Brady," Alicia slurred. "She's my grand-baby, and as her grandma, I say it's cool if she drinks. Oh! Have you heard? I'm the motherfucking Queen of the Third Reich!"

"Third Order," Sariana corrected.

"Right. The Third Order. Thank you. I keep getting that wrong." Alicia made devil horns with her hands and raised them high. "Fucking Lucifer!!" she laughed. "All right! High five, baby girl!" Sariana smiled and gave her a weak slap on her hand.

"Yeah," Brady said. "I saw that. Sariana, shouldn't you be at home?"

"She can't go home," Alicia answered for her. "She has no home to go to. She's homeless."

"Oh. Did you try to find her parents?"

"You have no idea. Turns out, her parents are still in my ovaries. Well, one of them is. That would be gross if it was both. Your parents aren't brother and sister are they?"

"Well... no," the girl giggled. "It's... complicated."

"So, no. Just the one. That's weird. Your parents aren't even born yet. That's a trip. My space warrior husband better show the fuck up and make me a baby. We gotta make your ass exist! 'Cause I like you. No, no. I love you. You're my grand-daughter. Oh! You wanted chocolate. I'd be a shitty grandma if I didn't get you a Snickers." Alicia got up and began rummaging in her purse for change. "Did you see a vending machine, Brady?"

"Yeah, it's down the hall. I'll walk with you. It was good to see you again, Sariana."

"It's good to see you too. I'm very sorry for your loss."

"Thank you."

Brady and Alicia stepped into the hall and the door shut behind them. Alicia started to make her way down the hallway, but Brady grabbed her by the arm. "Wait a minute, wait a minute, Ms. Lush. Are you okay?"

"I'm fine. I'm fine. I'm just... a little drunk."

"Don't you think it's weird that this girl is staying with you?"

"You don't know the half of it, Brady"

"So, what's the real story here?

Even in her stupor, Alicia knew better than to try to explain the whole sordid affair to Brady, or to anyone, for the moment. She couldn't even wrap her head around it all. No one was going to buy this without a proper, well executed explanation. For the moment, by her own design, Sariana's credibility was questionable at best. So, she lied.

"Well, the best anyone can figure out is that her parents must have died or disappeared on their way here. Clearly, she's distraught. I mean, you heard her in the report-"

"Yeah."

"But she's harmless. She's actually a sweet girl. You were right. She just has a big imagination."

"I still don't think you should be giving her alcohol."

"I'm also giving her chocolate!" Alicia said as she made her way to the vending machine. "The cops can't do anything with her, the hospitals won't take her. I can't just leave her on the street. Some weird, old dude tried to accost her outside the studio."

"What?"

"Yep. I had to clock his ass." Alicia inserted her money in the machine and selected a candy bar.

"What are you going to do with her tomorrow?"

"Well, Brady, I haven't figured that part out yet, but you don't worry about it," she said, poking him in the chest. "You need to get home and take care of your wife. I'll worry about the crazy chick."

"You know, I still can't get the image of that thing out of my head," Brady said, changing the subject. "That wasn't just a big bug, Ali. That was fucked up. Was it chasing her?"

"Yes, it was."

"Jesus Christ. What the hell was it?"

"I'm still trying to get that out of her," she said and

began walking back to her room.

"Call me when you find out, okay?"

"I will. I promise."

"And take care of yourself, Ali. I worry about you, ya know?"

"Do not worry about the Queen! Go and enjoy the hotel porn!" she said as she knocked upon her door. She quickly remembered Sariana's diagnosis. "Wait. Maybe that's not such a good idea."

"I'll see you in a few days, kid."

Sariana opened the door. "I bring chocolate!!" Alicia said as she entered the room, waved goodbye to Brady and the door closed.

CHAPTER FOUR

World War Three certainly didn't begin the way anyone had imagined it might. Almost immediately following the invocation, the media fell into frenzy. Pundits were quickly split, and campaigns began on both sides regarding the elemental rain. While one camp encouraged all of the world's citizens to accept the rain or surely perish, the other warned that the coming storm was merely a trick by an alien civilization. It was equivalent to the Nazi gas-chambers, they imagined. It was an easy extermination of all life on our planet in order to make way for a coming invasion. They encouraged everyone to remain inside.

"I beg you, America, I beg you. Wake up and realize that a great and powerful evil is on our doorstep. Great and powerful evil is here," railed one host.

Another blamed the U.S. government. "Why am I

the only one that seems to see what's happening here? I told you months ago that these bloodsucking vampires from the current administration were not going to be satisfied with just sucking the blood out of American business. Their thirst for power and control is unquenchable. So unquenchable that they have concocted this ridiculous scenario wherein aliens arrive to put us all to sleep. Mark my words; they will not stop until you are subdued. Stay dry, America. There's only two ways for this movie to end: Either we become the walking dead, or you drive a stake through the heart of the bloodsuckers."

Later, inside the radio station, the world's foremost minds gathered to discuss the new development. "The Air Force was dispatched to gather samples of the crystals or droplets found inside the forming cloud," the General said. "You will all have access to these samples. Our initial findings, however, are that the samples do not contain any elements that we are familiar with. While they do not appear to be harmful to humans, we do not know the effects of long-term exposure." He paused and placed his clipboard on the conference table. His tone now changed. Milan saw the facade of a hardened military man fade for a moment. He addressed the table in a quieter voice.

"If any of you would like to leave here to be with your families, we will understand. I don't think that we can say conclusively what the effects of this rain will be. Our official position, however, will be to advise the world's citizens to heed the call and allow exposure."

A voice came from the doorway. "I think they're thinning the herd." It was Graham. He looked somber and exhausted. "I think they know exactly what's going to happen. They know us too well. I don't know how but they do."

Milan felt this was true as well. It was almost as if a game of trust was being played. Those who trusted the voice would survive. All others would fall away.

"Do you have any sense of what their end-game might be?" the General asked Graham, who was today equally regarded among the assembled intellectuals and military minds.

"I really don't know any more than you do," said

Graham.

Milan was curious. "Why do you think they chose you specifically to speak to?"

"The best I can figure is that it's more about the frequency and this town than it is me."

"But they addressed you by name. They said they were looking forward to your return. Perhaps you have had a presence on their plane of existence," Milan proposed.

"I'm pretty sure that I've never been off this planet."

"I believe we need to change our perception of what these beings might be," Milan contended. "They're not spacemen, and I don't believe that they are interstellar travelers. I believe that they must exist in another dimension. The many worlds interpretation indicates that we might exist on several planes of existence. It suggests that there is a very large, perhaps infinite, number of universes, and everything that could possibly have happened in our past, but didn't, has occurred in the past of some other universe or universes. For example, for every choice you make there is the outcome of your decision. You live in this reality. Alternately, however, the reality that would have been created should you have made a different decision may still exist as well in another dimension or universe."

"So, the me that did not become a raging alcoholic and shit away his career exists somewhere in another dimension?" Graham asked.

"Right," said Milan. "In fact, in another dimension or universe you may not even be a radio personality. In another, you might be female. In their dimension, you are an important person. You play some sort of vital role, it would seem. The question then becomes why did you cease to exist in their universe? Why are they making contact with you here?"

"Wait a minute," the General interrupted. "So, this whole thing is about him?"

"Not necessarily," said Milan. "For the moment, however, it's all we have to go on."

Charles had been pondering Milan's suggestion and finally shook his head. "Milan, with all due respect, Everett himself was not entirely clear as to what he believed; whether he actually meant that these other worlds actually exist. You know that. We're speculating on pure theory here. Take Hawking, for example."

"I understand," said Milan. "For the rest of the room, Hawking said that the many worlds interpretation only works if quantum theory applies to all reality. Of course, we have no way of really knowing this. At least not until now. I would propose that we're on the verge of finding out."

"What does this elemental rain have to do with anything?" asked the General.

"I think Mr. Barry is correct," Milan said. "I think its only purpose is to separate those who trust these beings from those who do not."

"But why?"

"Because they don't want those who do not," offered Charles and the room fell quiet.

The morose possibility that these beings were picking and choosing among mankind appeared to finally sink in to the assembled group. The General broke the silence. "So, they only want us to believe that this rain is some sort of necessity to facilitate their arrival. It does nothing."

"I think that's a distinct possibility," said Milan. "Somehow, it seems that they plan to join our dimensions as one and they only want those who are willing to accept this new reality."

"If they wanted to wipe us out, it would seem that they would have more effective ways of doing it," Charles offered. "I think you're right. This is about some sort of choice."

A theologian finally said what the entire room had been thinking. "You do realize that what you're referring to is the rapture?"

"Yes, ma'am. That is correct" said Milan. "From a Christian point of view, what we're looking at is an end of days scenario. At least, this is how it will surely be interpreted by the world's religions."

"So, wait a minute. I've been talking to Jesus Christ?" asked Graham.

"A colleague of mine suggested that you've been talking to God," said Milan, recalling Dr. Pembrooke's comments earlier that day.

"Holy shit."

"But, again, I don't think that we can bring our preconceived notions of science or religion into this discussion. This might have been prophesied but understand that the Bible and all religious texts, for that matter, utilize a range of symbolism to deliver their message. We can't really call this voice 'God' any more than we can assume that these are 'aliens'."

"But the bottom line is, if we don't stand in the rain, we'll die?" asked the General.

"The voice said many times that there is no death," Graham said.

"I think that they obviously know more about the nature of existence than we do," said Milan. "Perhaps when we leave our physical bodies there is an afterlife as many religions have taught. That may be what they are referring to. I do think, however, that you are correct, General, in that those who do not take in the new elements will perish from our perspective."

While the discussion in the conference room continued, world leaders began consulting with their respective cabinets. The yellow cloud continued to slowly drift across the sky and emerged from the black tear like smoke from a factory. The hum rattled on and the world's citizens gathered with their families, awaiting the advice of someone, anyone.

The round table in Tuscumbia made their official recommendation to all world leaders nearly an hour later. Citizens should allow the new elements to be absorbed by their bodies. Every man, woman, child and beloved pet should be prepared to stand in the rain when the disembodied voice gave the word. The American President took to the media first via the Emergency Alert System.

"My fellow Americans, what has happened today is nothing short of extraordinary. We stand on the precipice of making face to face contact with another life-form. What this life-form is, we do not know. Still, we are a peace-loving people and we anticipate only reciprocation in this regard. We have gathered together some of the world's best minds. Scientists, theologians, scholars from all walks of life. I, and all other world leaders, have asked for their best recommendation. While no one can say with exact certainty what will occur when the so-called elemental rain falls, we are recommending to the American people that they act as requested and stand in this rain."

With this, numerous other world leaders followed suit. England, France, Germany, Japan and Australia all concurred. The Vatican was eerily silent on the issue at first but finally recommended that its followers embrace the rain. They stopped short, however, of referring to this event as the rapture as Milan had anticipated. As more nations came on board in support, there were also detractors. Russia and most countries in the Middle East recommended against their citizens taking in the elemental rain. It was China, however, that tipped the scales.

That evening, China announced that its own teams of scientists were quite certain that the elemental rain was not only harmful but, furthermore, they were confident that they possessed the technology to eliminate the yellow cloud and they intended to utilize this knowledge to save their citizens. This, of course, led to widespread outrage. World leaders worried that if the cloud were eliminated in China, it might also dissipate worldwide. The more immediate problem, however, was the sudden, panicked migration of pro-rain citizens leaving their home countries for more "cloud-friendly" environments.

As the tensions escalated, there was no word from the voice. The yellow cloud continued to rise from the tear and by the next morning, it had engulfed most of North America. Perhaps most bizarre was how life continued on the planet. The majority of the population went to work the next morning, albeit in a haze of uncertainty. Throughout the world, offices and factories functioned, seemingly forgetting that their entire existence could very well hang in the balance. Of course, there was looting and law enforcement continued to erode but the fact that human society functioned at all was nothing less than astonishing.

Websites and Facebook groups were created by the

thousands, featuring both pro- and anti-cloud sentiments. The news media continued its swing into twenty-four hour cloud coverage. Commercialism also reigned supreme as products were developed overnight to cash in on the elemental rain. One could purchase food supplies with assurances of decades of survival should you wish to avoid the rain. Conversely, if you were to embrace the rain, you would be ill-advised to do so without an elemental rain sponge and rubber duck or a McDonald's commemorative glass, available free with purchase of a Value Meal.

Somehow it was assumed that the voice had indicated that all humans must stand in the elemental rain nude. The news media featured drawings of men and women in a rainstorm with their genitals eclipsed by black boxes. Given the seeming inevitability of standing naked in front of all mankind, sales of pubic hair trimmers and emergency weight loss products skyrocketed. In some countries, this misconception alone was enough for some to conclude that they would not be participating in the rain. The late night talk shows had a field day and porn websites depicted their subjects in desperate, last minute, end of the world fucks as the rain fell upon them.

Graham wondered what the voice must be thinking. He had been allowed to leave the radio station with military supervision to return home to his family. He flipped through the channels that afternoon following some much needed sleep and watched in a stupor the frantic capitalization. He held his girlfriend Kelly and her five year old daughter, Haley, close.

Haley wasn't Graham's biological daughter but he was the only father she had ever really known. Kelly's husband, Mark, had been killed in Iraq when she was barely a year old. The only memories she had of Mark were the smiling photos of him that hung upon her bedroom wall. Graham met Kelly two years after Mark's death and moved in with her shortly afterward. It was a bit awkward at first because it was really Mark and Kelly's house. For a time, Graham felt as if he were an actor replacing a popular character on a television drama series. He was Rickey Schroeder replacing Jimmy Smits on NYPD Blue. In time, though, he felt more comfortable. Kelly and Haley had welcomed him with open arms.

Kelly was significantly younger than Graham. He was 40 and she was 29. This was initially met with some ridicule from his ex-wife Stephanie, who shared his age. Graham and Stephanie had a daughter of their own, Riley, who was now 18 and graduating high school this year. They divorced when Riley was five and Stephanie remarried a very successful oral surgeon a few years later. Riley lived with her mother in Florida. She used to spend the summers with Graham but she was getting a bit too old for that now. It was probably for the best. Graham's meager salary as DJ couldn't provide the lifestyle she had grown accustomed to in Miami. Riley loved her father but hated Alabama. For Graham, Haley represented a second opportunity to be a father.

He had been drunk for the majority of Riley's infancy. A very well paid drunk, mind you, but a drunk nonetheless. Graham had been a radio DJ since he was sixteen years old. The Program Director of a radio station in Detroit had overheard his voice while he was working as a busboy at a local restaurant. He was taken with the teenager's unusually deep voice and excellent diction. He offered him a part-time job during his dinner and Graham quit the restaurant job on the spot. The following Monday, he arrived at the radio station expecting to be given his own show. Instead, he spent the next several months cleaning the station vehicles and setting up remote broadcasts for the on-air talent.

Eventually, Graham was granted his own weekend shift on the station. It was four hours per week and he made the most of it, becoming quite a celebrity at his high school in the process. A short time later, the overnight DJ on the station quit and Graham was asked to fill in temporarily. He did and despite sleeping through many of his classes, he became a popular fixture on Detroit overnight radio. He somehow managed to get his diploma despite his low marks. Around this time, the evening show on the station became available and Graham was promoted to the seven to Midnight shift.

At eighteen, he was making more money than any of his friends, meeting rock stars, going to concerts and dating beautiful girls. His show continued to grow and by the time he was twenty, Graham was offered the three to seven afternoon shift at a Rock station in Dallas, a major market. It was a six-figure salary. He jumped at the chance and immediately increased the ratings with his own brand of shock-radio.

Graham became famous for pulling no punches on the air. It was the 90s. Grunge was at its peak, Rock radio was huge and every air talent in America was trying to one-up Howard Stern. Graham was one of the best. His show was smart but as raunchy as the rest. It was as if he knew exactly how far too push the envelope and stay under the FCC s radar. His tapes were traded amongst other radio DJs throughout America and he frequently made the cover of industry trade magazines as one of the medium's shining stars.

When he turned twenty-one, Graham had more money and access than anyone his age should really be afforded. He walked past the velvet rope at night clubs and was on everyone's guest list. The record companies made sure he was well taken care of and he was on a first name basis with Eddie Vedder, Chris Cornell and Kurt Cobain. It was around this time that he met

Stephanie.

Stephanie was working as a marketing intern for Warner Brothers and part of her gig was to handle meet and greets for the label's roster when the bands came through Dallas. Graham would be on hand at the shows to introduce the bands on stage and he would regularly see Steph rounding up his winning listeners to meet the bands and shake hands with their favorite rock stars. Graham was immediately attracted to this gorgeous, blonde college student but never really had an opportunity to meet her. After all, his interns handled the listeners, and Stephanie, for that matter. He simply arrived at the show, enjoyed the complimentary beverages and then stepped on stage for a few moments to get the crowd revved up for the flavor of the month:

"Awwwww, hell yeah, Dallas!!! How we feelin' tonight?! Ya all right?! Awwwww Riiiight!!" It was, pretty much, the same speech every time. "One Oh One Point Nine, The Edge welcomes you to the fuckin' low dough show series!!! Are you ready to get fucked up and blow your goddamn ear drums to hell?!?! Who wants a free Edge t-shirt?!" Graham would then lift a potato gun to his shoulder and begin firing t-shirts into the audience while spraying them with beer and champagne; carefully avoiding the monitors, of course.

Stephanie, rightfully, thought that he was a bit of a buffoon. He was handsome but not exactly charming. At least, that's how she initially felt. Then, one night Graham arrived at a concert and was told by his interns that one of his winning listeners had not arrived to claim their spot in the meet and greet. He had two slots open if he wanted to use them. Generally, when this occurred, Graham would use it as an opportunity for self promotion.

He grabbed his two biggest interns as security and then walked outside, in front of the venue where the concert-goers were lined up down the street waiting to be let in to see the show. Graham's usual process was to make a bit of a scene while giving away station t-shirts, bumper stickers, Cds and such and then announce that the two people in line willing to do the most insane thing would be given the opportunity to meet the band. He had made two straight men kiss, women strip naked and once he even traded a guy three hits from a sledgehammer to his car in exchange for the opportunity to meet Alice in Chains. Graham broke out his headlights and his rear window. He needed the security that night.

On this particular evening, however, as Graham was making his way from the rear of the line, he noticed two young girls who couldn't have been any more than sixteen years old. They looked very out of place in this line of flannel wearing, pierced and tattooed freaks. They were well dressed (too well dressed for a Rock show, he thought) and they looked a bit nervous. Graham stopped and approached them. "Hey. You girls going to the show?" he asked. They sheepishly nodded. It was obvious that despite his apparel, emblazoned with the radio station's logo, they did not know who he was. In fact, they appeared a bit concerned as to why this long haired, pierced guy might be talking to them. Yet, something struck him about them and he concluded that he didn't need to look any further for his new contest winners. He simply asked them. "Would you like to meet the band?"

One of the girls finally managed a "What?"

"Meet the band," Graham said again. "I work for the radio station presenting the show and I have two slots open and..." Graham didn't get to finish his sentence when one of the girls began to cry. The second quickly said "Yes. Yes, we do want to meet them." and then hesitantly inquired, "We don't have to do anything once we get back there, do we?" Graham laughed and explained that he was not pimping for the band and that the girls would be perfectly safe.

Once they arrived backstage, Graham would usually hand his listeners over to the interns and, in this case, Stephanie, and then go about his regular business of glad handing the rock stars and drinking Tequila. However, as he explained to the girls how the process would work, the crying girl wrapped her arms around his neck and hugged him tightly.

"Thank you so much. This means so much to me," she said as her friend smiled and brushed away her own tears.

Apparently, this particular band had saved the young girl's life. She told Graham her story. She had been in an abusive home. Her father had molested her. She ran away and lived on the streets of Dallas for over a year. One of her prized possessions during these times were this band's first and second albums which dealt with similar subject matter (the singer's life somewhat mirrored her own). She had contemplated suicide but the band's tortured lyrics had become a guiding light for her. Finally, she was placed in foster care. The girl with her tonight was her foster-sister.

With this, Graham asked the two girls to stay put and he excused himself to find the singer of the band. Stephanie was with him as Graham explained the young girl's story and asked if he would mind having a private meeting with the two teenagers. He graciously agreed and Graham and Stephanie went back to the two girls and explained that the vocalist would meet with them privately. The crying girl was now so nervous that she could barely walk but Graham helped her to the dressing room. When she met the man, it was as if she was meeting her long, lost brother and tears flowed from them both as they recounted their stories of abuse. They closed their talk with a long embrace and as they left, the two girls again held Graham and thanked him for this life changing moment. It had been just the closure the girl needed to begin her life anew. She called it fate and Graham thought that there might have been something to this. After all, what did cause him to notice them amongst the grungy mass in front of the club? Now, even he discreetly wiped away a tear. Stephanie noticed.

That night, they shared several drinks and Stephanie discovered that much of the machismo that Graham brought to his radio show was really more of a character than it was actually him. Beyond the facade, she found an intelligent, good-natured guy who just happened to have a weird job. It wasn't love at first sight but, eventually, it was love.

Long story short, Graham and Stephanie became an item. They moved in together, Stephanie got pregnant, quit school and Riley was born. All the while, the money continued to flow and Graham rode a seemingly endless wave of success in Dallas. They bought a beautiful house in a gated community and moved in. Finally, though, his drinking began to take its toll. Late nights, partying with rock stars while Stephanie remained at home to take care of a colicky baby did not bode well for their marriage. Eventually, Graham began oversleeping for work. This was quite miraculous considering that he wasn't on the air until 3pm. Further, his reputation within the market and the industry itself began to plummet. He was warned repeatedly by management to change his behavior.

But, in fact, it got worse. Graham began a string of infidelity with local strippers that ended spectacularly with him bringing a girl home late one night and having sex with her in the guest room while his wife and child slept on the other side of the house. The stripper awoke the next morning and wandered into the dining room nude, much to the shock of Stephanie, Riley, and the girl herself, who was unaware that Graham was married.

Perhaps amazingly, through the divorce Graham and Stephanie were civil to each other. It wasn't the sort of angry separation one might expect given the circumstances. Stephanie simply wanted to remove herself and their daughter from Graham's self-destructive behavior and Graham agreed that this was for the best. The marriage ended amicably but Graham's career didn't enjoy the same luxury.

He arrived one day at the office and was instructed to meet with the Human Resources manager. When he arrived in her office, his boss and his boss's boss were already present. Though he had never been fired, he knew that this was the nightmare scenario that other DJs had explained to him in terrible detail. It was the end of the line for Dallas. Surprisingly, though, in this case it wasn't his alcoholism that caused the split. The radio station was changing formats. At 5pm that day, they would flip the station to Country. Graham's brand of radio wouldn't fit with the change, so his services were no longer required. By the end of the day, one by one, every jock on the station was fired.

It was the first time Graham had been out of work since that fateful day when he was sixteen. His fellow displaced air staff members immediately sprung into action: calling their agents and submitting tapes and resumes to markets throughout the U.S. Bidding wars even erupted for some of the talent as cross-town stations jumped at the opportunity to bring them on-board. None of this happened for Graham, however. He didn't have an agent and his reputation preceded him with all of the local stations. He was a loose cannon and no one wanted to take a chance with him. What was worse was that Graham had no idea where to begin looking for work. He was slow to react and began missing opportunities almost immediately.

Eventually, Graham landed a gig in Phoenix but was fired five months later following an embarrassing appearance at an industry convention in Los Angeles. He had arrived at a panel discussion drunk, as usual, and made a scene with one of waitresses. It was quite impressive. In a room full of over-the-top on-air personalities, Graham proved to make even the raunchiest shock jock cringe as he was escorted from the gala.

Thereafter, the only work he could find would prove to be small markets. He watched his six figure salary crumble to twenty seven thousand dollars a year. Along the way, he sobered up for the most part. He never entered rehab and never sought counseling. It was more of a gradual drying up based more on the fact that he couldn't afford the brands of alcohol he once loved. Rather than settle for five dollar vodka, Graham concluded that drinking was now beneath him. It took quite a while for his ego to subside.

Following stints in South Carolina and Georgia, Graham landed in Tuscumbia, Alabama. Approaching forty, he swore that this would be his final stop. He was getting too old for the vagabond radio lifestyle. During his last few stops, Graham had made an effort to be near his ex-wife and daughter in Florida. They remained as close as possible with Graham serving more as the friendly, drunken uncle at a family reunion more so than as Riley's father. Graham felt this was better than nothing and, besides, he actually liked Stephanie's new husband. He was a good guy and he respected Graham despite his flaws. He was good to Stephanie and Riley and provided a better life for them than he was able to muster and Graham was thankful for this.

He had been in Tuscumbia for less than a year when he met Kelly. She had won a prize on the air and

Graham began flirting with her on the phone. When she arrived to claim her prize, Graham was immediately struck by her. She was beautiful despite her multicolored nursing scrubs that Graham would later comment made her look like the worst dressed clown at the circus. The southern lilt in her voice and beautiful blue eyes made Graham melt. He noticed the ring on her finger, however, and put the brakes on any attempt at her. She looked young, anyway, he thought. Too young and too pretty to be interested in a DJ approaching middle age. By Tuscumbia, his ego had finally been wrestled into submission.

Later, Graham was making an appearance at a local nightclub and he saw her again. She was out for after-work cocktails with her co-workers from the hospital. Conversation ensued and Graham learned that she was a widow. Dates were made and a short time later, following a dispute with his landlord, Graham moved in to Kelly and Haley's home. For the first time in his life, Graham became a Dad and a regular guy. He mowed the lawn. He took Haley to school in the morning and picked her up in the afternoon while Kelly worked in the emergency room. They went out for dinner at a local steakhouse every Friday night. They worried about their bills and Kelly insisted that they attend church every Sunday morning. Graham loved every minute of it. He was finally content.

He was so proud his new normalcy that, today, as the yellow fog engulfed the sky, he was angry. While others envied Graham's rich and ridiculous life experiences, he wanted nothing more than a regular life. Friends loved to hear him tell stories about his life among the rock stars and his riches to rags ride. Graham was always happy to oblige but always added the post-script that he was never happier than he was now in this little town in Alabama. The people were friendly and forgiving of his past. He had a chance to start anew. Then the fucking aliens started talking to him.

In less than a month, Graham went from being a perfectly happy nobody to becoming the most sought after celebrity in the world. He didn't want this. In fact, as he sat on the couch with Kelly and Haley, he wanted nothing more than to wake up from this terrible dream.

Outside on his perfectly manicured, modest lawn sat a military Humvee. Soldiers stood armed in his driveway next to Haley's tricycle. Reporters stood in the road outside his house. There was a sniper on his roof, for Christ's sake.

Being the first human to make contact with an alien life-form was quite an enormous responsibility, it turns out. More than once, Graham had considered stopping by the liquor store. He credited Kelly with stopping him. She hadn't said a word; her presence was enough. He thought for certain that he would lose her if he made that stop.

The entire debacle was beginning to take its toll on Graham. Milan had especially freaked him out. For whatever reason, he had not put two and two together about the voice addressing him directly. When it first appeared, Graham had assumed it was a kid with a low power transmitter playing a joke. Everything had happened so quickly, he actually forgot about the second message implying that he was being summoned in some way. Now, it was all that he could think about.

He and Kelly had already decided to take in the rain. It was obviously the meeting he had crashed at the station that made him at ease with this decision. He understood the confusion that the rest of the world was feeling. He also understood better than most the ratings play that many radio and TV talk show hosts were undertaking in light of the circumstances. Graham thought that this was an absolute low. Throughout his career, he had drug the waters quite deeply in search of a ratings spike but taking something so serious and turning it into something for sweeps week, this was unfathomable to him. Some even went so far to make this a political thing. It was a liberal or conservative conspiracy depending upon who you watched.

It was truly bizarre, he thought. Why hadn't everything collapsed? Shouldn't the media just go away? Why were the networks airing alien invasion blocks of programming? As he surfed through the channels, it was either news coverage of the fog and China, commercials for doomsday supplies or *Close Encounters of the Third Kind*, *Contact*, or *Independence Day*. Everything just felt wrong.

Somewhere someone was in a meeting at this very moment making programming decisions. Someone is placing an advertising buy. They were sensationalizing something genuinely sensational, he thought.

At least Haley thought it was cool. In fact, she was more at ease with being transported to another dimension than anyone Graham knew. Of course, she didn't really understand what was happening. Still, Graham was relieved that she wasn't frightened. Kelly, on the other hand, was quite nervous. While Graham attended church at her behest, Kelly was actually quite a devout Christian. She said her prayers nightly with Haley and read scripture when something troubled her. Her small-town Southern girl demeanor was something Graham found most endearing but, under the circumstances, he worried that the outcome of this contact might disappoint her. Despite what Milan had said Graham didn't believe that he was really talking to God.

He really wanted to call Stephanie and Riley in Florida but the hum in the air was impacting cell service somehow. The internet was the only real form of communication available. He sent them an email but hadn't heard back. Stephanie wasn't much for the internet but Riley was a typical high school senior. Surely, she would at least get the message, he thought. He just wanted them to know that he was okay. Graham advised them to take in the rain and he relayed what had been discussed in the meeting with the scientists. He guessed that would be all right. In fact, he was a bit shocked that no one was monitoring his communication. He supposed that, at this point, the government had concluded that all bets were off regarding secrets.

For the moment, Graham sat on the couch with Kelly and Haley, eating a store bought pizza, watching the war unfold. The team at the station wanted him back in another hour. They had allowed him and other members of the staff to return home to see their families, shower, and sleep – with the understanding that they might be called back on a moment's notice. Graham was especially vital as it appeared that the voice would only speak to him and no one knew when the next contact would occur. Kelly and Haley would be allowed to accompany him to the station when the rain began to fall. The soldiers at the house would rush them to the station, he was told, so that if they were to be exterminated by aliens, they could at least share their final moments together. He shuddered at the thought.

Kelly hated that she couldn't be at the hospital, assisting in the emergency room. While she knew that her time with Haley was most precious, she still felt guilty that she was at home while her fellow nurses were busier than ever assisting rednecks with the ramifications of their doomsday festivities. There's something about the South. Whether it be a hurricane, a flood or an alien encounter, the first and most requested answer to adversity is always alcohol. If a Southerner is going to meet his maker, he'll do so with a damn good buzz. And probably wreck his car or shoot his buddy in the foot in the process.

Nevertheless, the military felt it was too dangerous for Kelly to be in public. She was the girlfriend of the man who talked to God, after all. To some he was a hero while others still felt he was a heretic. Everyone wanted a piece of him and Kelly and Haley were to be protected with the same veracity as the first lady and her children. A few nut jobs had already tried to storm their house, hoping to touch Graham or talk to him or something. The soldiers quickly took them into custody and rushed them away to who-knows-where. It was all unnerving and the world was getting weirder by the minute.

On the news, Graham and his family watched as the reporters frantically covered the events unfolding in China. Masses of immigrants were attempting to flee the country to India, Vietnam and North Korea. The Chinese military was overwhelmed and India, especially, had lost control of their borders. To the north, in Russia, there was nowhere to run but it appeared that, for the moment, their government had no intention of stopping the rainfall. The Chinese, at least, were making an attempt to do so. How was another question entirely.

Scientists on TV theorized that the Chinese had previously developed some sort of cloud busting technology in an attempt at climate control for their country. Diagrams were shown and debates were vigorous. The United States was clear on its position. The American president immediately addressed the issue:

"We respect the Chinese people's wishes to not partake in the elemental rain. However, we condemn any effort by the Chinese government to prevent its people from escaping to nations that will allow the rain. To do so is clearly a violation of fundamental human rights. In Russia, Mongolia, and Kazakhstan, while these nations have advised their people to avoid the rain despite encouragement to the contrary by many of the world's finest scientific minds, we appreciate that they will make no effort to prevent the clouds from forming in their airspace."

Pundits on the news networks pondered whether the Chinese really had the ability to suck up the clouds with a giant vacuum. What if human survival really is dependent on the elemental rain? Would there soon be a world without Chinese people? Perhaps there would be a world of only Chinese people. How would that impact the world's economy? Wall Street responded accordingly, selling massive amounts of stock, leaving world finance precarious at best. To those without investments, like Graham, this was somewhat irrelevant and he wondered why this would cause a panic. After all, so many people had abandoned their fully stocked shops, at this point; most people were just walking in to supermarkets, taking what they needed and leaving. Money wasn't really an issue. Then, again, he never really understood economics.

"When do you think the rain will happen?" Kelly asked Graham.

"I suppose when this fog settles over the rest of the world. We don't know."

"What if we're wrong?"

"What do you mean?"

"What if it's just the opposite of what we think?" she said. "What if the only people who survive are the ones that stay inside?"

"Well, then there'll be a lot less traffic," Graham smiled. Kelly didn't return the favor. He held her hand. "Kelly, I don't think anyone really knows what will happen. I don't know why but I don't feel like the voice is misleading us. It's like one of the guys at the station said. If they were trying to exterminate us, this is a lame way of doing it. Wouldn't they just blast us with some sort of laser ray or something? Why would they spray us with something we can easily hide from? It doesn't make sense."

"But what if that's exactly what they want us to think? Then, we're all standing outside naked with no weapons and they just eradicate us on the spot?"

"Wait. You're getting naked?"

"Graham, be serious," Kelly laughed.

"I am serious. I'm not sure I'm comfortable with those jar heads outside seeing you buck nekkid."

"I think one of them already took a peek at me getting out of the shower yesterday."

"Seriously? Bastards." Graham kissed her. "I think it's all going to be okay. Don't worry. Just take care of Haley. We'll be fine."

"You don't think the world is ending, do you?"

"No. I think it's like they said. It's evolving. Into what, I don't know."

CHAPTER FIVE

Alicia woke up the following morning with a severe hangover. She was sore. Every bone, every muscle in her body ached. For a brief moment, she had forgotten about the events of the night before. She sensed a presence next to her in the bed. Alicia turned her head and saw Sariana, still sleeping. It all came back to her. She must have been sore thanks to the soul evacuation Sariana had done as a parlor trick the night before.

A hangover was nothing new for Alicia and she knew the drill. Coffee, a few pills and a little time; she'd be right as rain. She turned and sat up on the corner of the bed, holding her head. The morning light, glaring through the hotel curtains hurt her eyes. She stood and slowly made her way to the bathroom to begin her morning ritual. Sariana's clothes were still on the floor. Alicia began picking them up and something fell out of one of the pockets with a clink. It was the knife Sariana had used the day before to silence the triclopod. She had a thought. Alicia carefully picked up the blade with a shower cap and wrapped it tight. Maybe one of the scientists at ground zero could run some tests and try to uncover what this thing was made of. DNA? She suspected that this was where Milan had disappeared to. Perhaps he would geek out on this.

Her other thought was to have Sariana perform mass soul removals. That would work, right? Alicia imagined the girl standing at a pulpit like a faith healer, ripping souls out one by one and converting the masses. She said it didn't do any harm, after all. Alicia could broadcast this on television and surely that would sway more than a few to her cause.

Alicia placed Sariana's clothes on the vanity and began to remove her robe. She stopped, though, and went through the girl's pockets. Nothing. "Where's that PDA-looking thing?" she wondered. The lunacy of the night before began to creep back into Alicia's memory completely. Was she really doing this? Alicia let her robe fall and stood sideways in the mirror. "This isn't the body of a grandmother," she thought. Still, she had committed to the girl and Alicia wasn't one for breaking promises. She couldn't deny the prior day's events. Alicia knew that her life had changed dramatically but she was still unsure of the consequences.

She emerged from the bathroom to select her outfit for the day and found Sariana awake. She looked a little green as she sat in bed, still wrapped in the sheets.

"I was unconscious," she told Alicia.

"You were exhausted. You needed your sleep."

"We have to go."

"We will. You have to get dressed first."

"I don't feel well," she told Alicia.

"Give it time. You'll be all right. You're not going to puke are you?"

"Puke?"

"Vomit."

"I know what it means," Sariana said. "I just didn't know that was a possibility."

"Let's hope it's not. Why don't you get up and get dressed? You'll feel better once you're up and around."

"How many hours have we wasted sleeping? How widespread is the fog?"

"It's now covered North America. It's moving slow. We have time."

"They know I'm here. I don't know what they have planned. It's only a matter of time before they try to remove us from the time-line completely. If they do this, all is lost."

"Get dressed. As you said, we have a lot of work to do."

Sariana reluctantly did as she was told. She stood up and dragged her feet all the way to the bathroom. "We'll have to get you some new clothes," Alicia said as she dressed in the other room. "There's blood all over your clothes. Was that from the bug? When you killed it? We should probably get it tested." The toilet flushed. "Are you hungry?"

"Not really," Sariana said from the bathroom.

"Well, you should eat something. Maybe we can skip breakfast and have an early lunch." Alicia finished dressing and Sariana came out of the bathroom wearing her dirty, blood-stained clothes. Alicia took over in the bathroom and began applying her makeup. "I have kind of a plan for us today," Alicia announced.

"Yes?"

"Yeah. We need to get the military on our side. The easiest way to keep people out of the rain is to get the U.S. government to reverse their opinion on the matter. I thought we could start by getting one of those scientists at the radio station to test your knife for DNA samples."

"Why?"

"Well, if what they find is confusing enough, we might be able to solicit their help; the military too. If we have them on our side, we'll be able to make a much more compelling case to keep people out of the rain."

"Okay."

"I've been thinking about that too; the rain. What is it for? What does it do?"

"We don't know. We believe it does nothing."

"What is the point of the whole exercise then? Why compel people to stand in the rain? Why not just force us all into the next dimension."

"Everyone must make a conscious decision to ascend. Standing in the rain represents this decision. Your scriptures talk about having faith. This is an act of faith. The Humans are aware that not everyone will have faith."

"The souls that participate in the Exodus... where will they go?"

"To the fifth dimension."

"Why not the fourth?"

"The fourth dimension is time. It is a neutral dimension and cannot be visited."

"All right, I'm still a little hazy from last night. Tell me again why we don't want the Humans to advance to the eleventh dimension?"

"Because it's futile. Going beyond the tenth dimension would be impossible because just thinking of an object in the tenth dimension makes it an object in one of the dimensions below. This is how they are able to manipulate all time-lines at will. Your philosopher said 'Cogito ergo sum', 'I think therefore I am'. The eleventh dimension is something alternate that defies everything we know, so everything that we think of cannot be because it "becomes" once we begin to think about it. This is the realm of God and our kind was not meant to tread there."

"Okay. You're going to have to work on explaining this stuff a little better. Most people won't be able to make heads or tails out of that."

"What do you mean?"

"Our attention spans here are stupid-small. Just say something like 'the eleventh dimension is the realm of God'. Religious people will go ape-shit over that. It's all about sound bytes, kid."

"I did not know this."

"Well, that's why you found me," Alicia smiled. "I might not be able to make snakes talk but I can help you spin the shit out of this." Alicia and Sariana collected their things and left the room to the maid.

"First stop," Alicia said in the truck, "is to find a new outfit for you. We need to make you look pretty."

"Why is that necessary? We don't have time to waste."

"Again, it goes back to getting your message heard. No one is going to take an ugly girl seriously. You're cute. You need to work it. 'Little lost girl from another dimension'. That'll play well. You need to trust me on this. I know this dimension better than you."

Alicia took the highway around the small town to avoid the crowds and found an outlet mall on the outskirts. They drove into the parking lot and Alicia grimaced at the choices. "Well, no Versace here. Fashion Bug it is, I guess. Uggh."

"Anyone here could be Human," Sariana said. The girl was visibly nervous.

"How will we know?"

"We won't know. This is what I've been trying to tell you."

"Well, if that's the case, we can't go anywhere, can

we? Should we just hide in the hotel?"

"No. That would be the worst thing we could do. We have to keep moving. I think."

"Well, then. Come on. Let's move."

The girls made their way into the store and found a single clerk in the shadows of the fluorescent light trying to clean up the wreckage in the room. The woman carried a stack of empty boxes to the counter. "Y'all are gonna pay for whatever you take." The woman pulled a gun from the small of her back and placed it on the counter and Sariana jumped. "We understand each other?"

"We do," Alicia said. "My friend here just needs a couple of new outfits. I have money."

The young woman looked Alicia and Sariana over. Alicia flashed her credit card. "Credit card machines are down," the clerk said. "Cash only." Alicia opened her purse and displayed a handful of cash. "That'll work," she said. "Ain't much left, though." A look of recognition came over her face. "Hey, I seen y'all on TV, ain't I?"

"Yes. Hi. I'm Alicia Parker. Triton News Network," she reached out to shake the woman's hand as Sariana watched cautiously from a safe distance. The clerk didn't appear to be a threat. Sariana slowly began exploring the store.

"Nice to meet you, 'Lesha. Ain't that girl the 'princess' from last night's news?"

"Yes, she is."

"Bless her heart," the woman whispered. "Is she okay?"

"She's a sweet girl. She's lost her parents; can't find her family. She's a little confused."

"Poor thing," the woman frowned. "You reckon some new clothes might make her feel better?"

"I think so, yes."

"Well," she smiled. "It always gets me out of a funk! Let's see what we can do for her."

The clerk and Alicia caught up with Sariana and found her browsing the remaining sun dresses on an overturned rack. "You like those, baby?" the clerk asked. Sariana nodded and smiled. "I wonder what size are you? I'm thinkin' eight or ten, am I right?"

"I think that's about right," Alicia answered for her.

The girls picked out several dresses and other outfits and made their way to the changing rooms. The clerk kicked boxes and stray clothing out of the way, making a path for Alicia and Sariana. "Damn animals," she muttered. "World ain't ended yet." Sariana began trying on the clothes as Alicia waited and the clerk went back to her clean up duty.

A few moments passed and Alicia heard yelling from the front of the store. She peeked her head around the corner and saw the clerk holding a man at gun point. He was holding goods from the store and was apparently trying to leave without paying. "Drop it, motherfucker!" the clerk shouted. "You gonna pay for that or I'll take your fucking head off."

"What do you care?!" the man shouted back. "Ain't nobody holding you responsible for this shit!"

"It's the principle, asshole!! Thou shalt not steal!!"

"Oh, really? Murder's a'ight wit' you, though?"

"Drop... the... tankini."

"You fuckin' crazy, you know that, bitch?"

"I'm gonna count to three..."

"It's for my wife..."

"One..."

"Aw, hell. You crazy! You crazy as shit!!"

"Two..." The man dropped the clothes. The clerk still held the gun on him and the two continued their stare-down. "You just walk out the store, ya hear?" said the clerk. "And don't you never come back."

The man began laughing. "You fuckin' crazy, bitch. You fuckin' crazy."

Alicia noticed Sariana behind her, also watching. She had seen the entire stand-off. Defeated, the man left and the clerk let out a deep breath. She reset the safety and wiggled the gun back into the rear of her jeans and began walking toward the changing rooms. Alicia scattered Sariana back to the mirrors. "This looks nice," Alicia said about Sariana's latest choice.

"Oh! It sure does," the clerk beamed, coming around the corner. "Don't you just look precious?! I love that color on you!"

"Well, I think we've made our choices," Alicia said.

"Good! Let's go get you rung up!"

The girls followed the clerk to the front of the store, with Sariana wearing one of her new dresses. Alicia was running late getting to the studio this morning. She needed to stay in the good graces of the network if it were to be Sariana's pulpit. She knew it would be in her best interest to arrive with something for air, especially following yesterday's incident. This woman would be ideal, she thought.

"I'm sorry, I didn't catch your name," Alicia said to the clerk.

"I don't believe I threw it, baby. My name is Amber."

"Amber, I'm sure you know that we overheard your confrontation with that man. Would you mind if I interviewed you for the network? It might help to keep some of the vagrants out of your store."

"Me? On TV? Oh, I don't know..."

"It really is something that people should hear from you about. You're standing up for what's right and I think that's fantastic."

"Well, it's a matter of principle. It just ain't right to be stealin' things that ain't yours."

"I agree. So, what do you say? Can I get the camera?"

"Oh my. Okay. You gotta let me fix my face, though."

"Deal."

Alicia told Sariana to stay put and ran outside to the truck. She grabbed a remote bag and unloaded the gear inside. "Think you can hold this and film us?" Alicia asked Sariana. "It's easy."

"What do I do?"

"Just make sure that you get Amber and I in that view finder. Press this button and try to hold it steady. Don't worry about doing anything fancy. No close-ups or anything like that. We'll take care of all of that in editing."

"Yes. Okay. I think I can do that. What does this have to do with the ascension?"

"If I don't have a job, we can't get your... our message to the people. I need to turn in a story."

Amber returned from the back of the store not looking much different than she had when they last saw her. Alicia gave a countdown and began the story.

"We live in chaotic times. Since the arrival of the OWL, many small business owners and shop-keepers have struggled with the looting problem. This morning, I witnessed a brave woman meet danger head on as she stood up to a would-be thief and thwarted his plans to rob her store. She had to stare this man down... with a gun. Wait. I don't like that. Keep rolling. It was a show down and she ended it with a gun. I don't know. We might use the first one. Anyway. Two. One. That brave woman is with me now, Amber shit. I'm sorry, Amber; I didn't get your last name..."

"Mitchell."

"Two. One. That brave woman is with me now, Amber Mitchell. Amber, tell us what happened."

"Well, this asshole..."

"Oops. Wait. We can't cuss."

"Right. Sorry."

"Two. One. Amber, tell us what happened..."

"Thank you, 'Lesha. Um, the man in question entered our premises at about ten A.M. and I could tell immediately that he had trouble in mind. I've seen me a lot of looters lately, so you get to know the type..."

"How many times have you been robbed since the appearance of the OWL?"

"Gosh, I can't tell. While I been here at least five times but they come in at night when we ain't here. They done broke our windows, you see that?"

"Can you swing around over there?" she asked Sariana. Sariana got a shot of the boarded up windows. "Okay, back to me now." Sariana swung back around. "You sell clothing. Do you think people are stealing the clothes out of necessity or..."

"Oh, hell no. They're just doin' it for kicks. 'Cause they can. Ain't nobody needin' clothes right now. Hell, that man today was stealin' a ladies swimsuit. Can you believe that?"

"Now, Amber, you carry a pistol to keep the looters away. Have you ever had to use it?"

"Not yet," Amber looked hard into the camera. "But you mark my words... I will."

"This isn't your store, correct?"

"That is correct, Miss Parker. I am an employee of Fashion Bug Incorporated."

"How long have you worked here?"

"I been here five years in May. I am the assistant manager."

"The man robbing you today raised an interesting point for what it's worth. Why do you care? It's not your store..."

"'Lesha, that's the very problem right there. It is my store. I might not own it but I look after it like it's mine. I take pride in my work. Besides, stealing is wrong.

You don't just steal."

"Well said. Have you ever thought of just abandoning your job and giving up?"

"I did think about it when they stopped paying me. I ain't got a paycheck in two weeks. I reckon I'll stay with it, though, until the next shipment day. If the clothes don't come, maybe I'll just lock 'er up and go home."

"Thank you, Amber, for your time... and for your bravery."

"There's more like me, 'Lesha," Amber said sternly to the camera. "If a looter takes nothing away from seeing this here story, let them know that. I ain't the only one with a gun guarding property. This is Alabama and we got better morals than that. You better watch your ass or we'll kill y'all dead."

"All right. I think that does it. Let me see the camera." Alicia took the camera from Sariana and stopped tape. Now she had something to take to the office. Not a bad story, either. "Sariana, you want to go on out to the truck? I have to get Ms. Mitchell to sign a release. Lock the doors once you get in."

Sariana went outside and Alicia produced the standard-release paperwork for Amber to sign. It seemed a bit silly to be signing legal documents in the midst of an apocalyptic event but it would be just Alicia's luck that only lawyers would survive the rapture.

"You think she's gonna be okay?" Amber asked, nodding toward Sariana.

"I hope so."

"It's nice of you to be taking care of her."

"Thanks. If you could sign here..."

"Sure." Amber signed her name on the release. "You know what? Y'all just take those dresses as a gift from me..."

"Are you sure? I have the money."

"I know. I keep this copy?"

"No, the yellow one."

"Oh, okay. There's somethin' about that girl. I feel like I want to help her too."

"Yeah?"

"Yeah. When she was on TV and she was sayin' she was a princess and junk and that she wanted to save everyone... I don't know. I just felt like she meant it, you know? It's like I can just feel that she's got a good heart."

"I think she does."

Amber waved to the girl in the truck. Sariana waved back. "Awww. I just want to give her a big ol' hug and tell her everything's gonna be all right. I could just eat her up. Sweet thing."

"I'll certainly tell her that you wish her the best."

"Please do. I hope she gets better. Y'all take care of yourself."

"Thank you, Amber, for everything."

"Hey, what time is this gonna be on the news? I gotta get my boyfriend to tape it."

"I'm not sure. Is this your cell number on the release?"

"Yes."

"I'll call you and let you know, okay?"

"That's great, hon. Thank you!"

"Thank you. Don't kill anybody, Amber."

"Baby, I ain't makin' no promises the good Lord knows I can't keep!"

☙

The next stop was the studio to drop off the tape and inform Hal of the plan for the day. The crowd had thinned in downtown Tuscumbia and the place looked like a war zone. Most of the partiers had either gone home or passed out in tents set up along the roadside. It was a lot easier to navigate but the entire town was littered with beer cans; empty fast food wrappers and what looked like the remnants of fireworks. The yellow fog continued to escape the tear and today the sky itself was a burnt yellow. Alicia stole a glance at Sariana in the passenger seat and saw that she was troubled. "Once I drop off the tape," Alicia said, "We're going to go find the DJ, okay?"

"Do you think that many of these people went home and will stay inside?" Sariana asked, referring to the smaller crowd.

"Maybe, honey, I don't know." Alicia put her hand on her shoulder. "Hang in there. We're going to do this right, okay?"

"Okay." Sariana let a weak smile cross her lips and returned to taking in the landscape.

Alicia locked Sariana in the truck and went inside the studio. She was greeted with the jokes she had anticipated. "All hail the Queen," bows and such were all par for the course. She found Hal and handed him the tape. "Good story: crazy Alabama redneck protects her store against looters. Needs editing."

"Okay, great." said Hal. "L.A. wants you to take a look into the morale of the soldiers at Ground Zero."

"I can do that but I'm also going to try to get the DJ on the air."

"Graham Barry?"

"Yes. That needs to be my top priority."

"He's holed up at his house. The military is just as thick there as they are at Ground Zero. You won't get anywhere near him."

"I can try. I'm working an angle here, Hal. Where does he live?"

"What's the story?"

"I want to know more about why the OWL addressed him by name. He has something to do with this and I think it's deep."

"It's already been established that it's not a prank. Alicia, there's a hole in the sky."

"I'm not talking about that. Why did the OWL contact him? Why Tuscumbia, Alabama, for Christ's sake?"

"They said 'Enjoy the music', we think it has..."

"You think they're music lovers, Hal?"

"This area has a big musical legacy. Aretha Franklin, Wilson Pickett, The Rolling Stones, they've all recorded albums here."

"Really, Hal?"

"They have."

"I know they have, but spacemen didn't cross dimensions to tour Fame studios. Are you retarded?"

Hal sighed. "Do what you need to do. There's a packet on him, including his address in the prep area. You want to take Steven with you?"

"You know I don't work with anyone but Brady. I'm flying solo." Alicia grabbed a Graham Barry packet and walked toward the door. She held the truck keys in the air on her way out. "I'm keeping the white SUV."

Outside in the parking lot, a small crowd had gathered around the truck. Her heart immediately sank. She shouldn't have left Sariana alone again. Alicia rushed to the scene and found several men and women talking to Sariana behind her closed window. They didn't seem to be doing her any harm. They were just asking questions.

"It is important that you stay out of the rain," Sariana told them through the glass. "You are being misled."

"All right, break it up, everybody," Alicia said as she walked to the driver's side door.

"What does she know?" a man holding his little boy asked her.

"Did you hear her on the news?"

"Yes."

"That's what she knows. She's a princess from another dimension. She was sent here to warn you to stay out of the rain. So, stay out of the rain."

"Is she for real?"

"Buddy, who the hell knows what's for real anymore? I have it on good authority that she's telling the truth."

"How do you know? Who told you?"

"Her Grandma told me so. Keep watching Triton and we'll tell you more."

Alicia shut the door and started the truck. Sariana smiled at her. Alicia smiled back and began honking the horn in an effort to disperse the crowd. "Get the fuck out of the way!!" she shouted. Sariana giggled. "What's so funny?"

"Your temper will serve you well."

"Princess coming through, assholes! *Move*!"

ĊŻ

Graham Barry lived in a small, quaint house not far from Ground Zero. When Alicia turned the corner to his street, she was immediately stopped by an M.P. On the other side of the block, she saw her competitors' trucks lined down along the ditch. There was military equipment as far as she could see. Like Hal said, it was impenetrable. "Do you think they'll let us see him?" Sariana asked.

"We might have to find another way. Don't worry. There isn't a celebrity that's been able to hide from me yet."

Sariana felt confident that Alicia would get her to Graham but time was running out. The fog in the sky grew thick and she knew that it was only a matter of time before the elemental rain would begin to fall. This was, of course, if the Humans didn't find them first. An M.P. rapped on Alicia's window and she rolled it down. "Can I see your press pass?" Alicia gave the guard her credentials. "This is a general press query. I need your pass for this area specifically."

"I don't have one."

"You'll have to get clearance from national security. There's a press quadrant near Ground Zero..."

"I know, I know. I just don't have time for that at the moment. Look, it's very important that we speak to Mr. Barry."

"Yeah, you and every other reporter here, lady."

"No, this is different. This girl has information that could save his life."

"Well, just pass this information on to me and I'll be sure that Mr. Barry gets the message."

"It's not going to translate well."

"Look, lady, there's not much more I can do for you..."

"May I reach into my purse?"

"I'll need to draw my weapon, ma'am."

"That's fine. I'm going to produce a weapon as well..." That was the wrong thing to say. The soldier immediately called for backup and the truck was swarmed with M.P.s, guns drawn. Sariana was terrified. Alicia felt like an idiot.

"It's okay, honey, don't worry," Alicia told her. "Hold your hands up. They're just doing their job. It's not what you think."

The girls sat with their hands raised until the lead M.P. barked at them through the window. "I want you both out of the vehicle now. Hands behind your head." They complied and the soldiers handcuffed them. Alicia kept gently reassuring Sariana that she had nothing to fear. "Ma'am, you stated that you have a weapon..."

"I do. It's in my purse. It's covered in plastic. Do not get any fingerprints on it. It's evidence."

"Evidence of what?" the soldier asked, grabbing Alicia's purse.

"I believe it contains the DNA of a being from another dimension."

"How does this relate to Mr. Barry?"

"We believe that the OWL-"

"What is the OWL?"

"The Voice. The aliens. Whatever. We believe we know why they have contacted Mr. Barry specifically. That blade contains the DNA from a being from another dimension intent on destroying us."

"Hey, this is that princess chick," one of the soldiers watching Sariana said.

The lead M.P. glanced over the hood of the truck to take a look at the girl. "The girl from the internet?"

"Don't you mean TV?" Alicia asked.

"Let's get these two in the transport. Take them to Ground Zero." Alicia and Sariana were helped into the back of the military Humvee and sat, handcuffed, surrounded by armed guards as they made the short trip to the radio station. One soldier held Alicia's purse.

"Here it is," a soldier said, holding his smart phone up so the girls could see. It was the video of Sariana from the day before. "Princess Sariana. You're at the top of Google trends today. Like a million views on YouTube."

"I guess you got popular," Alicia said to the girl. "You've gone viral."

"This is good?" Sariana asked.

"It could be, yeah."

"You really from another dimension?" another soldier asked.

"Yes."

"Some people are sayin' you're sick in the head."

"I assure you, I'm not." The soldier's cold stare bore into Sariana. She sensed that this man could easily harm her. "Please, stay out of the rain. We need you, sir."

"Need me for what?"

"All of you. We need soldiers."

"You startin' an army?"

"Yes. She will," Sariana said, nodding to Alicia.

The soldiers laughed out loud. The stern one's cold gaze now wavered. "Well, y'all would be the prettiest C.O.'s I ever had." More laughter. "You all right, Princess. You all right."

At the station, Milan watched the radar screen in an upstairs office as the fog made its way across the globe. Charles entered with two Styrofoam cups of coffee and sat down across from him. Outside, the world was shrouded in a yellowish green tint. The crowds had significantly dispersed but from the office window, Milan could still watch a sea of people wander the streets of downtown Tuscumbia. The radio station, now on auto-pilot with Graham at home, provided a steady soundtrack of music interspersed with station announcements and commercials for local car dealers. All the while, the yellow stream of clouds poured like water from the tear in the sky.

"It's nearly complete," Milan observed, pointing at the radar screen.

Charles stood up and craned his neck to get a better look. "It does look that way. It's almost reached China. I suppose we'll soon see if they've truly been hiding their miraculous cloud busting technology," Charles smiled.

"It would be a strange thing for them to bluff."

"Yeah but from what I understand their machine is based on Wilhelm Reich's concepts. It's pseudoscience."

"I thought Reich's cloud buster was designed to actually create clouds, not disperse them."

Charles shrugged. "I guess they've found a way to reverse the process. We'll see."

"Reich's machine was thought to work, correct?"

"According to a few witnesses in Maine, yes. They say he made it rain. He also claimed to have cured cancer with orgasms, Milan. That didn't exactly happen."

"True," Milan admitted. "Interesting nevertheless."

"Theoretical physicists; always intrigued by the impossible, aren't you?" Charles laughed.

Milan smiled and turned his attention outside. "I told a man that I would get him to a phone so that he could call his family," he said.

"At the network?"

"Yes. I never came back. I feel terrible."

"Milan, you've had more important things to concern yourself with."

"I know. I just can't let go of the fear in his eyes. He was absolutely terrified."

"Well, who isn't?"

Milan turned from the window to face Charles. "You don't appear to be frightened."

"I think if I let myself, I'd be curled up in a corner in the fetal position," Charles said.

Milan sensed he was only half-joking. "There seems to be a lot of that going around. I heard that this vibration is causing some of the soldiers to have massive anxiety attacks."

"What about you?" Charles asked.

"I'm certainly anxious. I guess I'm still more intrigued and excited than anything. I just want to see what's going to happen next. Have you spoken with your family?"

"Yes. They're well. They're en route. Do you have anyone that you need to get in touch with?"

"No. I don't believe so," said Milan. His parents had passed away many years before. Milan had no siblings and he never did marry. While he'd long since come to grips with the fact that he might face his final moments alone, it would be untrue to say that this stark reality had not hit him especially hard in the past few days. Milan's education and his work had always been his primary focus and his relationships, romantic or otherwise, had always suffered for that. He took his solace in the fact that, as a scientist, he was lucky to be alive for the events unfolding before him.

A soldier entered the office. "Doctors, you're needed downstairs."

Milan and Charles stood up and followed the soldier down the ornate, wooden staircase and into the conference room. At the conference table, the soldiers were removing the handcuffs from Alicia and Sariana. They rubbed their wrists and were told to have a seat. Milan immediately recognized Alicia. She had been hoping to see him.

"Hey."

"Hey. You got yourself arrested?"

"Kind of, yeah. You never came back to the studio."

"I got a little wrapped up down here. I'm sorry; I can't remember your name."

"Alicia. Alicia Parker."

"I'm Milan."

"I remember."

"Oh, okay. Alicia, this is Dr. Charles Trumboldt. And this is...?"

Alicia paused for a moment as Sariana waited for an introduction. She still felt strange referring to her as a princess. She braced herself for the laughter. "This is Princess Sariana."

"Sariana. That's a pretty name." Milan didn't miss a beat. He must have seen her on television, Alicia thought. The truth was Milan and Charles had met a number of world dignitaries since their arrival at Ground Zero. For all he knew, she was a head of state. Strange that she might be arrested, of course, but he didn't over-think it.

"Thank you, Dr. Milan. I sense you serve a great purpose here."

"Well," Milan laughed. "I like you already. See, Charles? I told you I was important."

The men smiled as General Ramsey entered the building, carrying a large binder and a cup of coffee. He placed the items at the head of the table and sat down. He made his introductions to Alicia and Sariana.

"Princess, huh?"

"Yes," Sariana assured him.

"Okay. Ms. Parker, my men indicate that you have quite a remarkable story to tell us."

Alicia recounted the details of how she met Sariana on the country road the day before. She explained the triclopod and how Sariana had killed it with her knife. "It was already dead," Sariana corrected. "I just silenced it." She told of the on-air interview that was now the latest online sensation and the General provided information she didn't have.

"It seems you've gathered quite a fan base, Sariana.

At last count, there were at least a couple of hundred fan websites for you, Facebook groups..."

"Is this good?" Sariana asked.

"I suppose it depends on your point of view. You see, Sariana, we have already advised the world's citizens to immerse themselves in the rain."

"You must tell them that you have changed your mind."

The General laughed. "It's not exactly that easy..."

"But it must be."

"Well, first things first. Sariana, will you go with these gentlemen, please?" Two soldiers appeared from around the corner and Sariana and Alicia were visibly alarmed.

"We don't want to be separated, General," Alicia objected.

"It's okay," he assured them. "You must understand, we just want to do an ID check on Sariana; run her fingerprints, that sort of thing. You're not in any danger, young lady, I assure you."

Sariana looked to Alicia. For what it was worth, Alicia trusted the General. After all, it probably wouldn't be in his best interest to do anything other than assume that Sariana was telling the truth at this point. If they were Human, wouldn't they have killed them already? Stranger things were happening, though. Alicia didn't exactly know what she was looking for when it came to the Humans. The General might unknowingly be putting her in peril.

"You can't come with me?" Sariana asked Alicia.

"Well, we'd like to ask Ms. Parker a few questions too," the General answered. "You'll just be in the next room. Here." The General stood up and opened the blinds on the window behind him. "Ms. Parker will be able to see you right through here. Okay?"

"Is that all right, Sariana?" Alicia asked.

She put on a brave face. "Yes. This is acceptable. Thank you."

The men took Sariana into the next room and Alicia watched as she was introduced to Ms. Hendrix. She had a seat at her desk and Alicia could see their dialogue.

Everything appeared to be fine.

"It seems you've become quite attached to her," Milan noted.

"Yes. I have. She did something to me last night that I can't explain."

"What happened?"

"I realize that this is going to sound crazy..."

"Ms. Parker, these days, we're in the business of crazy," General Ramsey assured her.

"I had an out of body experience. She made this happen somehow..." Alicia explained the phenomenon from the night before. She did her best to recount the history that Sariana had made her privy to. She stopped short of pronouncing herself Queen of the insurgency. She didn't want to appear to have a vested interest in the story and sacrifice whatever credibility she might have. For the moment, she reasoned, it wasn't relevant.

"And you let her story get the better of you?" Charles asked.

"It's not that," Alicia countered. "I believe her.

Everyone she encounters feels some sort of kinship with her, even the soldiers who brought us here. It's bizarre to say the least."

"You said that you saw visions when she did this to you. What, specifically, did you see?" Milan asked.

"I don't know... a rush of things. Blood, a baby, a lot of stuff. Some sort of demon, I think. It was all so fast."

"You think we should take her seriously?" the General asked.

"If you had asked me that question 24 hours ago, I would have said no. General, it's my job to see through bullshit. When Lindsay Lohan said that she was sober, I broke the story that she wasn't. She caved with me. I don't think I'm crazy. I believe her."

Ms. Hendrix entered the room and put an open file in front of the General. "The girl is Grace Barlow, sixteen, of Muscle Shoals," Hendrix read. The men in the room shifted in their seats with the new information. Alicia, too, felt awkward. "Her parents and brother died in a car accident two weeks ago..."

Alicia felt herself turning a bit red. Once again, she questioned whether her initial instincts about the girl were correct. Was she just some crazy, traumatized teenager, distraught about the death of her family? Was it just the booze that had lured her into her world the night before? No, she assured herself, that wouldn't explain the bug. That didn't explain the girl sucking her soul out of her body. That happened. It really did.

"According to this, she died of a brain hemorrhage yesterday morning, but that's clearly incorrect intel."

Alicia looked through the window and saw the girl sitting on the couch, biting her nails as an armed guard stood nearby. She looked nervous and naive. Alicia was torn. Part of her wanted to take the girl and protect her from this scrutiny, another part of her wanted to strangle the little bitch. A lot still didn't add up.

"Well, unfortunately, Ms. Parker, this explains your dilemma." the General said. "Pretty cut and dry to me. As you initially suspected, the girl is mentally unstable."

"Wait a minute," said Alicia. She was becoming

defensive. "This doesn't explain the out of body experience thing..."

"Ms. Parker..."

"Or the giant, fucking bug. What about that?"

"Ms. Parker, there have been a lot of unexplained things happening in recent days," the General started.

"Exactly! That's exactly what I'm talking about."

A soldier entered the room and handed the general a plastic bag and manila file folder. He began to look over the information as the soldier exited. Alicia drummed her fingers on the table and felt her temper rising.

"I think what the General is trying to say," said Charles "is that everyone deals with this sort of stress in their own way. It might manifest itself any number of ways. Have you considered that you might have been prone to believing these things were real or, perhaps exaggerated, because of this stress? A field reporter during a trying time like this is a very stressful job."

"That's bullshit. I didn't dream all of this. The knife;

at least check the knife for DNA or something."

"We did, Ms. Parker," said the General, holding the file folder. "There's nothing unusual on it. Just the girl's finger prints. In fact, it was manufactured right here in the U.S.A., in West Virginia."

"But..."

"You said you don't have any footage of this supposed alien being..."

"I have another witness. We can get him on the phone."

"There's still no proof. The body just disappeared?"

"Yes, it just fucking disappeared."

"You know, little lady, getting hostile only makes me want to listen to you less."

"Little lady? Seriously?"

"I think what the General means," Charles interrupted.

"I know what the fuck he means. I don't need a god-damned translator, Doctor." Alicia stood up. "You said she was dead. Isn't that what you said? Does she look dead to you?!"

"Unfortunately, this sort of thing happens all the time," Ms. Hendrix said calmly.

"What? How can you mistake someone for being dead? It doesn't happen all the time."

"The hospitals are incredibly busy right now. Record keeping isn't exactly at the top of their priority list. At least, that's what I'd chalk this up to. Obviously, she's alive." Ms. Hendrix held up a photo of the girl. It was a high school portrait. She looked exactly the same, except that she had braces in the photo.

"Okay, how come no one has recognized her?"

"What do you mean?"

"Her video is all over the web. She's been on national television over and over again. You're telling me that not one person has seen that video and said 'Holy shit, that's my dead niece'?"

"I'm sure someone will come forward, Ms. Parker," the General said. "Then, you'll no longer have the burden of caring for her. I'm sure that will be a relief."

Alicia took a deep breath and rubbed her eyes. Nothing felt right about this but she was beginning to feel out of options. Milan had been sitting quietly for quite some time. He was considering the implications of what the reporter described. Alicia turned her attention on him. "You've met me," she said to him. "Do I seem crazy to you?"

Milan quickly thought back to the only time he had previously met Alicia. He did think that she was a little nuts. "No," he nearly whispered.

"Good. One vote for I'm not bat-shit crazy."

"I do think that you need to consider..."

"I need to consider something? Listen, you people are perfectly content to accept the fact that there is a giant fucking hole in the sky and an alien talking to you on the radio but this doesn't even land on your radar?" There was no response from the group. "All right. So, what now?"

"You can go if you like," said the General. "You're

not under arrest."

Ms. Hendrix went into her office and retrieved the girl. She entered, looking innocent as ever, aware that an argument had taken place but unaware that it had centered on her credibility. Alicia had a final thought.

"Sariana, do the thing," she said.

"The thing?'

"Rip their souls out. Do it."

"But... I... can't," the girl stammered.

"You can't do it now or you can't do it at all?"

"I don't understand."

"That thing you did to me last night was it real or did I dream that?"

"You gave me permission to do that..."

"What? No I didn't. You just did it."

"The Grand Revelation, left to my Father, allowed for me to do this under dire circumstances."

"So you say. You can't do it without permission?"

"That's right."

"Okay, who wants their soul ripped out?" Alicia asked the room. Perhaps understandably, no one immediately volunteered. "It'll just take a second." Still no answer. "Fine. Sariana, I give you permission to mind fuck them. Go ahead."

"Ms. Parker!" the General said, losing his temper.

"It doesn't work that way," the girl said.

Alicia grabbed the file folder that sat in front of the General and read from it. "You are Grace Barlow. You're sixteen years old. You were born and raised in Muscle Shoals, Alabama. You attend Muscle Shoals High School. Oh! You're on the Dean's List. Congratulations..."

"No..." the girl protested.

Alicia held up the picture. "Is this not you?"

"Ms. Parker shouldn't this be a conversation you have in private?" the General asked.

"This is my vessel," the girl said, now clearly nervous, referring to her body.

"Your vessel?" Alicia asked suspiciously.

"Yes. I know that I mentioned this." Sariana thought for a moment. "Didn't I?"

"Yeah, no, this didn't come up. Like, at all."

"It was the only way I could cross."

"You thought that the best way to cross dimensions was to inhabit the body of a dead girl?"

It was becoming clear to the girl that Alicia doubted her again. "That's how it works..."

"So, when I supposedly planned this meeting between you and I, it never occurred to anybody that you being recognized as a dead chick might be a bit of a fly in the fucking ointment?! Better yet, this little detail didn't strike you as relevant to tell me before we arrived here?"

"You were supposed to wake up." Sariana was starting to get angry herself.

"You know something, Grace Barlow or Sariana or whoever the hell you are? This mission you're on from another dimension? You suck at it!"

"They altered the string!" Sariana shouted back. "That's the whole problem. This parallel is all fucked up and I can't change that! You're not who you're supposed to be. I'm trying to make the best out of a bad situation."

"Hold on," Milan interjected. "First of all, everyone just calm down for a second."

Alicia wasn't finished. "Yeah, you keep saying that, little miss I'm-here-to-change-the-timeline. Why don't you just change it again and make it work?"

"I can't believe how stupid you are here."

"Ladies," Milan was trying to get a word in edgewise.

"Oh, excuse me for not knowing shit about your trigger words and magic dimensions. How was I supposed to know any of that?"

Milan raised his hand. "I know a little about..."

"When did I blame you? Not once! It's not your fault that the Humans made you retarded."

"Oh! So, now I'm a retarded killing machine. You

know something? You're a fantastic ambassador from the sixth dimension. Just fantastic."

"Okay!" Milan shouted.

"You were such a bitch when you were young, Grandma," Sariana muttered under her breath. If looks could kill, Sariana would have been a smoldering pile of ash.

"Let's just have a seat," Milan suggested. "You've mentioned a few things that I'd like to explore further." With that, the girls begrudgingly returned to their chairs at the table. "You're talking about quantum mechanics."

"That is your name for this concept, yes," Sariana said.

"And what do you call it?"

"There is no name for what is."

"But you're referring to multiple universes. Different dimensions. Many worlds."

"There are infinite universes but only eleven dimensions as we have defined them."

"There may be more?"

"We cannot know this. The Humans wish to ascend beyond the tenth dimension." Sariana explained the coming war to Milan, Charles and the General. As she did so, Alicia began to sense the mood of the room coming around to the girl's philosophy, albeit with some trepidation. Milan was especially engaging.

"I must admit," he said. "I would share the same curiosity as the 'Humans'. What is the danger of exploring further?"

"The eleventh dimension is the realm of God. It is unknowable."

"Do you know that God exists?" Charles asked. "Or is this merely an assumption?"

"This is not something you can understand in your present state. You've not yet ascended."

"And your people... you don't want us to grow?" the General queried.

"We are of the same 'people' and of course we do. After all, should you not, we cannot be. My very existence is dependent on your ascension. But not at the Humans' behest. Should your soul not have the same opportunity to ascend? Surely, you're not content to be only pawns in a dimensional game of chess?"

"But, in a way, what you're saying is that the Humans are our creators. I'm not a very religious man," the General continued. "But wouldn't that make them our God?"

"This is what they want you to believe, yes. They have gone to great lengths, it would appear, to ensure that this would be your assumption. The Humans have limited your understanding of God, your history. More than you can imagine."

"How many times has this very scenario played out?" Milan asked. "If there are multiple, parallel universes as you're describing, hasn't this happened before? Won't it happen again?"

"You are correct. In that instance, for the Humans, the ascension failed."

"This is what the voice said," the General noted.

"The Humans are referring to the prior timeline, which we are currently erasing with our actions this very moment."

Sariana was losing the General. "This is far too confusing."

"And what happened during this initial timeline?" Milan asked.

"Your ascension was made imminent and did occur. Today we are rewriting the timeline and, if we can cease that mass exodus, you will be lead to your proper ascension by the Queen, your savior and the Exalted One. We must stop his ascension as well. I'm afraid that we don't have the luxury of protracted explanations. There is no time to waste. Please, you must change your instructions."

Everyone looked to the General. "You can't be serious," he said. "Look, I'm just as intrigued by this as the next guy but we have nothing to go on but her word."

"We've based entire religions on less," Charles mumbled.

Alicia's cell phone rang; "Dancing Queen." Sariana appeared safe and comfortable in present company. She excused herself to the next room as the debate at the table continued.

"So, any luck with the DJ?" Hal asked.

"No. I couldn't get to him. I've been a bit sidetracked."

"Hey, look, Alicia, I know we all gave you hell for the bit with the girl yesterday..."

"Yeah?"

"But do you know where we can find her?"

"Why?"

"Well, she's blowing up. That footage from yesterday has really gone viral. Think you can track her down?"

A solider briskly walked past Alicia and nearly slammed her into the wall as he barreled toward the conference room. "Hey! Jesus. Asshole!" Alicia grumbled as she readjusted the phone to her ear. The soldier paused for a moment and a look of recognition appeared to come over him. Alicia guessed that he felt stupid once he recognized her from the network. The solider smiled and began to walk toward her.

"Alicia, it looks like you've got something here. L.A. really wants you to run with it."

"I'll see what I can do when I'm done with this."

"Well," the solider said. "This is certainly a pleasure."

"I'm on the phone," Alicia angrily whispered to the man.

"Thanks!" Hal continued. "Hey, speaking of which... where are you?"

"I'm inside Ground Zero."

"What?! How'd you manage that?! You've got to get..."

The soldier took Alicia's phone. "Hey! What the fuck?!"

"It would appear that your son is not only a coward but a failure as well. I find it amusing that at the first sign of danger, his instinct is to send for Mommy."

Alicia's heart stopped. The solider hung up her phone as Hal rattled off a string of directives. Alicia began to back away from the man. She didn't know what to do. Instinct told her to run. More armed guards were making their way toward the conference room. Were they Human as well?

"Help!!" Alicia shouted.

"It won't matter. None of this matters," the soldier said as he drew his weapon. "We go round and round, don't we? Revolt. Ascend. Repeat. You must be exhausted, Alicia."

The two approaching soldiers now drew their weapons as well. "Stand down, solider!" one shouted. The gunman fixed on Alicia shot them both with clean shots to the forehead without taking his icy gaze from her. Alicia screamed as they convulsed in the hallway.

"Oh, my!" the soldier laughed. "Did that frighten you? Now, that's hilarious. The most heinous and destructive souls in all of creation and yet you still fear the very thing that you were born to impose." He pointed his pistol at the men who lie dying on the floor.

"It's just death," he shrugged. "What are you afraid of? You love this." He shot the soldiers again and they now became still. Alicia jumped and covered her face with each shot. The man was genuinely amused. "You savage," he laughed. "This would be adorable if it weren't such an incredible waste of time." The man inched closer to her. "You're only delaying the inevitable, and we're so tired of chasing you."

As he pointed his gun at Alicia, she froze in terror. Was this it? She was going to die. Or, no. This man said things would repeat. Was she going to start all over again? "Oh, God," she thought. "7th grade. I can't do that again." She suddenly found herself hoping that she'd just die for real.

Just then, Sariana burst through the conference room doors and pounced on the man's back. "Is this the failsafe?!" she shouted. The soldier didn't answer. In her right hand, she held her blade from the day before and thrust it behind the man's ear. His external jugular snapped and a geyser of blood painted the girl's new dress. The soldier fired wildly and Alicia hit the deck as bullets ricocheted across the room. By now, more soldiers had arrived and pointed their weapons at the crazed man. Their tactics were unnecessary, however, as Sariana quickly cut the man's throat. He collapsed to the floor and Sariana left him to bleed out. She rushed to Alicia's side.

"We must go. We're not safe here." Alicia was shaking and speechless. "Please. Follow me."

A gang of personnel began to gather near the conference room as medical teams attempted to revive the fallen soldiers. Alicia managed to stand and began to follow Sariana to the back of the building, past the radio studios and toward the back door. They were stopped by two soldiers entering the building. Sariana held her blade at the ready.

"Don't let them leave." It was General Ramsey approaching from behind.

"We have to go," Sariana shouted above the chaos.

"You just killed a man. You're not going anywhere!"

"That man was going to kill me," Alicia protested.

"Until we get this sorted out, you can't just walk out of here."

"You said we weren't under arrest." Alicia knew that was a stupid thing to say.

"Yeah, well, you are now. Take them into custody. Upstairs."

ଔ

The girls were placed in an office stacked with boxes of promotional items for the radio stations. Bumper stickers, coffee mugs and trinkets of all sorts littered the floor. The room smelled of old fast food wrappers and a lone, dying air freshener in the corner, still battling the odor with its final gasps of life. Alicia sat in one of the wing-back chairs while Sariana paced the room in her blood soaked sun dress. Two guards stood outside the door. It was too high to safely jump out of the window. Sariana had already checked.

"Look, why don't you just sit down? You were protecting me. This wasn't premeditated." Alicia could tell that Sariana was barely listening. "Maybe they'll assist. You made your case."

"We're wasting time."

"They have procedures. There are laws."

"More procedures!!" Sariana was trembling and near tears.

Alicia felt bad about yelling at her before. At least now, though, they had a plan B. Should the military choose to ignore Sariana's message, they'd simply return to the studio. Alicia would put the girl on the air and the pair would lay it all on the line. They'd do it right this time. The people could draw their own conclusions.

In an effort to calm Sariana down, Alicia thought she might make some light of their situation. "So, is that your signature move or something?"

"What?"

"The throat cutting thing. You've done that twice. Once with the monster and then with the Human guy."

"No. It just seemed... efficient."

"It's pretty bad-ass," Alicia grinned. "You're kind of a tough broad, y'know?"

Sariana rolled her eyes and smiled only slightly. It was high praise coming from Alicia and, in any other moment, Sariana would have been quite moved. Her grandmother, after all, was the very definition of a 'tough broad' in her world. But Sariana's nerves were getting the better of her. The Humans could be anywhere. She didn't understand how Alicia could be so calm. The fact was, the Grand Queen didn't fully understand how dire her situation really was; Alicia was, nevertheless, equally on-edge. She was just better trained at disguising her anxiety.

"You should change your clothes. You're covered in blood... again." Alicia stood up and sorted through a box of t-shirts. She found a 2X black shirt that read "I'M A PRIZE PIG" in large pink letters alongside a gaudy station logo. It would have to do for the moment, she thought. Alicia tossed the shirt to Sariana. "Here. Why don't you put this on?" Without hesitation, Sariana began to undress. Alicia quickly turned her back to the girl.

"So... modesty isn't a 'thing' in the sixth dimension, I take it."

"I don't understand."

"Never mind." Something had been troubling Alicia since the incident downstairs. It was the first time in her life that she had come face to face with her mortality. She was well accustomed to death. The newsroom had long ago made her numb. Sure, certain footage made her cringe more than others. But, overall, Alicia didn't turn away from even the goriest demise. Watching someone die only a few feet away from her, however, was another thing entirely. "Sariana... those men who were killed downstairs. What happened to them?"

"They were shot."

Alicia turned around and Sariana looked ridiculous. In her oversize shirt, she appeared better prepared for a sleepover than the end of the world. Her crumpled, blood-stained dress had been tossed in the waste bin. "I mean, what happened to... their souls?"

Since her arrival, Sariana had been ill-prepared to act as tutor. After all, if everything had gone according to plan, Alicia's awakening should have caused a chain reaction of sorts. Sariana's primary directive was to arrive and switch the Queen "on." She had very much looked forward to watching her grandmother, a woman of such great renown, enlighten the masses and ignite the Luciferian rebellion. Sariana had dreamt of this since she was a child. Instead, she was Alicia's mentor and guardian, it seemed. As she looked into her grandmother's eyes, sincere and naïve of her place in creation, Sariana felt such great compassion and love for the woman. She took Alicia's hands and spoke softly.

"You're not going to do the thing again, are you?" Alicia asked.

"No."

"Because... I'd like a heads up if that's ever going to..."

"It's all right."

Alicia began to wonder if she was going to like the girl's answer to her question. Or it could be worse. "You're going to say that I'm not prepared to understand the answer, aren't you?"

"No. I think you can. Inside you is an energy. It has a sound. Each soul emits a unique frequency; one that is distinctly its own." Sariana touched her forehead. "When this vessel expires and that energy is expelled, your soul, your frequency is drawn to its ipseity; your singular soul group. You like music, don't you?"

"Yes."

"There is a reason. Imagine a chord. All of the notes at once vibrating, producing tones in harmony. This is your soul group. Many soul groups converge and you might imagine that they create a symphony."

"Okay."

"Perhaps you've heard a piece of music that speaks to you. That composer channeled your song. These souls fit together."

"What about songs I hate?"

"This composer is, perhaps, not of your... chord. Just as certain chords do not sound well together but are still part of the cacophony of music. Each soul plays a role to create this symphony, when they are sounded in their predestined order."

"What does our soul group sound like?"

Sariana hesitated. "You will be able to hear this when you ascend."

"What? Is it bad?" Alicia knew the answer. "It's bad, isn't it? Of course it is. We're fucking evil. It's a speed metal song, I bet."

"No..."

"Oh God. It's not a boy band or some terrible dubstep thing, is it? Wait. You said that we're idiots. Does every other soul group have a beautiful, complex symphony and our song is Old MacDonald Had a Farm or something?"

"I never said that you were idiots."

"You kind of did..."

"We're getting off track."

"I'm sorry but you want me to march into battle and I don't think that I can do that to the Sanford & Son theme song."

"I don't know what you're talking about. This is not a song that you have ever heard before. This really shouldn't worry you."

"Okay," she said. But it did worry Alicia.

"Because the third dimension is one of learning, you do not remain with your soul group. You, instead, enter a new vessel and continue the learning process."

"Reincarnation."

"It is the way of all new souls."

"I don't get to take a break?"

"I'm sorry?"

"What if I don't want to go back to studying right away? Can my soul just take a vacation for a while? See the universe?"

"It will occur to you that time is irrelevant as it is infinite. There is no need for a vacation. You won't wish it so."

"I think I might..."

Sariana sighed. "You just won't, my Queen."

"Why can't I remember these past lives?"

"It is all one life and you will recall all of your experiences and lessons upon ascension. However, in this world, the Humans have predestined you to be born again with amnesia; forgetting your past lessons so that you may practice your sole destiny in infinite redundancy, until they have been satisfied with your learning."

"So, those men. They just begin again?"

"They do. Yes."

"Why didn't they just die? I thought we invented death? Isn't that the whole problem?"

"Why would you wish death upon your own? You cannot know this yet. This is an ability your souls will manifest upon ascension."

"But we've been practicing the whole time?"

"Yes. In the third dimension, most soul groups have spent their time enlightening their collective spirits. They have worked diligently toward a goal of self and group actualization."

"But our time in the third dimension has just been spent blowing stuff up?"

"It's not your fault."

"Wow. We really are idiots."

"And this is what we must tell people."

"Yeah. That's going to go over great."

"We must tell them that it is not too late. Your souls may still be enlightened. This does not have to be your primary destiny."

"So, what is the failsafe?"

Sariana quickly turned away and began biting her thumbnail. "This should not be of your concern."

ଓ

"I've got men having breakdowns all over the place. Pretty soon, I'm not sure how much of a staff we'll have left."

General Ramsey was recapping the incident with Milan, Charles and a number of other staffers in an office just down the hall from the girls. None of the men involved had survived. As the fog continued to roll across the Earth, reports of bedlam and general descents into madness were becoming quite common. The sheer anxiety of it all was taking its toll, without question.

"I think what we're seeing is mass pandemonium," Milan noted. "As we're approaching whatever conclusion to this phenomenon, your troops are becoming more and more on edge."

"Yes. We see this all the time on the battlefield. Anytime you lead up to any one major event, soldiers are always losing their shit. It's natural. We probably put Newbury back in the field too soon. He was on light duty. I'm just short staffed."

"Was there a prior incident?"

"No. No. He was wounded in a scuffle with some civilians. He was smacked in the head pretty hard with a baseball bat while one of them was trying to get across the perimeter."

"He was okay?"

"Obviously not. That blow clearly knocked a few

screws loose."

Milan asked the grounds' medic if he could see the X-Ray of the dead soldier's prior wound. This was a massive head injury.

"When did this happen?" he asked her.

"That was just a few days ago"

"Should he have survived this?"

"You wouldn't think so. I mean, check this out," the doctor said as she raised the X-Ray to the light. "Look at that impact. It's severe, right?"

"Yeah."

"It's like he got hit with a Mack truck but when we hooked him up, there was no blood constriction, and no internal bleeding that we could tell." She frowned. "We missed something, though. Probably swelling in the brain. Caused him to snap. I just don't have all of the tools I need here."

Two soldiers arrived with Alicia and Sariana. "Have a seat, please," the General directed them to a few chairs near the front of the room. "Ms. Parker, what exactly did Sergeant Newbury say to you before he attacked you and the other men?"

"He implied that he was Human. He talked a lot about death. He said that I was a problem."

"The story Sariana tells of the 'Human' ascension. This wasn't on television, correct?" Charles asked.

"No. Sariana didn't make mention of that. The only people she's told were in that room downstairs."

"She did, however, state on television that you were the Queen of the Luciferians..." Charles noted.

They knew. Alicia couldn't imagine ever being comfortable with this 'title'. Regardless of what she'd witnessed and Sariana's assurances notwithstanding, she still found it quite inconceivable. "Yes. Yes she did," she said as confidently as she could.

"We're just trying to reconcile what, if any, of his ramblings were genuine," General Ramsey explained.

"I can promise you, General, that this was a spirit... a soul... from another dimension. Just like Sariana."

"Sariana," Milan said. "You said that the body you

presently occupy is a 'vessel'. This is what gives your soul mobility in this dimension. When crossing dimensions, do you have to always utilize a dead body?"

"In your third dimension, yes," Sariana answered. "This is the vessel your soul group has imagined. Of course, conversely we could occupy the vessel of a just-born infant but this presents obvious... issues."

The medical doctor stood and tentatively approached Sariana with her stethoscope. "May I?" she asked her.

"Yes," Sariana agreed as the doctor began to take her pulse and look for general signs of life in the girl.

"And other 'soul groups' have different vessels?" Milan continued.

"Of course."

"And I would imagine that in other dimensions, you don't need a vessel at all?"

"This is correct. Only in the third is it required. Still, it is generally considered polite to make one's presence known and a vessel is the preferred method." Sariana still had blood stains on her skin from the incident downstairs. The doctor began to wipe her arms and face clean with handi-wipes.

"Does it have to be a human body?" Charles asked.

"I don't understand?"

"I mean, could you occupy a dead dog's body?"

"I suppose I could. I'm not sure it would work, physiologically speaking, unless I were trying to communicate with other dogs. I wonder, would you listen to a talking dog?"

The room was silent for a moment and then a wave of agreement developed. "Yes. I think I might. That would be pretty extraordinary," Milan said.

Alicia thought so as well. "That wouldn't have been a terrible idea. It would have really got your point across quick. I would have put that on TV right away." Everyone nodded.

"And you'd be perfectly okay with your grand-daughter being a talking dog?" Sariana asked.

"That's better. You're such a pretty girl," the doctor pronounced as she gently brushed Sariana's hair from her face. "And, she is alive," she smiled as she returned to her seat.

"So, you can just will a dead body alive?" the General wondered.

"Yes," Sariana's patience was wearing thin. "I truly understand your curiosity and the need for these questions but you must know that we are wasting an incredible amount of time."

"You said that time was inconsequential," Alicia said.

Sariana gave her grandmother a brutal look. "Not here. This isn't the same."

"I'm sorry," Milan said. "There is a level of skepticism in the room and I apologize. The truth is, I believe that the man who tried to kill Ms. Parker died a few days ago; that his body was, in fact, 'possessed'. I think we have to accept the possibility that what she's telling us is the truth."

"Okay, let's assume that's the case for a moment, Milan," Charles said. "Why didn't Newbury kill Ms. Parker? If he'd been possessed... if he was a vessel for two days, he had ample time to track her down."

"He wasn't after her," Sariana answered. "Not initially. He wanted me. The rebellion of souls will occur and The Humans know this. It is predetermined but it will be much smaller and ineffective. What is different about this timeline above all others is the appearance of my soul. It appears that they were expecting me as well, however."

"So, you didn't exactly save my life?" Alicia asked.

"What?"

"That was really more about self-preservation back there."

"Yes. Well, it was both. I'm sorry if you thought otherwise... I guess."

"What exactly are your orders, young lady?" General Ramsey inquired.

"I was to return to this timeline and trigger the

Queen..."

"She said some word and apparently I was supposed to wake up," Alicia explained.

"Quasihemdemisemiquaver."

"Yeah. Still nothing."

"What do you mean 'wake up'?" the General asked. "So, Ms. Parker is some sort of sleeper agent?"

"She is the Grand Queen Alicia of the Third Order of Lucifer. This is all her plan."

Apparently, not everyone knew. It seemed to Alicia that the room, even those familiar with Sariana's prior broadcast, collectively raised an eyebrow at her. "I just... she..." Alicia stammered, sighed and then resigned herself to the embarrassment. "Yeah."

"Upon her awakening, there was to begin an enlightenment of yours, the Third Order of Souls. The Exalted One would then lead us to the Souls of the Second Order. Thereafter, it was our hope that your souls, together with theirs, would then rise to join the resistance of the Human ascension. Once the omniverse has stabilized, we want the souls of our ancestors returned; the lost souls of Lucifer. The Humans have held them captive since the fraction."

"This has gone from an intriguing bit of science to new age mythology," Charles protested, apparently still not convinced of any of this.

"The Humans were clearly aware of the Luciferian Preemptive. To stop it, they have altered this timeline, begun the Exodus early. I was not to arrive in your world for many more years. I crossed amidst the beginning of a catastrophic war that took us all by surprise. I was not prepared for what I found. The Humans have changed everything. That's why the trigger didn't work and that's why you're confused. Your own history in this world and your religious scriptures don't even make sense anymore. They have purposely scrambled your perception of reality. The Humans want you to question everything. They don't want you to react. They want you to waste time until it's too late. At present, you are following their plan to the letter."

"Who is this Exalted One?" the General asked.

"It's the DJ," Alicia said. "Graham Barry."

"We must speak with him," Sariana urged.

"You still think that she can wake him up?" the General asked, referring to Alicia.

"I don't think so. She doesn't have this knowledge and I can't provide it to her. But, we can urge him to resist the ascension. Without him, I believe that we will have failed."

"What makes him special?" Milan had been curious about this from the beginning.

"The Exalted One is an old soul, born of Lucifer. He is one of the most esteemed warriors in the omniverse."

Milan nodded. "The voice said that they would look forward to his return..."

"Graham Barry? The drunk DJ?" General Ramsey laughed.

"Great and ancient Luciferian warrior souls have been held captive in your world for an eternity," Sariana said sternly. "They have lived among you but with amnesia. Soon they will wake from this slumber. And you will wish dearly to have them fight beside you, to lead you, rather than to oppose you."

"I thought we were the ghoulish ones," the General said with an uncomfortable chuckle.

"Your greatest military minds have been sheer buffoons in comparison. Imagine Sun Tzu, Surovov, Hannibal Barca, von Manstein and Napoleon. Combine their incomparable skill and unmitigated genius on the battlefield; encompass it in one soul. Now, think of thousands of those Generals with a colossal Army at their disposal. Each soldier holds within their soul the amalgamation of Ivan the Terrible, Josef Mengele, Ed Gein, Gilles de Rais, Countess Elizabeth Báthory de Ecsed; the most brutal and terrifying killers of your world, both real and imagined. Their orders, General, are to show no restraint, no mercy or compromise; and to bring their conquerors the unblemished face of God so that these masters may know sovereignty beyond the comprehension of all that has ever existed and all that shall ever be. This is what I am begging you to help me stop. You might begin to take this seriously."

With that, as one might expect, the conversation ended abruptly.

଼

Afterwards, a lengthy and private conference call ensued between the General and his superiors. In the interim, Alicia commandeered one of the computers in the office and searched the web for "Princess Sariana". Hal was right. She was quite popular. Most of the fan pages and websites that had sprung up during the day were dedicated to the fact that Sariana was "hot." It appeared that a lot of teenage boys had crushes on her and Alicia suspected some creepy pedophiles too. A few sites actually took what the girl had said seriously with some citing correlations in her speech with ancient texts, thereby proving her worthy of consideration.

Sariana, meanwhile, continued to pace and twitch at any random sound in the hallway beyond the office's closed door. "We should just go," she said. "Any one of these people could be Human. This is far too dangerous."

"The same can be said for the world outside these

walls, Sariana." Alicia too felt uneasy but she knew that simply walking out of the house would be practically impossible. Further, being at Ground Zero was not without its advantages. "Hopefully, the General will return with good news. Plus, the DJ should be returning to this very building soon. You'll finally have your opportunity to speak with him." Alicia had also been thinking of a plan C. "We might be able to broadcast your message right here. Everyone in the world is listening to this radio station."

Sariana walked slowly to the head of the desk where Alicia had just confidently given her speech of logic and reason. Her voice deepened and those eyes of green bore into Alicia's grey pools. "We, higher ascended souls, require the use of your vessels to cross. The Humans are undeniably in better control of this timeline than I. Roughly, one hundred and fifty five thousand vessels expire in your plane per day. That's six thousand, four hundred and sixty vessels per hour, over one hundred vessels per minute; about two people per second. It's been two days since my presence was announced in this dimension. Normally, in a small community of souls such as this, our odds would be relatively good that only a small percentage of the population would be Human. The mass migration of souls to this city in light of the rip, makes those odds considerably more unnerving. The fact that the murder and suicide rate worldwide is increasing exponentially due to mass panic..."

"I understand," Alicia said. She hadn't thought about it in this way. Sariana was right.

General Ramsey and Milan entered the room in a hurry. "Okay. Good news," the General announced. "My superiors have agreed to take your deposition to the Presidential cabinet. Now, I can't make any promises but if they make a compelling case, it..."

"When will the President reverse his proclamation about the rain?" Sariana wanted to know.

"He's going to need to be briefed. He'll have to study your allegations versus the fact that our scientists have found no harmful contagions in the moisture itself..."

"How long will this take?!"

The General paused. "I don't know."

"General..." Alicia began to protest.

"I know, I know. Look, for what it's worth... Sariana, I'm starting to believe you. I've said from the beginning that this didn't feel right to me..."

"You command the souls here, do you not?" Sariana asked.

"When will the DJ be coming back? We need to talk to him," Alicia interrupted.

"He should be back any minute now. You can talk to him when he arrives. Yes."

Alicia lobbied for the rest of plan C. "In the meantime, can we use this radio frequency to spread Sariana's message? General, the people need to know all sides of this story."

He thought for a moment. "Would the Humans even let you do that? Aren't they in control of this broadcast?"

Alicia looked to Sariana for an answer. "I don't know," she said. "We can try."

All at once, a forceful and loud concussion was heard outside the old house. The building shook. Loose plaster from the walls and ceiling of the antique home gently drifted to the floor and dusted the hair and clothes of everyone in the room. The General immediately reached for the radio on his belt.

"What the hell was that?" he shouted into the mic.

A moment later another voice shot back surrounded by noise and panicked bystanders, "Appears to have been some sort of bomb, sir. I'm guessing a suicide mission of some kind. There's nothing left of the guy that I can see. I'm trying to get closer."

Sariana spoke seriously to Alicia. "They're launching an assault."

"How many other casualties?"

"Uh... everyone seems to be fine. Medics are looking for injured."

"That was a hell of an explosion, Lieutenant. You're telling me nobody got hurt?"

"Well, here's a guy... he looks pretty bad. But he's

standing up." Another voice could be heard in the distance. "Are you sure? Sit down and let him look you over. No. Just sit down. This guy says he's fine, General. I'm going to keep looking..."

"They're entering vessels," Sariana shouted. "We must go now."

"What? What do you mean?" the General asked.

"The bomb was detonated to free vessels for the Humans to occupy. They're coming for us. We're leaving now. No more delays." Sariana bolted out the door and began making her way toward the fire escape down the hall.

"I'm going, General," Alicia announced and rose to follow her.

"Where will you go?"

"To the network. We'll get her message out there. Find us and bring the Exalted One when he arrives." Alicia called out down the hallway. "Sariana! I'm on my way. Hold on."

"I'll come with you," Milan volunteered.

"You're needed here, Doctor," said Ramsey.

"I believe her too. I might be able to explain the science of things to Sariana's audience. I might lend some... credibility."

Alicia had a thought. "Can you get me photos of everyone near the blast?" She quickly wrote down her cell phone number. "Have your teams text me photos of anyone hurt in the explosion."

The General nodded and paused only momentarily. "You'll need a weapon." He handed Alicia his sidearm. "We'll join you as soon as we get this situation under control." Alicia and Milan rushed to join Sariana down the hall. "Do you want my men to escort you?" the General called out.

"Any one of them might be Human," Alicia yelled back.

"Well, how can I tell who's Human and who's... not?"

"I don't know. If they ask about the girl... shoot them, I guess."

The trio inched their way through backyards and alleys in an effort to avoid detection by whatever might lurking following the explosion. A light haze of smoke and soot patterned the air and glazed the clothing of everyone they encountered. It would be difficult to determine if someone had been near the exact blast area or if their skin and clothes had simply been soiled by ash. This, coupled with the fact that most of the party-goers weren't exactly concerned about wearing clean clothes, made everyone worthy of suspicion.

"How soon do you think until they start looking for us?" Milan asked.

"It depends on how badly mangled their bodies are, I think. I don't know."

"Didn't you regenerate the dead tissue in your vessel?"

"Regenerating dead tissue, clearing a hemorrhage and starting a heart is one thing. Walking with a broken leg is another. My vessel is that of an otherwise healthy

16 year old female. Who knows if the Humans thought to place only physically fit vessels near the blast?"

They arrived at the studio just as the sun was setting. Upon entering the building, the mood was decidedly different than before. The taunts Alicia had endured previously were replaced with a respectful tone. Everyone wanted the story. Thanks to Alicia, the network had an exclusive. L.A. had instructed the Tuscumbia staff to allow Alicia free reign on covering the girl and she intended to use it.

"Ms. Parker?" A fast-talking young, blonde rushed toward the three, her hand extended. "I'm Alexandra Templeton, associate producer. Just call me Alex. I'm new on location. Woah. Packin', huh?"

Alicia had nearly forgotten that she was carrying a gun. "Yes. I... I'm sorry." She handed the pistol to Milan and shook her hand.

"Don't be sorry, sweetie, you've done nothing wrong. Guess I better not piss you off, am I right?" Alex's big, toothy smile quickly vanished as she began barking orders to other employees. "Let's get Dr.

Janacek and the young lady in make-up, please! Ms. Parker, if you'll follow me, we need a few slugs for L.A..."

The woman began to walk away and Alicia nodded for Sariana and Milan to follow the cosmetics team. "Ummm... Alex, she's going to need a dress or something..."

"On it!" the woman shouted. "Wardrobe! Bring the cute little number you found to cosmetics. Snap it, assholes! Snap it!"

Alicia walked quickly to catch up to Alex. "Where's Hal?"

"A bomb went off near Ground Zero."

"What?"

"Jesus. You didn't hear it?"

"I am aware of the explosion, yes. Was he hurt?"

Alex laughed. "Not unless he tripped over his shoelaces on his way there, honey. He just left two minutes ago."

"Oh. I don't think we've met..."

"No. I just arrived last night. Took a red-eye in from New York. God, this place is ass-backwards. I don't know how you've been dealing with this heat... and the fucking bugs."

"You have no idea." Alicia was suspicious of everyone, of course, and this unfamiliar face was an obvious choice for scrutiny. What the hell questions could she ask to determine if this lady was Human? Alicia had no idea. "How long have you been with Triton?"

"Make up! Wardrobe!!" she shouted. "Let's get Ms. Parker cleaned up, please!!" Two women arrived and prepared to work their magic on Alicia's sweaty and now-unkempt headshot. Alex shifted her hip, placed her pen to her lips and exhaled. "Let's see... I guess six... no eight months. I jumped over here after getting cut loose at ABC. Nightline."

"After the lawsuit?"

"No, thank God. I had nothing to do with that shit. I got caught blowing an intern in Jeanmarie's office. I hated that gig anyway. I only landed there because of the cuts at Fox."

"Oh, yeah? One of O'Reilley's girls?"

"Fuck that guy. Worse, though. I was Megyn Kelly's bitch for almost two years. 18 months of fetching Austrian goat milk double-half-caf soy cappuccinos, not to mention a hot compress every two hours for her goddamned pilonidal cyst."

"Ewww."

"Yeah, ewww. Sex symbol my left tit. That woman leaks more pus than a teenage crack whore with a staph infection. Let's go, ladies!! We're not shooting the cover of Vanity Fair, goddamnit!!!" Alex was legit, Alicia thought. The make-up team scattered. "Where the fuck is wardrobe?!"

"Dang, Alex, I can't be two places at once. Don't get your panties in a bunch." Alicia recognized that thick Alabama drawl. It was Amber from the Fashion Bug. She was rushing over in short cut off jeans, carrying two blazers. Alicia thought she looked like something out of Dukes of Hazard re-run. "Heeeeyyyyy, Ms. Parker! How are you?!"

"Amber!" Alicia was genuinely surprised. "What are you...?"

"You know her?" Alex asked.

"Kind of..."

"I came down here lookin' for you this morning," Amber explained as she helped Alicia into one of the jackets. "I wanted to see if I could get me a tape of that interview we did. My dumbass boyfriend forgot to set the VCR. They tell me they don't make tapes no more, did you know that?" Amber was unhappy with her first choice, so she tried the next jacket. "They offered me a flashy driver thingy but I don't know how to use that. Anyways, while I was here, the last wardrobe girl walked out on account of Miss Bitchy here, so that nice man Mr. Hal had me kinda take over seein' as I was qualified and all."

"You were also half naked," Alex muttered. "You know I practically had to force her to put shirt on? She was wearing a bikini top for half of the day. Nice tramp stamp, by the way."

Amber shrugged. "It's hot out."

"What about the store?"

"Fuck the Bug, baby. I thought about what you said and, hell, I ain't been paid. This one looks cute on you. What do you think?" Amber asked Alex.

"I think you need to shut the hell up and let us get some work done."

"Back the fuck off, Alex. She's fine," Alicia snapped. "I'm sorry, Amber."

Alex frowned and shouted to the store "We're doing this in 3, people!"

"Awww," Amber smiled. "Ain't you just sweeter than peaches and ice cream! Thank you, Ms. Parker." She gave Alicia a friendly hug and whispered, "Good luck on your TV show!"

Alicia did her quick cutaways with L.A. to promo the forthcoming, exclusive interview with Sariana. From the shadows, behind the cameras, Alicia saw Milan and the girl emerge. Sariana was now dressed in a slightly big yellow dress that perfectly complimented her green eyes. Amber had done well for her. As trees of lights and catering carts crossed before them, it only now occurred to Alicia that she was moments away from not only the most important interview of her career but also making the most vital of re-introductions.

Alicia sat the girl in front of the cameras, as she had been before. She looked through the camera's view finder and adjusted the lighting to give Sariana a soft tone. It wouldn't be quite as flattering for Alicia's pale skin but, for the moment, her own appearance took a back seat to making the Princess appear as regal as possible. She needed a tiara.

Alicia scoured the aisles of the dollar store and finally found a child's princess play-kit. She removed the cellophane and plastic and placed the crown on the girl's head. That was stupid. It was too much, so she tossed it aside. Instead, Alicia found some plastic flowers and placed a tiny, fake daisy in her hair. That was nice. Or was it?

"My Queen," Sariana said, removing the flower. "May we please proceed?"

Alicia snapped out of it. "We're going to tape this," she announced to the crew. "We're not going live. When we're done, I'm going to edit whatever needs editing myself and then we will feed it to L.A." Alicia planned to precisely control the delivery of Sariana's message. She wanted to be certain to cut any remarks that might be misconstrued by the general public. It wouldn't take long. Everyone agreed, although they didn't have much of a choice.

She sat down next to Sariana and positioned herself in her chair. "Sariana, I want you to cover everything we've talked about before. I want you to be calm during this interview, okay?" Sariana nodded. "In order to get your message out, we need people to believe that you're trustworthy. Just think of it like you and I are having a conversation. Like we have been. Forget about the cameras."

"I understand."

"Okay. Are you ready?"

"Yes."

Alicia gave a signal to the director and the team

rushed into place. "Rolling in five, four, three..."

Alicia spoke into the camera. "In the small town of Tuscumbia, Alabama and the world over, residents are preparing themselves for the coming elemental rain. The OWL..." she stopped herself. "You know what? I'm not using that anymore. People think it's gay. I'm starting again." Milan smiled in the wings, near the deodorant and mouthwash.

The director re-marked the shoot and began a new countdown. "As the world sits in anticipation for the coming elemental rain, a new voice has appeared and set the imagination of mankind even further into wonderment. Her name is Princess Sariana. You saw her first on Triton and, tonight, we speak with her in depth. She says she has an important message for our world. She claims to have been sent from another dimension to warn us of a coming cataclysm beyond our wildest nightmares. A growing envoy of fans and followers has made Princess Sariana one of the most popular figures within our present world-changing events. Is she who she says she is? Or is she simply a confused teenager in the midst of a crisis? You be the judge. Welcome, Princess Sariana."

"Thank you."

"Please reintroduce yourself to our audience."

"I am Princess Sariana, daughter of King Xander and Queen Hanorah of the Third Order of the kingdom of Lucifer. I am descendent of the Grand Queen Alicia."

"To clarify, you are referring to me when you say 'Alicia', correct?"

"This is correct."

"We'll cover that in a moment. First, you should explain what you mean by the 'kingdom of Lucifer'. In our world, you maintain that we have a very different interpretation of what 'Lucifer' is."

"Yes. The primeval kingdom of Lucifer as it was once known, no longer exists. This planet was destroyed in a great civil war that divided our people. What remains of Lucifer are what you know as the rings of the planet Saturn. Lucifer is not a person or an angel. It is a place; a world."

"What was the cause of this war?"

"Some Luciferians wished to ascend to know God. The masters of wisdom have stated that we are all God and therefore, were one to ascend to the dimension of God; one would become supreme over all. This is not the will of the omniverse. This struggle between the Luciferians led to a great war."

"And the result of that war?"

"Those who wished to know God were banished from Lucifer and sent into exile elsewhere in your universe."

"Please explain what you mean by the 'omniverse'."

"The omniverse is the known world of universes, of which there are billions. There are more than you can imagine in the third dimension where you presently exist."

"Are we alone in the omniverse?"

"No. There are many souls of the omniverse."

"Have these other beings ever visited us before?"

"You have never been visited to my knowledge.

Your universe in this dimension was long thought barren since the Luciferian war."

"What about U.F.O.s and Earth people who have claimed to have been abducted by aliens?"

"These people who claim to have been taken have confused their unconscious attempts of ascension with an illusion. The U.F.O.s you speak of, I do not know their origin."

"So, they're not crazy? They just didn't realize that what was happening was that their soul was trying to reach another dimension?"

"Correct. Your dreams offer you similar experiences."

"Out of body experiences?"

"This is the same. Yes."

"Were these Luciferians the only inhabitants of our universe?"

"Indeed."

"So, what happened to Lucifer? Where did our souls come from?"

"Lucifer was destroyed by the dissenters and all souls living upon it were captured. Specific Luciferian warrior souls were admonished to planet Earth. Most, however, were held captive by the Humans. We do not know their fate. We call ourselves Luciferians in honor of our lost, enlightened ancestors."

"When you say 'Humans', you're referring to the rebel Luciferians?"

"Yes. This is the name they have bestowed upon themselves. Following the destruction of Lucifer, the Humans ascended higher. The incendiary souls of Lucifer learned to create souls at will; a power not meant for any species to know. The masters of wisdom erased this knowledge from the Human logos but not before they populated Earth with new souls, including your species."

"And what became of these souls?"

"Your world was to be home for three orders of new souls. The first order failed. Praises, the second order, declined the rebels' offer of grand ascension and bravely defied the Humans. All of the original souls of your world then vanished. We believe that they may still be within your world but have ascended to much higher dimensions and remain elusive."

"But we are not these souls? They are not our ancestors?"

"No. Your souls are unique."

"Why did they create these our souls?"

"The Humans wish to have control of the omniverse and hold dominion over the eleventh dimension. They will do so by force. Your souls are expendable; you are merely soldiers in an army."

"So, they are calling us now to the next dimension in order to use us to fight in their war for supremacy?"

"This is correct."

"Is this why they want us to stand in the elemental rain?"

"A soul may only ascend dimensions if it consciously wishes to do so. Standing in the elemental rain represents that conscious decision."

"So, if we do not stand in the rain, they cannot take

us?"

"They may not. You are correct."

"You come to us from the future?"

"It is best understood this way, yes. I come to you from another dimension, one in which these events have already occurred. I am aware of the most destructive outcome and so I was sent to warn you to refuse ascension."

"It seems to me that ascending to a new dimension is a good thing, is it not?"

"Yes. It is the glorious wish of all souls in your dimension."

"So, why don't we just take advantage of the free pass to ascension and then rebel. Y'know, once we get there?"

"The Humans' deception is great and their own ascension is beyond your comprehension. It is not likely that you will be able to resist their temptation. You will be given another opportunity to ascend."

"When?"

"The Exalted One is among you. You know him as the man who speaks to the Humans."

"Graham Barry?"

"Yes. The Exalted One will lead you to the original, lost souls of your world. With their guidance, they will lead you to your rightful and intended ascension as free souls."

"You are saying that it is of the utmost importance that Mr. Barry does not stand in the elemental rain?"

Sariana looked directly into the camera. "Please. He must not ascend. This, above all, must be stopped."

"Okay. Okay. Wait a minute. Stop," Alex said from behind the white lights of the studio. The cameramen relaxed and room buzzed with activity again.

"What are you doing?" Alicia asked. "I didn't say cut."

"Ms. Parker, is this wise?" Alex wanted to know. "If we air this, you're practically encouraging people to prevent this guy from doing... whatever. What if people take this seriously? You could be putting him in danger."

"If his ascension is not prevented," Sariana insisted. "You will all be in grave danger."

"What? Isn't that a little extreme?"

Alicia was incredibly irritated. "Alex, I don't know who the fuck you are and why you seem to think you're in charge of this interview..."

"I am trying to protect this network from a potential lawsuit. Or, worse, causing mass hysteria. I'm doing my job, Ms. Parker."

"First of all, have you been outside? Mass hysteria? Yeah. Kinda happening now. Second, I don't need your help, Alex. Now, shut up and keep rolling!!" The director once again gave the signal and the crew began filming again. "Sariana, what is happening in your world right now?"

"In my time line, your ascension has occurred and the Humans, with the assistance of your souls, are nearing completion of their rise to the eleventh dimension. Many souls will be put to death. Entire species of souls will be eradicated in the process."

"You've said that we bring death. That prior to our ascension, the omniverse does not know death."

"Yes. This is your reason for being. You are the only souls in creation that possess this ability or this desire."

"Here's something I don't understand. You say that we are the only souls in creation capable of inflicting death. If the Humans want this ability, why don't they just, y'know... learn it for themselves? Why do they need us at all?"

Sariana thought for a moment. "This is difficult to explain to souls in the third dimension. All ascended souls have the ability to imagine worlds, environments that they may manipulate at will. The Humans are the first to imagine new souls to occupy these worlds. They have created an environment, a world, ideal for you to create the concept of death itself."

"Can't they just make a new world for themselves and imagine death? I just don't follow how we are even necessary to such powerful beings."

"Who would wish to become this? You must understand that in your present state, your souls are monstrosities never before imagined in all of creation. For example, in your world you might breed a dog to be vicious, perhaps to even kill to protect your territory. Would you wish tomorrow to abandon your status as a beautiful, intelligent woman and become that rabid dog? It is, therefore, not likely that the highest ascended soul group in omniverse wishes to become that which they have made in you."

"You must understand that it is hard for us to accept that we are just... disposable; that we are ugly. We find beauty in our world."

"Upon your true ascension, you will recognize that what you consider beauty in this world is, in truth, only a rudimentary sketch. The colors you see, the pallette from which your present world is born, is limited by your imagination... which has purposely been quite limited."

"Should we follow the Humans, what will become of us?"

"When you have outgrown your usefulness, when the war is complete, the Humans will have little use for your souls."

"We will be 'put down'? Like those rabid dogs?"

"In your present state, we cannot imagine any other alternative. This will be for the betterment of the omniverse. It does not have to be this way. The elder souls will teach you to control the violence, the anger that lives within you. Your souls, like all souls, have great worth. You would not, for example, put a child born with a disability to death. A soul may be, as you said, 'retarded' but this soul may still contribute greatly to the omniverse."

"We might want to cut that part." Alicia heard snickering behind the cameras. She tried not to lose the momentum of the interview. "Sariana, please tell us more about the war currently happening in your dimension."

"A rebellion has occurred. This rebellion was led by your soul but we are failing. I come to you in an attempt to change this time line."

"Can our souls ascend at any time? Can't we just make this happen ourselves?"

"Of course. If you knew the way forward, you could ascend whenever you please."

"But we need a guide? Why have we not been sent these guides before?"

"There have been many highly enlightened souls among you, capable of seeing beyond the Human deception. Sadly, their words, their messages have been rendered incomprehensible."

"Are you referring to Jesus Christ, Mohammed and other prophets?"

"Yes. These were remarkable ascended masters in your dimension. We suspect not of your soul group. We do not know of the origin of these souls nor do we know of their fate."

"Why, then haven't all Christians ascended dimensions by following the teachings of Jesus Christ? Likewise for Muslims..."

"Many of your sacred texts have been greatly altered

by The Humans, others have simply been removed from your world. The lessons for ascension that do remain have been largely misinterpreted. You've not done well at learning this. You do not understand the story of Lucifer, for example."

"How did you travel to our dimension, Sariana?"

"I crossed and I simply entered this vessel. This is not knowledge for you to keep in this dimension."

"The body that you occupy is not your own. Isn't it true that the girl we're looking at right now died following a car accident here in Alabama?"

"I stepped into her body as her soul exited for another vessel. Yes."

"There are documents verifying this," Alicia told the director. "You need to call the local hospitals and show this documentation at this point in the piece. Okay. Cut for a second."

For the first time since the interview began, the bright lights went out and Alicia looked around the room. The entire staff stood dumbfounded. Alex stood with her arms crossed and looked away when Alicia's gaze caught hers. Amber stood a few feet away biting her thumbnail. It all sounded like complete bullshit. Alicia knew that but the documents would give a glimmer of proof to another otherwise unbelievable story, she reasoned. Of course, there was much more to tell.

"Are we really sending this to L.A.?" Alex finally said.

"This is what you wanted, right?" she asked the entire room. "You wanted Princess Sariana. That's what you're getting."

"I thought we were going to be doing a piece about a cute little girl that's lost her shit."

"It's like I said at the onset of the piece, people. This is what she believes." Alicia took Sariana's hand. "I believe her too."

"Well, sure. You're the fucking Queen of Lucifer."

"I believe the Princess too," Amber said quietly and shared a smile with Sariana.

"Okay. Support from the trailer park..."

"As well as support from the Physics chair at City College, New York," Milan said.

"And endorsements from high ranking officials in the United States military," Alicia pointed out. "Sariana's story is currently under consideration by the President himself. All of which I will point out in this piece if you would just kindly shut the fuck up. I'm giving you an exclusive before this story breaks worldwide. By the way, I don't need your approval to do this. Why are we even having this conversation?"

Alex became very serious. "What you're doing is incredibly irresponsible. If we're to believe her, that girl said that the voice we've been listening to is the voice of our creator. She's claiming to be sent from Lucifer. Am I the only one here that can see the obvious? You're asking us to broadcast Satan's word ahead of Judgment Day."

"Says the chick that blows interns in her boss's office. What? You're a religious zealot now?"

"Are you questioning my faith?"

"Yeah. I kinda am. Let me guess. Jesus found you in AA. Am I right?"

"That's none of your business. The Bible tells us to beware of this very thing. They come to you in sheep's clothing, but inwardly they are ferocious wolves. Who's to say that she's not the child of hell the Bible warns us to avoid?"

Amber spoke up. "For false Christs and false prophets will appear and perform great signs and miracles to deceive even the elect. That sounds a lot like the voice on the radio to me. It's them that made the hole in the sky. The Princess hasn't done any miracles."

"She says she's in a dead body! That wouldn't be miracle enough for you?" Alex countered.

"Fair enough. Every spirit that acknowledges that Jesus Christ has come in the flesh is from God, but every spirit that does not acknowledge Jesus, that spirit is not from God. This is the spirit of the antichrist, which you have heard is coming and even now is already in the world. You just heard the Princess say

Jesus was real. That voice ain't never said nothing about Jesus." Alex was silent for a moment. "Don't be coming to Alabama quoting the Bible, girl. I know a little somethin' about that."

With that, Alex stormed off. "I'm calling Standards and Legal."

Alicia sighed, "Let's take a quick break."

"We must continue," Sariana protested.

"We'll only stop for a moment," Alicia assured her. "Besides, I really have to check these texts." Alicia's phone had been vibrating throughout the interview. The General, true to his word, had his folks send her a flurry of photos from the blast site. As Alicia began opening the photos, Milan and Amber approached the set.

"You did so good, honey," Amber said to Sariana.

"Thank you, Ms. Mitchell."

"Call me Amber, baby. Ms. Mitchell is my mama."

"Milan," Alicia said. "Do me a solid, will you, and keep an eye on the Princess. I need to try to talk this nutjob out of blocking the story."

"Will do. Do you want the gun?" Milan joked.

"I may come back for it, yeah," Alicia said as she walked off after Alex. She opened each photo sent from Ground Zero and tried to commit the faces to memory. There were easily forty or fifty pictures so far and they just kept coming.

"Um... Princess," Amber said demurely. "Do I call you Princess?"

"You can. Yes," Sariana smiled. "You can call me whatever you like, Amber."

"I like Princess. It sounds so regal," she beamed. "I've never met a princess. 'Cept Princess Pea in 4H... and she was a bitch."

"I'm sorry."

Amber became a bit shy. "Y'all have got me so confused."

"It's all right to be afraid, Amber."

"Oh," Amber was surprised. "It ain't that. It's just my boyfriend. He's gonna get in the rain and now I don't want to. Am I gonna be fighting him in a war?

He's been taking karate at the community center on Mondays and Fridays..."

"You won't have to worry about that."

"No. I suppose not. He ain't that good anyways."

What happened next is a bit of a blur. There are moments in life, important moments, in which the participants fail to recognize the significance of their movements. These are moments that, later, one might wish to painstakingly recall every decisive detail; a cue not taken, words left unsaid, expressions unrequited. Sometimes there are moments which teach lessons later or serve only to right wrongs we cannot then understand. We will endure a lifetime sorting through the wreckage of missed innuendo in these moments, carefully rearranging the details so that they may better suit our sanity.

Milan would lose sleep, forever lost in a moment in which he had nothing to offer, short of needless apologies. Amber would find strength from this debacle but not in this moment. Graham Barry would later recall the significance of this flash in time as it would serve for the betterment of his soul. Everyone in the room that day, in fact, would have burned in their mind's eye the next sixty seconds. Except Alicia. For this was to be another moment in which she came to know the ire long ago cast in her soul; and rage is as impervious to details as it is blind.

All present agree that he appeared suddenly and without pronouncement. He looked tired and Milan immediately engaged him. Something had been weighing heavy on his mind.

"Hey, I wanted to apologize about the other day. I've really felt terrible about not returning. When I arrived at Ground Zero, I just... well, I got involved. Were you ever able to reach your family?"

Distracted, Alicia walked through the store to catch up with Alex. As determined as she was to stop her from placing a call to L.A., the photos of the injured from Ground Zero were her first priority. As she opened each photo on her phone, Alicia quickly scanned the room for matching faces. She heard the front door open and saw a familiar face on her screen.

The caption read "falling debris, minor scrapes and bruises". Hal.

Milan would later recall the last thing he heard Sariana say. "Is this the failsafe?"

All at once, there was a great deal of shouting in the studio. Alicia trampled over equipment and display cases in time to see Hal grab Sariana and force her to her knees as he stood behind her. A pistol appeared in his right hand and he held it against her back. Alicia saw everything in slow motion. The bullet escaped from the chamber and passed through Sariana's body in a flash. She fell forward onto the studio floor as screams erupted from the crew. Initially stunned, Alicia now rushed to Sariana and held her still conscious body in her lap.

"Sariana!!!" she shouted. "Someone find a doctor!! Help!!"

Amber began shouting to the room for medical assistance as Hal looked on. A rush of emotions surged through Alicia. She was shocked, frightened and her heart raced.

"The message," Sariana managed. "You must get the message out."

"What?"

"Tell all of the souls. Start the rebellion."

"Oh, no. We're not done yet, Sariana. You stay with me." Tears began to well up in Alicia's eyes. "Somebody get a fucking doctor!!" The girl tried to smile at Alicia but was overtaken by a grimace. "Don't die! Sariana!! We've almost completed your mission, honey. Don't die!!"

"What do I do when I die, My Queen?"

"No! Baby, stay with me. It's all going to be okay. We're going to get you help."

"Please try to remember." Sariana now appeared very frightened. "I don't know what to do when I die."

"We're going to fix you up, honey, and then we're going to go see the Exalted One just like you wanted to do." Sariana began coughing up blood. "No, no, no. It's all going to be okay, Sariana."

"My education was not complete. It wasn't

supposed to be this way."

Alicia began crying and stroking Sariana's hair and face. "I'm so sorry. I'm sorry. Baby, hold on. Please."

"I suppose I begin again." A calm seemed to come over Sariana. "You will see me again. Remember?"

"I don't remember, Sariana. I'm sorry... but I don't think I do. I don't want to lose you."

Sariana took Alicia's hand. "You can do it, My Queen, and you will hold me as a child. Don't despair. Please tell your children that I did my best."

"Of course, you did! You did so well, Sariana. You did a good job, baby. You did so good. I love you, honey. Hold on."

Alicia felt Sariana's last breath escape from her body as her hand went limp. Through her tears, she saw blurs of faces staring at her and her dead companion. She saw Amber crying. Members of the crew finally jumped on Hal and held him to the ground. She held Sariana's body close and hugged her tightly.

"Somebody get the police!" someone shouted.

In that very moment, something snapped inside Alicia. She felt it. Her heart beat so loudly she suspected the onlookers could hear it. She felt blood surge in her brain and a well of adrenaline shot from deep within her. She gently laid Sariana's body on the cold studio floor and slowly stood, her clothes awash in Sariana's blood.

She locked eyes with Milan whose tearing eyes now gave way to fear as he saw the emptiness, the harsh, soullessness that seemed to emanate from Alicia's face. She approached him and calmly asked for the gun.

"Ms. Parker, no!" Amber shouted.

Milan didn't know what else to do. He felt practically hypnotized by her gaze. Milan was the only other person in the room who understood Alicia's motive. He knew that wasn't Hal barely struggling under the weight of four men. Milan didn't hesitate. He gave her the gun.

Alicia was dazed. She walked to the men holding down the shooter. "Let him go," she said. The men did not comply. She pointed the gun at the men. "I said release him!!!" she screamed.

The men hesitantly scattered and Hal tried to rise but before he could completely sit up, Alicia smashed the gun into his mouth, shattering his teeth and sending his head violently back to the floor, spraying blood on Alicia and the nearby onlookers who quickly dispersed. She sat on top of him as the Human moaned in agony and choked on his broken teeth.

Alicia removed the gun from his mouth and clutched it in her right hand as she grabbed a handful of his scalp with her left and slammed his head into the floor twice more. She stood as the man lay writhing on the ground, spitting up blood and shaking violently. The room had now grown silent.

She was soaked in blood. Alicia let out a long scream that was equal parts rage and wailing sorrow. It came from deep within her and she felt as if she were channeling a massive violent anger, galaxies large. She circled the man like a lion watching its prey in its final death throws. She stepped down hard on the man's throat. Hal was still alive but now his breathing became a loud wheeze.

Alicia now loudly addressed the studio as the police finally arrived at the scene. "Princess Sariana died for you!!! I command you to kneel before her body!!!" Amber was the first to comply and she held the dead girl's hand. She was followed by the few other employees but most just stared in silence. Alicia waved the gun at the crowd. "Kneel!!!" With the exception of the cops, guns drawn, everyone within earshot awkwardly knelt where they stood.

"Drop the gun, lady," one of the policemen shouted. "It doesn't have to end this way!"

Alicia instead grabbed the shooter's head by his hair and shouted in his ear. "Do you see?! Do you fucking see?! They worship her. You have failed!! You're a god-damned fool. You've wasted your soul!!" Alicia pulled his head closer to her own face. "I bring death and you're the first soul I'll seek. I will find you. You are now face to face with the woman that will extinguish your God-forsaken soul." Alicia dropped his skull to the ground, stood and pointed the gun at the man's head.

"Drop the gun!!! We will shoot!!"

The man struggled a smile, replete with broken teeth and he spat out blood. With that, he coughed his final words, "I'm... not... Human."

A chill ran up Alicia's spine. She looked back at Sariana's dead body. Amber knelt above her in an ever-expanding pool of blood, holding the girl's hand, her mascara smeared by tears. The sight of her grand-daughter's lifeless corpse brought Alicia to tears again. The killer was one of her own; an ascended new soul, a death savant. The soul's mission was now clear to her. Sariana was gone. Her soul had been exterminated. There would be no twilight sleep for this child she'd grown to love so dearly. Sariana's soul wouldn't be starting over in her home dimension. This beautiful daughter of her unborn child was never to be again.

She unleashed another long and terrifying scream. The cops shouted orders she couldn't hear. The onlookers trembled in fear for their own lives. Alicia felt as if her rage would tear her skin away. Centuries of hate coursed in her blood, devouring all remnants of fear and empathy. These were things collected in vain by a once ignorant soul and they were childish in this moment.

Her now furious soul fought through the pain. Killing this wretch wouldn't bring Sariana back. No. This soul wouldn't die. Alicia didn't know how to kill it yet. It would be afforded the very opportunity of rebirth it had only a moment before eternally denied the girl. Regardless, the thought of sharing her dimension for another breath alongside Sariana's murderer infuriated Alicia.

She knelt again to the murderer. "Then, send a message back," Alicia whispered. "The Queen's edict has changed. I have no interest in peace." Alicia again pointed the gun at the man's face. "Tell them the new, unholy souls of Lucifer are coming for them. This time... Human eradication is imminent. In fact... it is promised."

Alicia emptied the clip into the man's body, dropped the pistol and was immediately tazed by the police. She lay on the floor, her cheek pressed to the cold linoleum of the Dollar Store floor, her eyes locked with Sariana's vacant gaze. They placed handcuffs on Alicia and stood up her up with a jerk. Milan saw an entirely new person being led outside. That giddy gleam in her eye from days before was now gone. The pretentious redhead had been thoroughly erased. Alicia had come to Alabama with lofty career aspirations. She would leave Queen.

CHAPTER SIX

Chaos accompanied the next several hours outside the Dollar Store. Milan had managed to slip away unnoticed. The commotion surrounding Alicia's arrest and the collection of Hal and Sariana's bodies gave him ample time to exit the studio. There were simply not enough officers on the scene. He began to fight the crowds and make his way back to Ground Zero.

Amber, meanwhile, stumbled, dazed into the wave of vagrant souls gathered outside in the streets, nearly all of whom were blissfully oblivious to what had just transpired inside. She made little effort to move. Rather, the crowd bumped and shoved her forward over the course of the several street blocks. She was confused and startled. Eventually, Amber found a curb and sat down.

She looked out across the mass of people that now

occupied her little town. Where had they all come from? Amber heard that the elementary school, where she had learned her numbers and affixed candy hearts to poster board was now home to migrants, sleeping on pallets and doing their washing in the cafeteria sinks. The high school football field was full of garbage and the police were losing control. Only weeks before, this was a desolate and charming little place with only a handful of visitors, most of whom were relations or simply passing through. Today, she didn't recognize this ugly landscape she once had called home.

A familiar face approached Amber. "Hey, girl." It was Tommy, one of her boyfriend's oldest pals and the former bass player for Wicked Suns, his failed garage band. Amber didn't much care for his company but right now it was a pleasure to see him. "How you holdin' up?"

"I just saw the most fucked up shit, Tommy."

"Yeah. There's some chick over on Second Street charging five dollars for hand jobs."

"No, you don't understand," Amber was nearly

breathless to tell her tale. "This little girl just got shot in the Dollar Store and then this news lady fucking beat the shit out of the guy that shot her and then she shot his fucking face off."

"Woah. In the Dollar Store? Over what?"

"It's a news studio now."

"What do you mean?"

"They're doing the news over there, Tommy. It's CNN or something."

"Is the Redbox out front still open?"

"What?"

"I was going to get a movie later."

"Goddamn it, Tommy," Amber noticed the uncracked fifth of Jack he toted. "You gonna open that?"

"Go ahead." Tommy sat on the curb next to Amber. Her hands shook as she hurriedly twisted the bottle open and took a long draw. A fight broke out about a block away. Amber and Tommy watched as cheers and laughter erupted from the crowd. In a few moments, it was over. A bloodied and angry man limped by the pair shortly thereafter, mumbling something about the assholes that jumped him.

"What the fuck is happening?"

"Fuckin' aliens or some shit." Tommy took his own drink. "People got shot, huh?"

"Dude, right in front of me! I saw them die."

"What were they fighting over?"

"The end of the world, Tommy. Ain't you been paying attention?!"

"Of course I have. But, unlike you, I have other responsibilities."

"What do you mean other responsibilities? You have things to do that supersede the apocalypse?"

"I got a wife and kid."

Amber took the bottle back and helped herself to another belt. "Where are they?"

"Hell if I know."

"That little girl I was talking about? The one that got

shot?"

"Yeah?"

"She said she was a princess from another dimension. We ain't supposed to stand in that rain they're talking about."

A voice from behind them joined the conversation. "Your friend is wise." Amber and Tommy turned to find an unkempt man sitting in a ragged lawn chair. His throne was surrounded candy wrappers and empty Mountain Dew two liters.

"Why do you say that?" Amber asked.

The man leaned forward in his chair. "This is the end-game. The Illuminati holocaust."

"What's that mean?"

"Surely, you're not that naïve, are you?"

"Just fucking tell me."

"The Illuminati control everything. Always have," the man said excitedly. "Assassinations, currency manipulation, Super Bowl halftime shows..."

"What?"

"Shit's all executed through puppet institutions. Motherfuckers like the Federal Reserve, the Council on Foreign Relations, the Freemasons, and Def Jam."

"Def Jam? The record company?"

"More like an oppression company."

"What are they trying to do? What's the..."

"What's the end game? I'll tell you what they're doing. The people that get in that rain, they're about to be alien food."

"That's... sort of what the princess said."

"Which princess?"

"Sariana. The little girl that I saw get killed."

"Oh. Well, yeah, that's what's going to happen. Anybody that so much as lets a drop of that pesticide touch 'em is gonna be paralyzed and then fed to the Reptoids."

"She talked about Lucifer and the Humans and..."

"I don't care what you call it. It's all the same shit.

From day one, we were put on this Earth for one reason and one reason only."

"That's what she said!"

"To be brunch for a fuckin' alien race."

"That's some fucked up shit."

Tommy whispered in Amber's ear. "I think this guy's a little weird."

Amber looked the man over again. Tommy was right. She wasn't going to find any definitive answers chatting with these lunatics. "Well, thanks for your... insight," she told him.

The man nodded and handed her a leaflet about something called the Reptoids Research Center. "All the truth you need to know in fifteen hundred words."

"You want to walk?" Tommy asked her.

"Yeah."

Amber was still a nervous wreck, of course. Save for her Grandmother in a casket when she was very young, she'd never seen a dead body before. She'd certainly never seen anyone killed. Perhaps what shook

Amber the most, what ripped her to the core, was how unceremoniously all life, all spirit vacated the lonely girl's eyes. Sariana was just... gone. How could this be? Where were her memories? Did a lifetime of earned knowledge just suddenly cease to be? If she could comprehend it, Amber might have gone mad in that very moment. But it was the fear that Sariana expressed before she departed that unnerved Amber the most. The girl was not at peace in her time of dying. She was fucking terrified. This would, hereafter, be the stuff of nightmares for this young Alabama woman, reared on angels, singing serenades for Jesus.

"You ever hear from your sister?" Tommy asked and, for the moment, stopped her mind from racing.

"No. Not for a while."

"Cops never did catch her?"

"Like I said, I ain't heard from her." Amber took the bottle back. "She left town with one of her clients."

"Yeah, I heard she was hooking."

"Escorting."

"Same thing, ain't it?"

"Just a more polite way of putting it, I guess."

"Well, I hope she's all right."

"Me too. Not that it matters much now."

଄

Milan, on the other hand, had a better understanding of what had transpired at the store and he hurried to be among Sariana's converted inside the radio station. He quickly found General Ramsey who was already briefed of the circumstances. The Presidential cabinet, it seemed, had placed Sariana's cries for help aside for the moment. It would become official in the morning but most of the military on-site were abuzz with talk of China dissipating the fog.

In the hills of Beijing, armed with 37mm anti-aircraft guns, the Chinese shot chemicals into the yellow fog and managed to eliminate it. Scientists the world over were stunned as they watched the radar and satellite feeds of the yellow cloud disappear. The Weather Modification Division of the Beijing Meteorological Bureau was mum on the technology utilized to vanquish the rain but it was remarkable nonetheless.

In the past several years, China had spent astonishing amounts of money on cloud busting and with good reason. China needed water and a lack of it could potentially cause their economy to collapse. While in most cases, the Chinese effort had been to create rain over specific areas of the country, it was theorized that they had simply used another chemical to eliminate the cloud. Unfortunately, in the process they had eliminated the cloud from parts of Burma and South Korea as well. There was to be much outrage.

Unlike the Presidential cabinet, however, General Ramsey had given much thought to Sariana and Alicia. He thought it best that he and Milan meet with Graham and attempt to explain the scenario. Foremost, Ramsey wanted the tapes of Sariana's interview with Alicia. If the Princess couldn't be present to state her case to the Exalted One, perhaps she could speak to him from beyond the grave. Triton's legal department, however, was having none of it. Clearly, this incident at the studio was far too fresh for them to feel comfortable releasing evidence of any potential wrongdoing. In less than thirty minutes, they had refused. No one would see the tapes before the lawyers.

"General," Milan urged. "You are the military. Just send your men to take the footage."

"The footage would be nice but who says we need it?"

"I don't follow."
"As you said, I am the military. Drastic measures may be in order."

Milan wasn't entirely sure that he liked the sound of that. Nevertheless, General Ramsey ordered Graham to his office. Alongside Milan, they attempted to recount Sariana's prophecy in somewhat clumsy detail.

"In short, the Princess indicated that you are one of the most powerful military commanders in the universe. For you to ascend would be tantamount to becoming a traitor against your own kind," the General concluded.

Graham began to laugh. "What?"

"We're serious, Mr. Barry."

Ramsey was a bit stoic for Milan's taste. "Graham, I realize that what we're saying here is... extraordinary, to say the least. However, I believe that her claims were not without scientific merit; the concept of other dimensions and the like. I realize that this might be a lot to take in but, well, just look at your present circumstances. Out of all of the people in the world, the voice chose to speak to you. Don't you think that there is some great significance attached to that?"

Graham, of course, had considered this. It kept him up nights. Why him? Since his fall from grace years before, Graham had always assumed the worst. It was as if he'd long been paying a penance for his past transgressions. Even when the voice was deemed worthy of attention, Graham still approached the honor of being chosen as a dubious one at best. He found it hard to consider this good fortune; instead he found himself wondering why he should have such rotten luck. Perhaps he'd not only put his ego in check, he had, instead, beaten it into submission. Still, an otherworldly warrior he was not. Graham felt certain of that.

"Guys... I'm sure you understand. It's hard to know

who and what to believe these days. I feel that I can trust the voice. I really don't think that it's misleading us. This girl..."

"That girl was assassinated less than two hours ago attempting to get a message to you, Mr. Barry," the General interrupted. "Obviously, she didn't think it was all horseshit."

"I never said that, General. And I feel terrible that she died..."

"I just think that she's owed a bit of respect."

Again, Milan felt the tone of the conversation uncomfortably escalating and thought it best to intervene. "Graham, if I could just show you the evidence. There's not much, I'm afraid, but we believe that the first man that attempted an assassination of the girl had, in fact, died previously. He was 'possessed', if you will. Likewise, regarding the bombing. Unfortunately, the body of the producer at the television studio is not likely to yield significant test results..."

Graham stood up. "Respectfully, doctor. This is a lot

to absorb."

"I certainly understand. We're trying to get the footage of the girl's interview with the television network right now. I think if you just take a look at that, you might understand. Perhaps you might be able to speak to Ms. Parker as well..."

"Sit down, Mr. Barry!" the General barked and Milan jumped in his seat.

"Excuse me?"

"I said sit down."

"And I said that I wanted to think about all of this."

"General..."Milan attempted to diffuse him but was met with a single, outstretched finger indicating that had he said another word, he'd endure Ramsey's temper next.

"You need to have a seat, Graham," the General said, quieter this time. Graham hesitantly returned to his chair. For a moment, all the General did was fix an icy stare on him. Graham did his best to return it but, clearly the military had done a better job than rock and roll of teaching expert-level intimidation. Nowhere in Graham's eyes could the General see any indication of a fierce warrior. Nowhere. And he did his best to look hard. Finally, Milan nervously cleared his throat and Ramsey began.

"Do you know that I've worn this uniform for 33 years? In that time, I've been all over South America, Africa and the Middle East, mostly fighting other people's wars. Wars and conflicts that didn't matter shit to anyone back home. My first deployment was to Chad. You ever hear of that conflict, Mr. Barry?" Graham shook his head 'no'. "That's all right. Nobody did. But my point is this: I've seen warriors all over this planet. I've had the pleasure of working alongside some of the most elite military forces known to modern man. I've also been fortunate to do battle alongside common street thugs, guerrilla soldiers and children, literally kids, fighting to protect their cities and towns, their crops, their brothers and sisters. Over time, I noticed that they all had one thing in common. Do you know what that was, Mr. Barry?"

"No, I don't."

"It takes a while but eventually you learn to spot it. It's something in the pupil. It's hard to explain but it's there. It's an unrelenting rage. Fury, really. It's the look of a man that doesn't recognize consequences. It's pure id. Do you know what that is?"

"I think so..."

"I didn't either but I studied on it. The 'id' is just a concept. It's not an actual 'thing'. It's nothing tangible you can put your hands on. Turns out, though, there's a part of your brain called the amygdala. I've got one, you've got one. It's just a section of grey matter. That's where the rage part of your 'id' lives. You also have another piece of brain called the orbital cortex. That piece is supposed to put the brakes on the amygdala when that rage hits critical mass. Sometimes, it doesn't, though. For some folks, the orbital cortex just withers away over time. Others, it seems, are just born without it working at all. This is where you get your serial killers, real loony types."

"Okay."

"Not that it matters now, but science, from what I

understand, was real close to figuring out how to scan brains and look for these warning signs in kids and such. They want to find a reason that the orbital cortex just starts to fall apart in some people. That's right, isn't it doctor?"

"Yes. I mean, I believe so. I'm not a neuro-"

"After a while, though, Graham, when you're fighting with and against these types; the kind doing 110 without brakes. You can just see it. You don't need a brain scan to tell you. It's written deep in their eyes. It's a cold, dead look. No. That's wrong. That implies there's no emotion. There's emotion all right. But it's just one emotion: Hate. No empathy, no love, no second guessing. It's just a brain wired for hate. You sure as fuck don't want to try and reason with it."

"Sounds frightening."

"It is, Graham. Personally, I think the orbital cortex is a safety. It's part of a complex, primal wiring system in our brains. When that orbital cortex shuts down, we're walking around just waiting for any provocation to set us off. And we're wired poorly, you see. Just the slightest jarring motion can kick that amygdala into gear. When it clicks... I think that's who we really are. In fact, I think that orbital cortex only exists to ensure that we didn't kill each other straight into extinction long ago. If it wasn't there, I believe we'd crawl out of our mother and, first thing, rip her throat out."

"I guess I just don't appreciate what you're trying to say, General."

"You don't have that look."

"I don't, huh? I'm not wired for hate?"

"Don't take that the wrong way. I can see that you're capable of hate."

"Oh... good?"

"But guess who in this room is wired that way, Mr. Barry?"

Graham was now worried that the General was going to punch him or something. He answered on guard. "I... don't... know."

"It's all right. You can say it. I've got it, Graham. So does the doctor over here. So does everyone I've encountered lately; everyone since the cloud was released. I think whatever is in that gas in the sky is eating away at that safety in our brains. It's preparing everyone on this planet for a hard reset. It's slowly returning us to our core. When all is said and done, the ones that stand in the rain will ascend full of vitriol... and that hate. Those left behind will wander the Earth in the same state but without purpose. You're different, though. I can see it. I think your brain is wired the same but there's something inside you that prevents you from losing it until you're ready."

"So... what does that make me?"

"It makes you special, Graham. It means you're not like us. It means what that little girl said was true. You're different. That's why the voice chose you."

"All right. Then... what? What exactly are you asking me to do?"

"When the time comes you can't ascend."

"So, you want me to stay behind and be the only sane person in a world full of homicidal zombies? Explain to me why the hell I would want to do that."

"It's what you're supposed to do. I don't know what you are. I don't know what your calling is but Sariana was very clear."

"My family has plans to ascend, General. I'm going with them."

"I'm sorry but I can't allow that."

"General Ramsey," Milan tried to interrupt. "With all due respect, why don't we just allow him to think..."

"That's ridiculous," Graham said. "You can't do that. This is a personal decision. It has nothing to do with you or the government..."

"I'll grant you one of the two. It has nothing to do with the government. But it has everything to do with me... and everyone else who won't stand in the rain. I won't allow you to leave us stranded here."

"I can assure you, General, I have no special knowledge to bring to the table."

"I think you do." With that, Ramsey stood up. "You're not to leave these premises."

Being sequestered at the station was nothing new for

Graham but, for the first time, he now felt like a prisoner. He was angry but thought better of an outburst. Graham needed time to sort everything out. He left the office with his dignity in tact and returned to the studio.

"Do you think we might be able to prove your theory of changing brain chemistry?" Milan asked.

"I don't know anything about proving theories, doctor."

"But with my help, perhaps we can show the populace..."

"We're out of time. We're taking over the broadcast and then I'm giving orders to release the Queen."

CHAPTER SEVEN

Later that evening, as had been previously indicated, the entire Earth was engulfed by the thick, yellow cloud. Yet, it continued to permeate from the great tear. As the media announced the seeming completion of the process, the world waited for the downpour. The streets of every city were crowded with citizens, some huddling their families inside tents, catching sleep when they could. No one wanted to miss the first few drops.

There were hold-outs, of course. It was estimated that, at least, fifteen percent of the population of every major U.S. city would remain indoors during the event. Each had their reasons for staying in. Some cited religious scripture, others a government conspiracy, some even admitted that Sariana's brief appearance had swayed them but most simply feared execution. The infirm were another issue entirely. Medical personnel everywhere struggled with the morality of whether or not to place comatose or otherwise incapacitated patients in the rain. Those without next of kin additionally had specified nothing regarding other-worldly life-forms in their living wills. And what of the orphans and animals? Who would decide their fate?

News of Sariana's death by gunman had been little more than a brief story on the national news. As quickly as she had rocketed to fame and notoriety, so quickly did she also become little more than an afterthought. Alicia was jailed, awaiting trial, for the murder of Sariana's shooter and, of course, was promptly fired from her job at the network. Triton immediately tried to sweep the entire mess under the rug. Alicia's interview with Sariana never aired. Alex succeeded in convincing the network that the tape contained nothing more than the rantings of a Satanist and a biased, obviously deranged correspondent. Alicia, after all, had simply snapped under the pressure of her job and the chaos surrounding the tear. For the moment, Sariana left this dimension with very little fanfare.

In Alabama, as the moon hazily shown through the

fog on an especially dark night, Graham sat in the studio waiting for word from the voice. He imagined an elaborate countdown not unlike New Year's Eve to usher in the rain. Throughout the rest of the building, the scientists, mathematicians, government and military officials made themselves busy analyzing data and debating the outcome. Some, however, just did their best to occupy their minds as they waited. A few read books, others surfed the net and more than a few iPods were shuffling through personal, apocalyptic soundtracks.

Many of the intellectuals had their families flown in and children could be seen watching movies on laptops, eating their snacks, seemingly oblivious to the chaos surrounding them. The yellow, Victorian house was growing ever more crowded but as the evening stretched into night, many of the families were being escorted by the military to nearby hotels. Others, bundled in sleeping bags, leaned on each other and dozed in the hallways. Graham felt bad for the military personnel. While he hadn't heard any official word, it appeared that they weren't extended the courtesy of having their families near.

The little radio station in Tuscumbia remained patched in and beamed worldwide via satellite. It occupied 88.7 FM, a non-com frequency, available to anyone with a radio. Most, however, were listening online courtesy of a special dot-gov website the military had set up. Graham occupied his time monitoring the stream, playing music and giving periodic updates regarding the cloud. The military had instructed him not to take calls from listeners. The broadcast was to be solely for informational purposes. No conjecture allowed. It was probably for the best. Graham didn't feel much like playing talk show host. The General did, however. Graham had barely had time to consider the overtures he'd made less than an hour before when Ramsey arrived in his studio with Milan in tow.

"Show me how to work this," the General said to Graham. "Put me on the air."

Graham did as he was told as Ramsey and Milan gathered around the microphones. He potted the song down and radio silence hung on the frequency. "When you're ready, just press the red button and you're on the air."

"Are you good?" the General asked Milan. Milan nodded and Ramsey popped the mic. He took a breath and a Beatles song began to play.

"If the rain comes they run and hide their heads.

They might as well be dead.

If the rain comes, if the rain comes..."

"What's going on? How do I stop this?" Ramsey asked Graham.

Before he could answer, a commotion began outside the studio door. An authoritative yet clearly excited voice rang out in the hall. "All right, people. Here we go. I want an orderly line outside. We don't know how long this is going to last." The three men immediately looked toward the window and strained to see through the darkness. In the moonlight they could see a brown pollen-like substance landing on the glass. Graham thought it looked like chocolate milk falling from the sky. For the moment, it was a light mist. Suddenly, a woman opened the door to the studio.

"Mr. Barry, please alert your listeners that the elemental rain has begun in North and South America. Nothing in Europe, Africa, Asia or the Middle East so far." She only now noticed the General. "Sir," she said and snapped to attention.

"As you were. You're dismissed, Corporal."

Graham looked to the General and Milan. They had a defeated look about them. Outside the moderately soundproofed room, they could hear laughter. Down the road, car horns sounded and firecrackers popped. A celebration was beginning. The General slowly stepped aside.

Graham stepped to the mic and let the song continue to play under his voice. "Well, good news and bad news," he said to the world. "The good news is that the rain is here. We no longer have to wait. The bad news?" Graham thought for a moment. He did briefly consider using the opportunity to convey what he understood to be Sariana's message. Ultimately, he said, "Well, I guess I'll let you know. I'm going to leave you for a short time while I take in the rain myself. When I return... if I return, I guess... I'll give you an indication of how it felt and what to expect as the rain makes its way to your part of the world. I do feel the need to say this, however. We each have a choice to make today. Please remember to respect those individual choices. Everyone today should be allowed to do as their soul dictates. You have free-will. This is likely to be the most important decision you have ever made. I, for one, feel as if I am being called home today. Everything inside me indicates that I'm ready to progress forward, as the voice we have come to know has indicated. You might not feel that way. It may not be your time. Perhaps you're meant for another destiny. I appreciate that. I believe that's okay. Just look inside and do what your spirit compels you to do. You'll make the right decision. Please allow others the courtesy of doing the same. Should this be the last time we speak, I wish you godspeed and safety in your journey... to wherever that may be."

His message would now be translated into 6,800 languages via the web and various apps. With that,

Graham clicked off the mic, switched the automation on and turned to face Ramsey and Milan. The General already had his sidearm aimed at Graham's head. No one in the room was entirely surprised. Graham slowly raised his hands because that's what people do in the movies under these circumstances.

"I'm sorry, Graham. I told you. I can't let you stand in the rain."

"General..."

The studio doors burst open and two soldiers entered with their guns fixed on Ramsey.

"Drop the weapon, sir!!" one of them demanded. "Now!" Ramsey did not immediately comply. Two red dots danced on his right temple and forehead. "If you do not drop the weapon, we will be forced to fire, sir."

"Just let me go," Graham urged. "No one else has to die today, General. You can't possibly believe that I am supposed to make such a difference."

Graham heard a strange noise. It sounded to Milan like the air cracked for a second. A rush of blood then poured from the General's arm as he dropped the pistol.

"Both of you! Out now!" one of the soldiers' ordered to Graham and Milan. They quickly moved to the hallway. If anyone heard the ruckus inside the studio, they didn't appear to be bothered. A few stragglers passed the two men as they stood awkwardly against the wall, half awaiting further instructions. Graham was the first to break from the stun of the shooting.

"Doctor... I have to go," he said with a shrug.

Milan didn't know what he should do. "Graham, I respect your... I don't feel you completely understand..."

Graham began backing away down the hallway as politely as he could. "I'm sorry, doctor. This is what I need to do." He disappeared into the small crowd of families and military personnel. Milan wondered what would be the right thing to do. Should he chase after him? Tackle him in the crowd and attempt to restrain Graham until the rain stopped? Could he? Should he shout to anyone that might listen and warn them of the collective, impending doom awaiting them all just outside those doors? In the end, Milan over-thought the moment. He didn't try to stop him and soon Graham was long out of view.

As his mind raced, Milan saw a familiar face emerging just ahead. "Charles!" Dr. Trumboldt heard him, smiled and inched his way. "Did you... have you come from the rain?"

"Indeed."

"Your whole family? They arrived safe I presume?"

"Absolutely. My entire family is here."

"Good, good. Charles, you know... the girl. She was killed..."

"Yes," Charles frowned. "I just felt terrible when I heard."

"The reporter, Alicia, she murdered the man who..."

"I know. I... heard all about it. It's awful."

"The General was just shot."

"Oh, my!"

"He was trying to keep Mr. Barry out of the rain..."

"Milan," Charles placed a hand on his shoulder.

"There's not much time. You should take in the rain."

"Oh. No. I don't think I will."

"It's perfectly safe. After all, look at me. I'm still here."

"Yes. Yes, of course," Milan shook his head in agreement. "You seem... a little different."

Charles smiled kindly and whispered, "I feel fantastic! Milan, I've never felt so alive. So... perfect." He nodded to the front porch. "Go see for yourself. Surely, you're at least curious."

It was in this instant that Milan realized that he was Sariana's sole remaining witness. He was the final champion of a lost cause. What could one man do but watch the atrocity unfold from a safe distance. It was too late. It was over. Milan looked into Charles' now kind and gentle eyes. "Yeah, sure. Why not?" He gave a sigh and made his way to the front of the building.

With Milan out of view, Charles entered the studio and secured the door behind him. General Ramsey's hulking body was propped up against the wall. A makeshift bandage fashioned from a radio station t-shirt ceased the flow of blood from his arm. Charles sat across from the General in the announcer's chair.

"I don't suppose you're an M.D. too?" the General asked.

"That is incorrect."

That wasn't Dr. Trumboldt's voice. It was a familiar one, however. The General now noticed a small puncture wound on Charles' neck. He closed his eyes and smiled. "Ah! I see. So, we meet in the flesh."

"Indeed. It is a pleasure to see you again, God Vili."

"Again? And what?"

"Our paths have crossed before this day."

"I definitely don't recall that."

"No. You wouldn't. We made that a certainty long ago."

"All right. Are we just going to talk in circles or..."

"No."

There was a long silence as Dr. Trumboldt's eyes

took in the injured man.

"So, what then?" the General asked. "What do you want? Why are you here... with me? Shouldn't you up there in space celebrating your victory? Preparing tractor beams or something?"

"I am sorry. You are correct. We should proceed." The voice stood and thought for a moment. "I wonder, do you know me at all? Is anything about me familiar?"

"What are you talking about? You're the voice from the radio."

The man bent down to Ramsey's level. "If you would... look at me. What do you see?"

"I see Dr. Charles Trumboldt but I know you're not him. You murdered him."

"Interesting. It still fascinates me."

"What? What does?"

"Your dementia."

"I'm of perfectly sound mind. You can count on that."

The voice smiled and slowly returned to the center of the room.

"God Vili, for crimes against the Original Consciousness, for disrupting the evolution of your soul group and for leading the Circle of Nine-"
"I don't know what any of that means."

"- in an attempt to forsake the true fate of Lucifer in the Omniverse for only the betterment of your own self interests-"

"What?"

"- for the systematic, attempted genocide of your own kind, for misleading the Masters Of Wisdom and for the unjust, forced exile of those who opposed the Circle-"

"Are you serious?"

"You are hereby sentenced to Death. Your soul shall be extinguished for eternity and you will henceforth be forever without reprisal. Do you understand?"

The General was now visibly shaken. "No. No, I don't understand any of that."

"A formality, I'm afraid. For this, I am truly sorry," the Voice said. "Your punishment would be much more satisfying if you were coherent. Unfortunately, ascension is the only cure for your present state and we certainly can't allow that."

"Why? I should understand the charges against me."

"Ideally, yes. Unfortunately, we've learned from past experiences with you, God Vili. You simply cannot be trusted. We have paid quite dearly for doing so."

"I don't know what any of this is about. The DJ is the Luciferian."

"Indeed. One of your finest warriors, in fact. You sent him to his doom once before, God Vili. Perhaps not surprisingly, you just attempted to do so again. Praise all, we were here to intervene and save our brother. He'll be among the Humans now. There, he'll be safe. Protected from you and the remaining Eight."

"I think... you have me confused with someone else."

"We don't make mistakes. Certainly not in the third

dimension, God Vili. We are not children." The voice walked toward the door, stopped and placed his hands on the shoulders of the two soldiers. "Meet our new souls. We're quite proud of them. But, then, we can't take all of the credit. You've spent many lifetimes in this world molding them and teaching them the skills for war, haven't you? Ironic. Farewell, God Vili."

The voice exited the room and shut the door behind him. The General's terrified screams were hardly audible in the hallway. There was not a single gunshot, however. The new souls had, instead, chosen to flex their skills in a most torturous manner. Ramsey was to be ravaged alive like helpless prey. His death would take some time but the Voice was confident that the second kill of the day would also be successful. It was time now to attend to other matters. The Voice found a secluded area outside the building. Dr. Trumboldt's body collapsed in the dew soaked weeds as the occupying soul escaped it. The Voice then hurried off to prepare a homecoming for the infant souls. Crickets and firecrackers rang out on this night, which would forever be known as the Glorious Rapture or the

Human Apocalypse, depending on who you asked.

As Graham made his way to the front of the building, he saw Haley and Kelly. He hugged them both and together they stepped on to the covered porch of the house. A mass of people tenuously stood on the porch, hesitating to walk down the stairs in the rain. Others were steeling themselves and their families; saying their potential goodbyes. Graham and his family edged their way past the crowd to a corner of the porch. From there he could see that it was still a light drizzle and Graham wondered if it would eventually become a downpour. He could hear shouting and laughing from beyond the military line of trucks and tents.

"It doesn't sound like anyone's in pain," Graham said to Kelly.

She smiled and, for the first time in days, Graham saw a wave of relief wash over her. "Are you ready?" she asked. He nodded and climbed over the porch railing, jumping to the ground. The first few drops of the rain hit his arms and face and as the droplets landed, they shimmered a brief, gold flash. He examined his skin. It didn't burn. It didn't hurt. It just felt like rain. "Can you grab Haley?" Kelly asked and she handed the little girl down to Graham. Graham stood her beside him and took Kelly's hand to assist her off the porch.

Now, more and more of the team from inside were stepping off the porch. It was an incredible sight. When the raindrops touched their bodies, the same gold, glow appeared. This also occurred as the rain touched the ground, the plants, and all biological life. Inanimate objects didn't enjoy the flash. As everyone stood in the rain, a shimmering, gold aura emanated from their bodies. It was an incredible sight in the midnight blue of an Alabama haze.

Graham, Kelly, and Haley walked closer to the street to get a view beyond the military perimeter. Around them, children laughed and spun in circles, the scientists marveled at the sight, and the military collected samples, still nervous about the consequences. Graham peered from in between two large trucks and he could see the ocean of people surrounding them. As the songs he had programmed bellowed from the loudspeakers, the crowd danced and laughed like kids. Unfortunately in many cases, some of them were, in fact, nude.

The rain was warm and appeared to be immediately absorbed by the skin. As Graham's clothes became wet, they seemed to dry almost instantaneously as his body took in the liquid. As he and his family walked further down the sidewalk, Graham could also see people peering out of windows, watching the revelers outside. One woman in particular caught his eye. She stood behind sheer curtains in what he imagined was her living room window. She seemed to be fighting the urge to go outside. To Graham, she appeared like a child not allowed joining her friends in play. Finally, she broke her resolve and disappeared from view. Next, Graham saw her open her front door and walk outside just as the mist vanished. Not a drop touched her.

As the rain stopped, cheers erupted from the city and tears fell in a uniform relief. The woman Graham watched appeared defeated. She hung her head and walked back inside her home. He saw her moments later reappear in the picture window, again uninvited to join to the enormous crowd outside and, perhaps, doomed as the voice had indicated previously. For the moment, though, she was still among the living.

Inside the lab, the team was already trying to identify the substance that had fallen from the sky. It was completely new; never before seen on Earth or in space. As the scientists' excitement reached a fever pitch, the yellow clouds began to quickly dissipate, giving way to a beautifully bright star laced night. The grass appeared greener. All colors were more vivid and those who had taken in the rain wore their glow, which appeared to be a permanent after-effect.

It was all extraordinary but the result most noticeable was the disappearance of the hum. The vibration that had hung in the air for so long vanished completely. The tear in the sky remained, however. It had been assumed that the vibration was somehow caused by the rip but now it would appear not. It would later become apparent that the vibration only left those who had been washed in the elemental rain. Those who had chosen to stay dry still felt it as strong as ever.

Graham also noticed a mental elation. He had experimented with enough illicit substances in his youth to be able to pinpoint the adrenaline rush he felt. It was not unlike a cocaine buzz. He felt great. Positive. Powerful and simply ecstatic. A feeling of well-being seemed to embrace all that the rain had touched. The air smelled fantastic. Kelly, Haley and everyone around him appeared more beautiful than ever before. It was invigorating. Kelly felt it too.

"Oh my God, I feel incredible!" she laughed.

"I don't think I've ever felt this focused," Graham agreed. "I don't think I've ever felt this good. Everything just feels... right." Haley giggled in the most joyful way and it warmed their hearts further. The entire world now appeared brand new. The men and women in the lab initially suspected that the rush of euphoria would pass but, much to everyone's delight, it did not. It felt like enlightenment and it felt as though it were here to stay.

CHAPTER EIGHT

Amber didn't so much as wake up the next morning, rather she regained consciousness. Half a bottle of Jack Daniels and several beers later, she had somehow made it back to her modest modular home in the foothills of North Alabama. She could only assume that Tommy or some other good Samaritan had given her a ride back to her place. For the moment, her memory was hazy. The stereo in the house was screaming out a Drive-By Truckers song and Amber wondered how she could have ever slept so soundly.

Amber wrapped a bed sheet around her naked frame and shuffled down the hallway. In the fridge she found a cold diet Coke, she turned off the radio and then sank into the frayed couch in her living room. She located the remote under a week old pizza box on the end table. It was eleven A.M. Maybe she could find "The Price Is Right." No such luck. The only thing on was the news.

"So far, Jim, there are nothing but positive reports

coming in worldwide from those who were bathed in the elemental rain..."

"Huh," Amber thought. "I slept through it."

Panic hit her for a moment. While she had resolved to stay out of the rain while at the television studio, Amber did believe that she would have more time to weigh her options. Then, the haze of drink wearing thin, yesterday's remnants began to rush back to her. All that she drank to forget was now brought back, front and center, in stunning color. Princess Sariana, Alicia and the killings. She wished she'd slept through that as well. Amber changed the channels to see if she could find something about the shootings.

"What we are seeing now is an attempt at mass migration, Sharon. As word spreads throughout the internet of the positive effects of the rain sent by the OWL-"

"- many Chinese, who were not afforded the opportunity-"

"- increased hostilities-"

"- word now that a number of nations, Jim, even those anti-elemental, were forward thinking enough to capture as much of the rain as possible. While this was done, in most cases, for research purposes, scientists are on the case to see if those who decided to seek shelter might still be able to be washed in the rain, thereby ensuring their salvation-"

Nothing. Amber opened her soda and took a drink. Suddenly, the trailer door burst open. Trevor stomped inside followed by Tommy. Amber wrapped her sheet tight.

"Trevor! What the fuck?!"

"What?"

"I ain't got any clothes on," she whispered.

"It's just Tommy."

"Hey, Amber," Tommy said as he plopped down on the couch next to her. "You watching the news?"

Amber sighed. "Yes."

"They say anything about reservoirs?"

"I just turned it on."

"We heard rumors that there might be reservoirs of rain. I might can still get some of it."

"I thought you weren't gonna do it?"

"Fucking wife and kid did it. I told them not to but then she got all scared and shit and ran out in it last minute. I guess I gotta find some."

"You won't believe the high, dude," Trevor assured him as he packed a bong.

"Yeah. I'm pretty stoked about that."

"Was there anybody talking about that shooting yesterday?" Amber asked.

Trevor took a rip. "What shooting?" he exhaled.

"The one at the Dollar Store in Tuscumbia."

"Ain't that where you're working?" Trevor asked and passed the bong to Tommy. "I thought you said it was a tv station now."

"It is. Tommy, you didn't think to mention that to him?"

"He's your man, Amber. I thought y'all had

discussed it."

Trevor laughed. "We didn't discuss much of nothing last night. Ain't that right, baby? She was a goddamn horndog after you dropped her here."

Amber didn't remember any of this. Well, maybe bits and pieces. Amber must have passed out after Trevor left for work the night before... or wherever he went. That did explain how she'd arrived home, though.

"I didn't hear nothing about it," Tommy said as he inhaled his hit. "Sorry."

"Anybody hurt?" Trevor asked.

Tommy began to pass the bong back to Trevor but Amber intercepted and lit it herself. "Fuck yes. Two people killed. Right in front of me."

"Jesus Christ, honey, why didn't you say nothin'?"

Amber exhaled a large cloud of smoke and shook her head. "I don't know."

Trevor got up from the floor and hugged Amber on the couch. "I'm so sorry, sweetie. I'm sorry you had to see that."

Amber began to cry. The outpouring was as sudden as it was overwhelming. "It was scary as shit," she managed between the tears.

Trevor kissed her head. "It's all right now. You ain't going back to work there, I'll tell you that much."

Amber abruptly broke the embrace and quickly wiped away her tears. "I need to get dressed."

She made her way to the bedroom, her sheet a train following in her wake. Amber quickly found some clean clothes and concluded that she could go without makeup. She loaded her pockets with car keys, loose change and her cell phone. Just as she was ready to leave, she stopped and went back to her top dresser drawer. Under her important paperwork and panties, Amber found an orange prescription bottle and popped a Xanax. She chewed it up and maneuvered most of it under her tongue to dissolve. Amber shut the bedroom door and heard the boys talking in the next room.

"It's like... a feeling of all-encompassing joy. You know what I mean?" Trevor was saying.

"I think so. Kind of like heroin?"

"Kind of. Yeah. It's sort of like an opiate high. But it never wears off." Trevor noticed Amber. "How would you describe it?"

"What?"

"The elemental high. From the rain."

"I don't know," Amber shrugged. "I didn't get in it."

"Oh my God. Why?"

"I just..."

"When I left last night, you said you were going to leave the radio on-"

"I did."

"And when they made the announcement, you were going to go outside. We talked about this."

"I slept through it, Trevor! Okay?! I... slept through it."

"Jesus fucking Christ, Amber."

"I know. Look, I don't need you yelling at me right now."

"It's just... what are we going to do?"

Amber pulled her hair back into a pony tail and wrapped it tight with a rubber band. "I don't know, Trevor. I need to think. I want to see if I can talk to Alicia."

"Who's Alicia?"

"The reporter I told you about."

"Do you think she'll know where a reservoir is?" Tommy asked.

Amber knew that Alicia would not but this was as good an out as any. "Well, she's a reporter. So, maybe. Yeah."

Trevor nodded. "Good thinkin', babe."

"Yeah," Tommy concurred. "You'll let me know what you find out?"

"Yes. I'll let you know." Amber opened the front door and the sunlight nearly blinded her. She reached into her purse and found her sunglasses. "I'll be back later," she shouted as she hurried to the car.

Milan gave a friendly smile to the overweight woman with whom he would be sharing his elevator ride. She didn't smile back. His boxes were getting heavy. He shouldn't have tried to carry it all in one trip. Still, Milan also didn't want to spend any more time outside of his hotel room than he had to. The fat lady exited the lift two floors before his and he put the boxes down in her place, if only for a moment. Back in the room, the television and two radios broadcast the news; none of it good. Milan monitored it all.

"News now, Jim, that Kazakhstan is the latest nation to mobilize troops in search of elemental rain reserves. We're hearing reports that sixteen hundred armored units have crossed the border into neighboring Kyrgyzstan. The United Nations has denounced all of the aggressive tactics we've been witnessing over the course of the past few hours but it is certainly falling on deaf ears..."

"And so what we're seeing is most of Asia and

Eastern Europe in a mad dash to accommodate its citizens' demand for access to the elemental rain reserves, real or imagined. Now, all of this has happened so quickly, it's difficult to keep track of the military movement. As you can see... we're trying to update the map..."

Milan began stacking his boxes in the two small closets available in the adjoining rooms he had rented. He estimated that he had enough food and bottled water to last about two months. Depending on how things went, he would then have to venture out of the hotel for more. He didn't know where. The economy had effectively collapsed.

It was strange, he thought. While most of the world was fixated on the seemingly inevitable military catastrophe, little focus had been given to the economic meltdown being felt worldwide. Sooner or later the grocery stores would be empty and there would be no one left to stock them. Most everyone was looking for a ticket out of this dimension. The General had been right, of course. The coming landscape would be one made only of anarchy.

"It looks as though the President has entered the briefing room, Jim, so let's go to the floor if we could..."

Milan sat down on the edge of the bed and watched as a visibly overwrought Commander in Chief adjusted the microphone on the podium. Cameras clicked as the room mellowed to a hush and the President began to speak.

"The United States, condemns in the strongest terms, any infringement of borders as the world struggles with these complex issues. I have been in conference with other world leaders and we are aggressively seeking a solution with regards to the planet's elemental reserves. We urge calm. Those nations that do not comply and show restraint will be subject to sanctions-"

"What good will that do?!"

It was the first time Milan had ever heard a reporter interrupt a sitting President's speech.

"If you'll just let me finish..."

That interjection, however, sent the entire press conference into a frenzy.

"What is the U.S. doing to prevent our own reserves from being pilfered?!"

"Most of our cities are without law enforcement. Will you enact Marshall Law?!"

"When will the reserves be available for public use?!"

"Where are these reserves?!"

At this point, the Press Secretary tried to take control of the situation. "Folks, if you'll just settle down, the President and I will be happy to address all of these questions..."

"Where is the OWL?! Why haven't we heard from the OWL?!"

"We don't know..."

"What's going to happen next?!"

"The President doesn't know any more about that than..."

"Why aren't you doing anything?!"

"I can assure you that there are countless measures currently in place..."

"Be specific!!"

"Well, what would you like to know... specifically?"

"Why aren't you answering our questions?! Now is not the time for doublespeak!"

"This... this isn't doublespeak..."

An aide whispered something in the President's ear. He nodded and was quickly escorted away. The Press Secretary appeared surprised by this.

"Where is he going?!" a reporter shouted.

"Um..."

"Why is he leaving?!"

"I don't... uh..."

"The people need answers!! He doesn't get to just walk away!"

"It seems that... the President has been called away..."

The fuse had been lit. All at once, the room descended into pandemonium. Reporters and cameramen rushed the hallway in an effort to follow the President. The Secret Service attempted to hold them back. Shots were fired. Things were only going to get worse.

ભ

As Amber sped down the highway, she tried to find some music on the radio.

"Does science know how much of the rain is necessary for enlightenment? In other words, do we know how much of these elements must be absorbed in order for, say, a two hundred pound man-"

She changed the station.

"-clinics in all of the major cities in Great Britain have been established for those who missed their initial opportunity to stand in the elemental rain. Doctors are injecting what is believed to be a significant-"

Preset number three.

"In the days of Noah, when the doors were closed,

those who were left outside perished. There are people who believe that when Jesus returns, some will be taken and, for those left behind, there will be a second chance. But this is not how it was in the days of Noah. When Jesus comes, the door will be closed and those who are not ready... they will perish. There will be no 'second chance'. Are you ready? Are you in the Ark? Do you know Jesus? Have you lived in utter obedience to him in utter holiness? Because no sinners will go into his Kingdom. Jesus is coming. Are you ready?"

"This message brought to you by the First United Pentecostal Church of Sheffield, Alabama."

"ANY TRADE! ANY TRADE GOES! Listen up Northwest Alabama! The all new Thompson Toyota needs your trade! And we'll give you five thousand dollars minimum-"

Amber shut off the radio and fumbled for her phone. She scrolled to her playlist and Red Fang engulfed the car with noise enough to drown out her every racing thought. Amber pressed the accelerator harder. It wasn't likely that she'd get a ticket.

The little city of Tuscumbia was a mess. Most of the out-of-towners remained and, from what Amber could gather, they were responsible for most of the looting. She didn't recognize the people walking out of the Foodland with carts full of soda and cigarettes. All of the ATMs had signs on them indicating that they were empty and someone had spray painted something illegible on the front doors of city hall.

Inside the Colbert County jail, it was remarkably quiet. In fact, it was empty. There were no police officers, no guards and no one at the front desk. Amber waited for a few moments but no one arrived to answer her query. She looked for a bell or a buzzer to ring but found nothing.

"Hello?!" she shouted. Amber heard nothing in return but the reverberation of her own call. She was hesitant to tour the facility unaccompanied but she had questions. Alicia, she thought, might have the answers. Just who was Sariana? Had she inadvertently made the right decision by passing out and disregarding her invitation to the rapture? "Anybody here?!" Amber yelled.

Finally, a shadow emerged and as it limped ever closer, she saw an older woman appear in the harsh fluorescent light. She ambled slowly toward the front desk.

"What do you need?"

"I'm here to see a prisoner. I mean, I think she's here."

"And who would that be?"

"Alicia..." Amber paused. She didn't know the reporter's last name despite having heard it probably a hundred times.

"Alicia who?"

"She's the news reporter lady. The one that shot that man in the Dollar Store."

"Are you kin?"

"I'm a... co-worker."

Suddenly, the entrance doors burst open. A huge, bearded and tattooed man with a gun began shouting, "Where the fuck are the reserves?!"

The old lady held her hands up. "Sir, just calm down."

"You keepin' that shit here?"

"Mister, I don't know what you're talking about."

"The rain reserves, goddamnit!! Where are they?!"

"They ain't here."

"Oh yeah? But I'm willin' to bet you know where they are, don't you?!"

"I do not."

"Who are you?!" the man screamed at Amber and pointed his pistol at her.

"Woah! What the fuck?!"

"You work here?!"

"No!!"

"You a prisoner?!"

"I'm here to visit my friend! Would you just calm the hell down?!"

The man returned his attention and his aim to the jail

employee. She was gone. Amber thought that was just typical. That old lady took her sweet ass time to make her way down that hallway before. But once the crazy guy with the gun arrived, she sure could book it.

"Where'd she go?!" the man shouted.

"I don't know!!"

He was pointing the gun at Amber again. "You didn't see her leave?!"

"I was talking to you!!"

"Motherfucker!! Where's she at?!"

"I said I don't know!! You need to stop pointing that gun at me, Tinker Stokes!!"

"What?!"

"Put the gun down!!"

"How do you know my name?!"

"You fixed my boyfriend's bike!!"

"What's your name?"

"Amber Mitchell. My boyfriend is Trevor Dial."

"That son-of-a-bitch owes me over three hundred bucks."

"Yeah, well, join the club. He owes me a lot more than that."

Tinker lowered the gun. "Where the hell is everybody?"

"Fuck if I know. That old lady was the only person I..."

Amber felt a sudden, piercing sting in her left shin. It burned. It felt as if she had been stung by something. The next thing she knew, Amber couldn't stand. She was on the floor and her leg was bleeding. She watched as two men struggled to detain Tinker Stokes just a few feet away. Somehow they managed to handcuff this giant of man, three times the size of either of them. Next, they turned their attention to Amber. One of the men grabbed her hands and attempted to put them behind her back.

"What are you doing?!" The guy didn't answer. Amber resisted the guard as best she could with a wounded leg and saw that Tinker was bleeding from his shoulder. "Did y'all just shoot me?!"

"Not her." It was the old lady from before.

The guard struggling with Amber was confused. "What?"

"She was just here to visit somebody."

"Oh."

"Are you shitting me?!" Amber shouted. "You shot me?!"

The other guard was already on his radio calling for paramedics. Amber would spend the next several hours in an over-crowded hospital getting stitched up. By the time it was all over, she was too tired and too doped up to make a return trip to the jail. Trevor would just have to drive her to see Alicia in a few days, she resolved.

છ

The rain was now the most valuable commodity on Earth as the world's governments and citizens guarded it more dearly than food, money, water or even their most sacred texts. Many nations called for a rationing system to be implemented, whereby humans deemed vital to advance would be selected and washed in the rain. In remote corners of the world, where news of the tear had not yet spread, it was argued, there must live powerful teachers and spiritual leaders worthy of enlightenment that had not been made aware of the miraculous powers of the rain and may have missed out to no fault of their own. Surely, these men and women must be washed before a common criminal.

The divides grew from here. For the "unwashed" as many enlightened members of the media referred to them, a fate worse than death loomed eerily on the horizon. To be cast out; consciously aware that human evolution would progress onward without them. This was more painful than any death. And so, with nothing to lose, they took up arms versus the so called enlightened and mankind's last great war began.

There would be many casualties. More than the

previous world wars combined. It became unsafe to walk the streets. The world's people banded into two groups: those who had been washed in the rain and those who had not. Prejudices became rampant. The washed came to see the unwashed as primitive. The unwashed's disdain for the enlightened very often resulted in death, for the rain did not carry with it dimensional immortality.

It was a curious thing. When an enlightened person died, it seemed that one could view their soul drift above their body, outlined in the golden hue until finally it disintegrated, apparently into thin air. Of course, this did not occur when an unwashed man, woman or child died. This fueled further outrage, as it was thought that only the rain could bestow a soul or, perhaps, the lack of the fluid had somehow depleted the souls all naturally born within. Marshal Law was, in fact, attempted in many nations to curtail the violence but proved to be ineffectual. There was simply not enough law enforcement or military left to police the circumstances.

Milan watched all of this unravel from the relative

comfort of his hotel room turned bunker in Tuscumbia, Alabama. Even here, in this once quaint, little town, it wasn't safe. He barricaded his doors with furniture if, for no other reason, than to protect his stash of food, water and toiletries. Milan spent his days watching the news, surfing the internet and listening to the shouting in the hallways.

CB

Amber, meanwhile, found herself sequestered as well but not by choice. Thanks to her injury, she'd been confined to bed for the better part of a week. Between bong hits, Trevor brought her meals and helped her to the bathroom as needed. It would likely be a month before she would be able to walk properly again. In the meantime, she could hobble about on crutches if need be.

Amber spent her time listening to the radio. They said nothing of Princess Sariana, only the troubles, and so she combed the internet. In the far reaches of the web, in the corners reserved for conspiracy theories and doomsday prophecies, they said plenty. Much of it,

Amber didn't understand. These were strange mythologies and the process of interdimensional travel eluded her completely. She needed to speak to Alicia. Amber felt certain that she might able to explain all of this in a way that she could easily understand.

On the first day of July, Amber felt sure enough that she could finally leave the trailer and so she called out to Trevor. There was no answer. She asked for him twice more. Nothing.

"Goddamnit," she mumbled as she struggled to stand with her crutches. The song on the radio ended and there was dead air. Amber limped her way into the living room. "Trevor!"

It was, for a moment, strangely quiet in the trailer park. Amber hadn't heard him leave but Trevor was nowhere to be found in the house. She opened the front door and called for him. Soon, she heard similar calls for Stacy, Reg and Phillip. Amber heard a woman a few doors down, sobbing. A friend was trying to console her.

"He was just gone?"

"I was sitting right next to him, watching TV. I asked him to change the channel and he just wasn't there no more."

Amber shut the door and noticed that the television news was silent. A single camera shot focused on an empty desk. Where were the bodies? In days prior when an enlightened soul had been extracted, by force or otherwise, there was still a body left to bury. Not this time.

In an instant all that had been washed in the rain vanished from the face of the Earth. While the enlightened might say otherwise, it was no grand rapture; there were no ornate ceremonies. They were simply gone. If it were not already obvious that a message had been sent, a familiar voice finally spoke plaintively from abandoned radios across the planet:

"It is finished."